"Mary tells it like it was—an
and funny re-telling of life i
from the perspective of a young
her career in the '70s. It is a must-read for any young woman
contemplating or embarking upon a career in law or business."*
Deborah H. Bornstein
Litigator and Law Firm Partner

———

"Courting Kathleen Hannigan is a wonderful, true-to-life
depiction of a female attorney's role in a large law firm—
complete with struggles, successes, relationships, self-doubt—
running the full gamut of personal and professional challenges.
This novel is for anyone who has experienced or who may face
gender issues in the workplace. It also beautifully explores
the effect—subtle and not-so-subtle—that a woman's professional
career has on her personal and family life. Reed's character
development is extremely detailed and realistic.
The book was a page-turner for me as I lived each day along
with Kathleen, her friends and colleagues."
Leslie Desmond
Attorney (retired)

———

"Mary Hutchings Reed, a highly regarded law partner herself,
has skillfully created a gutsy and appealing heroine.
Kathleen Hannigan joins a blue-stocking law firm,
shrewdly plays to win, makes partner, finds romance and then
faces her most crucial trial. If you want to know the truth
about the law firm game, read this book."
Enid Powell
Breakthru Writing

———

"Mary Hutchings Reed has written an insightful story
about the impact of women lawyers on the culture of a law firm.*
Unfortunately, the funny, strange and sexist situations
ring true, even in today's world."
Pete Wentz
Executive Vice President, APCO Worldwide
Former General Counsel, Helene Curtis

———

COURTING
KATHLEEN HANNIGAN

MARY HUTCHINGS REED

To Lisa —

*Because we accomplish
nothing important alone*

*Thanks for your help
and support,*

Mary Hutchings Reed

AMP&RSAND, INC.
Chicago, Illinois

ISBN 978-0-9761235-6-9

Design: David Robson, Robson Design
Cover Art: Darlene H. Olivo, Visual Artist
Published by Ampersand, Inc.
1050 North State Street
Chicago, IL 60610

ACKNOWLEDGEMENTS

It's all fiction and it's all true.

For those who've practiced law in Chicago, I assure you that while you will recognize every character, you will know none of them. I am grateful to my legal colleagues who read and commented on earlier drafts of this work, including Christine Albright, Deborah Bornstein, Leslie Desmond, Lawrence Gill, Deborah Haude, Jane Pigott and Pete Wentz; my friends Dr. Robert Rynearson, Marjie Rynearson, Sue Telingator and John Wood; and my late friends, agent Jane Jordan Browne, Sr. Gertrude Treybal and Alex Clark. I am indebted to Enid Powell, who has nurtured the writer in me since 1997; and to the supportive members of her workshop, including Wendy Grossman, Scottie Kersta-Wilson, Erin Goseer Mitchell, and Eric Sutherlin. I am grateful to Patricia McMillen, a lawyer, a poet, a friend, and an inspiration; to Lucia Blinn, who keeps the faith, walks the walk and is ever true to the writing process; to Julie Weary, who has shared many a frustration and every small triumph; to Anne Mini, whose friendship I treasure for so many reasons, including her ability to tell the unvarnished truth; to Barbara Lachenmaier Spangenberg, my most enthusiastic reader; and to Fred Shafer, whom I met after writing *CKH*, but who has taught me and so many others that every sentence has a plot, the long ones make the short ones possible, and every draft, like this one, can always be improved. My thanks to Suzie Isaacs and Ampersand, Inc. for helping to make this project a reality. And, as always, to the love of my life, William.

MHR
July, 2007

DEDICATION

*This novel is for every person
who has nurtured a creative spark wherever it was found,
and, in particular, for*

*my mother, Mary Jo Hutchings
and
my father, LeRoi Hutchings
and
my sister, Donna C. Steele
and
my career buddy, Christine Albright
and
my best friend and husband, William R. Reed*

"Nothing that is worth doing can be achieved in a lifetime;
therefore we must be saved by hope.

Nothing which is true or beautiful or good
makes complete sense in any immediate context of history;
therefore we must be saved by faith.

Nothing we do, however virtuous, can be accomplished alone;
therefore we must be saved by love."

REINHOLD NIEBUHR

ONE

The Oath

"To tell the truth, the whole truth, and nothing but the truth, so help you God?"

What was the truth? Even after analyzing months of truth (re-remembered) and truth (half-forgotten), attorney Kathleen Hannigan could not be sure she knew the truth, the whole of it or nothing but. What did her version matter, anyway? Her own lawyers had suggested that her opinion might be irrelevant, especially if she insisted on saying what she really thought. It was a defense lawyer's twist on her mother's adage: If she couldn't say something helpful, then she shouldn't say anything at all.

"I do," she said. She had sworn as much 15 years ago, when she had been admitted to the bar. It was, as to a marriage oath, the expected answer.

The case, pending before the United States District Court for the Northern District of Illinois, was captioned *Ann Rose vs. Albright & Gill et al.,* and Kathleen was one of 315 A&G partners listed as a defendant. She was the only A&G lawyer being called upon by Ann Rose to testify against her partners, in effect, against herself.

Just a year and a half ago, the plaintiff, Ann Rose, had been the law firm's star associate. Today, she was a public thorn irritating its venerable side. According to the allegations of the complaint, Kathleen and her law partners (all but 15 of them men) had discriminated against Ann because of her sex. She claimed that they had not elected her to partnership because she didn't wear make-up or jewelry. The Firm said it was because they simply didn't like her that much. Kathleen herself couldn't stand the woman.

Kathleen Hannigan was seven years senior to Ann Rose and had been a partner for eight years. She'd served on two important Firm committees and had set her sights on ascending to Albright & Gill's all male Management Committee. She persisted in believing that members of that Committee had the power to change things, for women and for others. Conveniently, this allowed her personal ambition to masquerade as political cause. Until Ann Rose sued the Firm, she had been on track.

Now, with her right hand raised for the oath, Kathleen's career was on the line for the sake of a detestable woman who once had found a fellow A&G lawyer dead in his office and had billed her time with the paramedics to "Firm Administration." Apparently, Helen Bornstein, Ann Rose's attorney, was counting on Kathleen to put her feminist ideals above her petty animosities and personal ambitions. At the same time, Bornstein was taking a chain saw to the ladder of Kathleen's career.

"Louder, for the record."

"I do."

"You may be seated."

She sat in the black leather swivel chair in the elevated witness box and crossed her legs at the ankles, forcing her knees together in a ladylike but uncomfortable pose. In real life, she always crossed her right knee over her left, and when nervous rotated her right ankle until a little crack betrayed her age.

The courtroom looked bigger from the witness stand than it had a few months ago when she and Marshall Long had argued a case for Anthony, the single named, legendary rock promoter who was Kathleen's most prestigious client. They had faced the judge from a podium 20 feet away from the bench, and, because the ceiling was twice as high as normal, he had been dwarfed by the great black iron seal of the federal court hanging on the wall over his head. It was not real cast iron, just as the courtroom's reddish-brown paneling was not real mahogany, but an obvious imitation. Since there were no windows, the room was like a very large cave laminated with the sticky paper Kathleen's mother used to line kitchen drawers.

According to the oversized silver-colored clock embedded in the paneling at the back of the room, it was about 10:00. Kathleen smiled pleasantly at the jury, comfortably seated in red plush theater style seats behind the railing below her and to her left. Waiting for Helen Bornstein to attack, she knew she would be tempted to say something nice, like she had been taught, to please her audience. If she could think of just the right thing, perhaps she could salvage her career. *Just the right thing* would punish firms that discriminated against women, but would not require them to offer the plum of partnership to the wrong women, women like Ann Rose.

A surprising number of her partners at Albright & Gill, one of the city's oldest law firms, were scattered among the courtwatchers, even though Blake Mills, the Managing Partner, had urged them not to attend. It would be unseemly, he had suggested, to show too much interest in the proceedings, akin to attending the taping of a daytime talk show. Nevertheless, at least half a dozen had found a convenient pretense that morning to stop in Judge Jasper's courtroom. Most of them, Kathleen knew, were present out of morbid curiosity rather than a desire to be personally supportive, and so she was all the more disappointed not to see her best friend in the gallery.

Jill had warned her the night before that she was having nanny problems. Dumbfounded, but unwilling to risk a confrontation, Kathleen had merely said, "Oh." After all, they had been there for each other through all the ups and downs of the 15 years of their careers. Perhaps they had drifted apart recently due to the changed particulars of their lives—Jill's life, with the baby, had changed the most—but surely she would be there, nanny problems or no.

Kathleen scanned the audience. No Jill.

For courage, she looked towards the defense table, where Marshall Long sat with Philip Darby, the Firm's attorney. Blake had asked Marshall to monitor the trial so that he himself could maintain a public distance from it. Blake probably wanted the jury to see Marshall's boyish face and mistakenly believe that they were all like him. In a skinny, intellectual sort of way, Marshall was quite handsome. He was in his mid-forties, but not yet graying, and his medium-length, brown hair had a friendly, windblown curl to it. Was it possible that while Jill had been busy mothering, Marshall had become, without Kathleen knowing it, her most dependable friend? So as not to blush, Kathleen looked away when Marshall winked, and, on the rebound, her eyes briefly met Ann's. Ann didn't flinch.

Dressed severely in a charcoal suit and a white shirt buttoned high at the neck, Ann sat rigidly at the plaintiff's table. Scared to death or superbly confident? So much depended on the jury's perceptions. Kathleen checked herself. She remembered the way her mother had inspected her every Saturday morning during high school debate season. Smoothing her collar, her mother would tell her that appearances mattered. Her mother said the appearance of confidence bred confidence. Kathleen had had to learn for herself that appearances could be deceiving.

That morning, she had stood in her walk-in closet in her high rise Chicago condo and fingered the outfit which gave her the most confidence—a hot pink brushed silk suit with a short, straight skirt. The stakes were high; she would be playing with the truth and with her own career. No, she decided reluctantly, hot pink was too hot, too controversial. Instead, she chose a gray suit with a skirt two inches above her knees, which added length to her legs and made her feel younger than her 41 years. Still, gray was the Albright & Gill party line, so she smiled a wicked smile when she slipped into her favorite shoes—horse hair dyed to look like leopard. Sexy. Strong. Savage. Confident camouflage for Kathleen's uncertain soul.

Helen Bornstein approached the wooden podium in the middle of the courtroom. A brilliant trial lawyer, she had brought one of the first sex discrimination cases ever in the federal courts in Illinois and had been consulted in some capacity in almost every significant one since. If Ann Rose had asked her, Kathleen would have recommended the 55-year-old woman, based on her reputation and the picture of her on the cover of *Chicago Lawyer* a few months back. With single cultured pearls piercing her ears beneath her short-bobbed blondish hair, Bornstein had stared off the page with a confidence Kathleen envied.

Earlier in the week, Bornstein had made an impressive opening statement to the jury. She had read them the relevant federal statute, and told them that "because of her sex" Albright & Gill had denied

Ann Rose partnership even though she had had more billings, more hours, and more responsibility than her male counterparts. Helen Bornstein asked the jury to pay special attention to what one Kathleen Hannigan had to say—she was Chair of the Evaluation Committee, and she had been the one to tell Ann Rose that she ought to wear jewelry and make-up and act more "femininely." The Firm's lawyer countered with a phony, home-spun approach about the Firm's founding in 1877. The partnership was holding its collective criticism, hoping he'd put on a more worthy defense.

After the opening speeches, Bornstein had called her first witnesses, and then led Ann Rose through her story. Ann displayed a credible, if uncharacteristic, civility, sprinkling her testimony with eager, "Yes, ma'am's." Kathleen fidgeted with a layman's annoyance and subtly but repeatedly jabbed Darby with her pointed elbow. She worried that the jury wouldn't know that this was the same woman who once had thrown a legal pad at a secretary, who had sat sullenly silent through an important client dinner, and who had rejected all the helpful suggestions Kathleen had generously offered. How were they to know the whole truth about Ann Rose?

Certainly not from the "character witnesses." Bornstein had called former clients and schoolmates—not fellow A&G workers—to attest to Ann's interpersonal competence and good manners. Then, a social psychologist explained gender stereotyping to a restless jury.

Finally, Bornstein called Kathleen. At the defendants' table, Kathleen tugged down on her skirt and rose. If she merely told the truth, just told the jury her personal experience with Ann Rose, then the Firm would be vindicated and Bornstein and her feminist comrades could not accuse her of being a traitor. Kathleen lifted her chin slightly and walked slowly to the witness stand.

There, she swore to tell the truth.

The argument could be made that Ann Rose should have hired a man, someone who looked like most of the defendants. She could have hired a senior litigator from a firm just like Albright & Gill, which might have diffused any notion that Ann's was a feminist cause *celébrè*. Perhaps a man would have made it strictly a contract case—a breach of promise to an employee—which had nothing whatsoever to do with sex. No doubt Bornstein had thought of that angle, too. Her two associates at the counsel's table were men, one in his early thirties with a jaw chiseled from the pages of *Esquire* and the other a fresh graduate whose face hadn't received the message that adolescence was several years behind him.

The poised woman from the cover of *Chicago Lawyer* casually adjusted the thin black microphone at the podium. Kathleen told herself she could go the distance with the famous Helen Bornstein if she kept it simple, if she didn't try to outsmart her at her own game.

"Ms. Hannigan, will you state your name for the record, please," Helen Bornstein asked.

"Kitty Hannigan."

"Is that your given name, Ms. Hannigan?"

It was going to be a tedious morning, the truth being picked apart like that. "Kitty" had slipped out. It was who she was when she was most herself. She had become "Kathleen" the day she started working at Albright & Gill.

"Let me repeat, Ms. Hannigan. Is Kitty your given name?"

"Kathleen Ann," she said. She reminded herself not to explain.

Bornstein continued with the routine: Address. Age. Education. Occupation. Marital Status. "Ms. Hannigan, do you know the plaintiff in this case, Ann Rose?" ("I do.") "And how do you know her?" ("I am a partner at Albright & Gill, where Ann Rose was an associate.")

"Were you a friend of hers when she was employed by Albright & Gill?"

Kathleen's mouth was again dry. "I would say we were friendly in the sense that we worked on some matters together," she stammered. "After that, I took an interest in her career." Darby had wanted Kathleen to position herself as a mentor to Ann Rose, someone who, as a friend, had been brutally honest in telling her the things the Firm now regretted had been said.

"Were you what one might call a role model for Ms. Rose?"

"You should ask her who her role models were," Kathleen said.

For the rest of the afternoon Kathleen Hannigan and Helen Bornstein wrestled with each other, with the truth, and with

Kathleen's career. Bornstein would take off her reading glasses, put them on, wave them like a baton at the jury. Kathleen would smile, cross her legs, uncross them, frown. Sometimes for substance, sometimes for show. The two women understood each other perfectly. They both knew it was just a matter of time before Bornstein asked Kathleen the one question Kathleen did not want to have to answer.

"Did the Evaluation Committee ever caution any of the lawyers against the use of sexually stereotyped comments?" Bornstein asked.

"We relied on the objectivity of the Evaluation Form," Kathleen said. In the audience, Marshall nodded his support.

"But under 'comments' they could say whatever they wanted, stereotyped or not."

Kathleen did not respond. There was no need to argue with Bornstein. All the lawyers knew she wasn't asking a question.

Bornstein asked if the Committee recognized the evaluations of four partners in particular (including Kathleen's) to be "stereotyped."

Kathleen looked at the defense table, but Darby didn't move. He apparently was saving up his objections, in an attempt not to alienate the judge or annoy the jury. When it was clear to her that Darby was going to let her answer, she said, "No. It agreed that Ms. Rose needed to work on her interpersonal skills."

"Ms. Hannigan, if the Committee had not received those four evaluations, would Ms. Rose have had a superior evaluation?"

"You mean, if you throw out the criticisms, are only excellents left?" She shook her head with a small laugh. She would get the better of Bornstein and her circular questions.

"I mean, if you throw out the evaluations which smack of sexual stereotyping, her evaluations are excellent, aren't they?" Bornstein said.

"Objection!" Darby finally said.

"Withdrawn." Bornstein paused as if to mark a victory. "You've said before that you feared the Firm would not make her a partner. Why was that?"

"Her interpersonal skills got in the way."

Bornstein referred to her notes. "When you spoke with the plaintiff, you used the word 'bitchy.' What exactly do you mean by that word?" Bornstein wanted Kathleen to admit that bitchy was a word ascribed most often to women—hard-driving, aggressive, ambitious women.

Res ipsa loquitur, she thought. *The thing speaks for itself.* Helen Bornstein herself might qualify as bitchy.

Bornstein seemed to have read her mind. "Would you describe me as bitchy?" she asked, flashing an eager, staged smile at the jury.

Because she saw the humor of Bornstein's question, Kathleen's own smile to the jury was genuine. She raised her eyebrows. "I don't know you well enough," she concluded. She was sorry to disappoint the courtwatchers, who would have found a "yes" answer much more entertaining.

"But you might?" Bornstein did not back down.

Kathleen saw an opening. "I might," she smiled, "if you were nasty to staff or younger people or if you screamed at them over things that weren't their fault."

"And if I were a man, and I was nasty to staff, how would you describe me?"

"Objection!" Darby was on his feet. "We're way off the track here, Your Honor."

"I am showing, Your Honor, that the words used by evaluators to describe Ms. Rose are the result of sexual stereotyping. *But for* that stereotyping, Ms. Rose would have been named a partner. That's what this lawsuit is about. Because of her sex, Ms. Rose was denied partnership."

Kathleen could read on Darby's face his regret at having given Bornstein an opportunity to make a speech.

"I'll allow it, but hurry it along, Ms. Bornstein." The judge nodded to Kathleen.

"Son of a bitch?" Kathleen paused. She meant for her answer to be humorous, and a couple of the jurors grinned. "Bitchy is naggy, unpleasant, difficult. It's not gender-based. I didn't say she *was* a bitch."

Helen Bornstein shrugged her shoulders and moved on. Kathleen felt she was holding her own. But there were several hours left to go before Bornstein would make her final point, and ask the question that tortured Kathleen's soul.

"Ms. Hannigan, I have one last question. Do you believe Ms. Rose should have been named a partner?"

TWO

Q: *Ms. Hannigan, will you state your name*
for the record, please?

At five to nine on the first Monday morning in June 1976 the elevator was crowded, and when the doors to the forty-seventh floor opened, a chivalrous centrifugal force plastered the eight men in suits against its sides to let the five women out first. Kathleen Hannigan stepped out second, a Coach leather briefcase, not a nick on it, hanging from a long strap over her left shoulder, and a matching zippered purse, showing signs of more use, slung over her right.

Albright & Gill occupied six of the higher floors of what was called First National Plaza, a stone and granite building on Madison Street that swooped 57 stories into the air from a great sunken plaza on its south side. It was in the very bullseye of the city, just one block west of State and Madison, zero-zero in the numbering system. Albright & Gill's main reception area was on 47, where a young woman sat behind a dark wooden desk with a marble top, looking up whenever one of the eight elevators opened in the wide hall in front of her. To her left were two U-shaped groupings of leather sofas and chairs facing floor-to-ceiling windows; the high summer sun bounced off the city's largest boat harbor and obscured the tops of office buildings below. A young woman sat on the edge of a chair in the first grouping, nervously facing away from the view.

"Kathleen Hannigan for Mr. Farnsworth," Kitty announced to the receptionist, surprising herself with her adopted formality. When had she decided to change her everyday name? "Kathleen" had come out spontaneously, as if "Kitty" were too casual and flirtatious to be a proper name for a lawyer. The receptionist told her, in a civil but uninterested tone, to take a seat. Kathleen chose a chair opposite the woman she'd noticed earlier and immediately recognized a law school interview suit. This one was navy, with a blue, gold and white scarf tucked modestly into the V. It was moderately, but not outrageously, expensive, crisply tailored. The woman's white knuckles betrayed another case of first day jitters.

"Are you new, too?" Kathleen asked, trusting her instincts.

"Jill Alton," the woman said.

Kathleen asked her where she was from. "From," among law students, meant law school, not home, and law school was an instant indicator of rank. Jill was "from" Michigan, which, in Kathleen's book, was a top five law school, but Yale, Kathleen's school, was number one. Before they could talk further, a plump, fortyish woman stood before them.

"Kitty?" she asked. "I'm Joyce, Chas' secretary. Good to see you. Come on in."

"Old nickname," Kathleen muttered to Jill, and followed Joyce.

On Kathleen's first day at Albright & Gill, Charles Farnsworth's desk was lined with vertical columns of papers on both sides, each document showing its identity only by its letterhead sticking out from the one on top of it. Charles Farnsworth was the head of a department, and therefore had a four window office, which he was, at that level, entitled to decorate with his own furniture and to his own taste. When Kathleen had interviewed at the Firm, she had noticed that all the attorneys' offices, except the four window and corner ones, had exactly the same wooden desks, credenzas and file cabinets of a recognizably early American style. The only difference was the relative degree of order or chaos, reflecting the personality of the temporary resident. Every year or so, she had been told, the office manager would announce the office moves, the attorneys would box their things, and over a fall weekend, a moving crew would shuffle the new attorneys from interior, windowless offices to their first window, then two, then window-post-window, then window-window-post, then window-window-window, and then window-window-window-window, where all but the anointed few members of the Management Committee of the Firm (who would get a corner) would live out their time on this earth. Some of the partners were stuck at window-window-window; all of the staff were stuck behind half-wall fabric dividers at metal desks. She had been told that A&G took a reverse pride in its comparative shabbiness. While other firms were gilded in South American mahogany, Albright & Gill tended toward the look of a prudent but smugly-prosperous insurance company.

Chas' desk was really a table and it was pointedly not early American. Instead, a heavy beveled glass straddled two oblong pillars of beige marble. Three modern, stubby green fabric chairs which looked as if they were meant for a living room were placed in front of it. His suit jacket was draped on the back of his black leather swivel chair. He stood up and absently ran his fingers through his thinning gray-brown hair before holding out his hand. She sat in the chair closest to his windows.

"Would you like some coffee, Kitty?" Joyce offered.

"Great," Chas said.

"Thanks," Kathleen said, and caught herself before she stood to get it herself. She was surprised that a secretary had *volunteered* to get the coffee, and not quite sure if she should let her, but Joyce seemed more friendly than servile, and Kathleen decided, despite her feminist ideals, to follow along, at least this once. She was, after all, an attorney now, and would have to watch carefully how attorneys were supposed to act. Like an immigrant, she would need to learn the local customs before she could change them.

Chas—he never used Charles—fumbled shyly for small talk. How was Yale these days? How many girls—women—were there undergrad, now? For the head of a group, Charles Farnsworth seemed to Kathleen to be not quite sure of himself, like the red hot lover the morning after. She knew there had never been a woman in his group, but she couldn't imagine that that was an issue. Wouldn't a male and a female attorney be treated exactly the same way on the first day?

"Isn't there an orientation or something?" he asked hopefully, although he could have been expected to know that. With 24 new lawyers—six of them women—joining the Firm that day, it was a reasonable assumption.

There were currently 236 attorneys—seven of them women—in the Chicago office, and on this particular Monday in June, even the office manager would profess not to know the precise number in the Firm, counting all four of its offices. One thing was clear: her class would nearly double the number of women in Albright & Gill. How that might change an institution that referred to itself, as if there were no other, as "the Firm," remained to be seen. In fact, many of the women, whose parents, like Kathleen's, were not lawyers or financiers, did not know themselves what to expect. Like a feeder lot, law school had pushed its best and brightest to the most prestigious of the country's law firms, but it had not introduced them to the day-to-day practice of law. The least Kathleen expected was to be treated like every other first-year.

"I think the orientation's at 10:30," Kathleen answered. "Is Brian in? I'd love to say hello again." She had met Brian Weissbord, the senior associate in the group, when she had interviewed last fall.

Chas brightened. Kathleen knew she'd helped him out and they strolled down the long gray carpeted hallway to a spacious window-window office. Brian was on the phone, his feet propped on his desk, a bit of white skin showing just above the ankle. His red club tie was inexplicably askew, the long part tossed over his right shoulder as if he were about to dig into a plate of spaghetti, and his forehead shone under the fluorescent office lighting. Brian was in his early thirties, but his hairline had already receded considerably. The phone was cradled between his neck and his shoulder, leaving his hands free. He twiddled his thumbs. Kathleen almost laughed out loud—Brian actually looked physically uncomfortable in his overdone caricature of "the boss." She knew from law school gossip that most first-year lawyers found themselves not working for the big names—like Charles Farnsworth—that had attracted them to their firms in the first place, but for lieutenants, like Brian Weissbord, who were, collectively, an anxious group teetering on the brink of partnership. A slip-up by a junior associate like herself—not catching a typo, mis-citing a court decision, failing to find out that a case had been overruled—could tip the scales of law firm justice against the 30-year-old on his way to easy street.

Of the more than 400 lawyers in all the Firm's offices, all the lieutenants were men. (It would have been the same at any of the other big firms in town.) A&G's two women partners were both in the probate and estate group. One was a 60-year-old woman named Miss Parsons who had never married and had no interest in younger lawyers, even young women lawyers. She practiced alone, without lieutenants. The other, Sally Streeter, was 40 years old. Unassuming and soft-spoken, Streeter seemed genuinely excited about the incredible number of new women joining A&G. When Kathleen had interviewed at the Firm, she had met Sally, who had graduated from Yale more than 20 years before. Sally had been one of only three women in her class, but had finished in the top 10. It had been tough in Sally's day for women to find jobs in law firms— there weren't even quotas for them, like there were for Jews. When her male host had taken Kathleen to Sally's office for an interview, he had said, "I don't know what she does, exactly, but I think old Mr. Taylor brought her in. She's very sweet." There had been just a hint of condescension in his voice, a whiff of a suggestion that Sally was the pet of "old Mr. Taylor," whose name had been fifth in Albright, Gill, Moss, Lieber & Taylor before the Firm streamlined it for marketing reasons.

Chuckling into the phone, Brian waved Chas in, gesturing with his thumb and forefinger that the call would end shortly. Brian was technically a lieutenant, but at her recruiting dinner last fall, both Chas and Brian acted as if partnership were a sure thing for Brian. He expected to be elected this coming December.

Brian's phone call extended beyond his indicated smidgen to at least an inch long, during which Chas and Kathleen admired the Chicago skyline. Finally, Brian hung up, addressed Chas in a kind of shorthand, "George says Tuesday," and then held out his hand to Kathleen.

"Welcome. I certainly could use some help around here," he said.

"Got time for lunch?" At the beginning of their second week at A&G, Jill's voice was a welcome interruption. "Meet us in the lobby in five minutes."

"Us?"

"Haven't you met Ned and Harry? Ned Hazelton is corporate and Harry Blomquist is antitrust. Ned has the office next to mine. You should know Harry; he was in your class at Yale. Maybe a little older—he was a Rhodes. Don't get excited, though. I think they're both married."

At lunch, Harry looked only vaguely familiar to Kathleen. She thought she knew all 150 in her class, but she wasn't sure she'd actually seen Harry, who, with his full head of brown wavy hair, goatee, and imposing six-foot-two stature, surely would have caught her eye among the law school's otherwise slim pickings. Not only was Harry good looking, in a faintly British, portly sort of way, but he had a weary cynicism that caught Kitty off guard and tickled her, both for its timing and its content.

"So, tell me why I had to come to Albright & Gill to meet my law school classmate?" she asked Harry. They were in the Double R Saloon, a dark basement restaurant that specialized in cheap burgers with too many onions and very hot chili peppers. Since Jill hadn't warned her, Kathleen was scraping them off, hoping they wouldn't infect the fries, which were extra crispy and extra salty. Ned and Harry were the only men in the place with ties. Ned and Harry had ordered beers, so Kathleen did, too. Jill had a diet Coke.

"What a terrible joke, the law school," Harry said. "Anti-intellectual mass pedagogy, incestuous jurisprudence, two-bit intellectuals sucking each other's... well, you understand my point. Being the Moot Court chair, I presume you loved it."

She laughed. He was trying to insult her, and she wasn't sure why—although aggression was said sometimes to show affection—but he had just admitted that he had heard of her, by reputation, anyway, and had told Ned and Jill that she was chair of the Moot Court, an accomplishment of some academic ranking—and at a school like Yale, no less.

"Adored it," she said. "But only because the men were so charming."

All through June and July, the would-be new lawyers of Albright & Gill reported to their new and uncluttered offices, hoping (although it would have been against tradition) that someone would give them some serious work to do, lunched on burgers and beers in the Double R, and whiled away their afternoons in the windowless ballroom of a third tier hotel. The Firm was paying them to take a cram course for the Illinois Bar Exam. Yale, Michigan, and the other "national" law schools from which A&G recruited did a poor job of teaching the nuts and bolts—sometimes called the "black letter"—of Illinois law, and when the instructor passed out four thick yellow books of subject-matter outlines, Kathleen saw she had a lot to learn, or at least to memorize. The material itself, stripped to simple declarative sentences setting forth supposed statements of immutable law, was excruciatingly tedious, and, according to Harry, designed for the lowest level of intelligence found on earth. In the middle of the second week of class, he said the whole thing would go down better with a bourbon and branch. The next day he brought a half-pint in a brown paper bag, and sat next to Kathleen. She was thrilled with the acknowledgment that they were kindred spirits. It was arrogant of them to drink while others were hanging on the instructor's every word and at least half of the 500 bodies in the room were in serious peril of flunking, but she could not honestly imagine—given that in Illinois more than 90 percent ultimately passed—that she would not at least squeak by.

The first day, the assistant professor type who gave the "how to beat the bar exam" lecture had offered a single piece of advice that she had taken to heart. "This is not an exam you want to ace," he'd said. "You want to get a 'C.' The questions are over home plate. There are no tricks. Do not complicate the question. If it looks simple, it is. A complicated answer will only confuse the grader. Don't try to get an "A," don't try to be smarter, don't try to give a unique answer. Unique is not good in this game. Do what's expected."

Kathleen understood: they would be fed the questions, and damn near the answers.

Jill was appalled that Harry would drink and tempt Kathleen to drink while their livelihoods were on the line, but Harry scoffed. He told her to lighten up. Rumor had it that only once in recent memory had someone from A&G failed the bar exam, and no one seemed to know what had happened to him. Hedging his bets, Ned, who had both an MBA and a JD from Illinois, nursed a short one during the entire three hours.

In anticipation of passing the bar exam and of continuing to be employed by A&G, Kathleen and Jill went about the business of filling in the material difference between dorm life and real life. Because each of them had lived their whole lives in their parents' home and dorm rooms, from the weekend after they first met, Kathleen and Jill regularly shopped for all the things such unattached women needed in order to set up a domestic life of their own.

Jill had a fine glass-and-polished-chrome vision and, luckily for her, a budget to match her tastes. Prior to accepting her offer, she had asked the Firm for an advance to cover the security deposit on her one bedroom Lincoln Park apartment, and had borrowed several thousand more without interest for the incidentals, like furniture, to go in it. Kathleen, who had relied upon her parents all the way through law school, had once again turned to them for help with the rent, but she had been reluctant to borrow much extra other than the price of a mattress and box springs. Jill urged her to ask the Firm or her folks for more, but Kathleen wasn't ready to commit to furniture that exceeded her modest credit limits, and besides, VISA, unlike her parents, never demanded input on how she should spend her borrowed money and, more importantly, never criticized her taste.

On the second Sunday in her new apartment, Kathleen's parents drove in from the northwest suburbs where they lived to deliver a carload of household items they had saved in anticipation of their daughter's first city apartment. She saw their contribution as a mixed blessing, like canned spinach in a food basket for the needy: a set of plastic dinnerware dating back to Kathleen's high school years; seven NFL promotional glasses from a gas station; a shiny metal tea kettle; three woven straw trivets; a mostly cherry end table from their basement recreation room that her father had made 15 years ago from scrap lumber; a bamboo floor lamp that her mother said would "do just fine" but which Kathleen knew her mother couldn't stand; an old, white knotted bedspread, smooth in two spots on either side, and a covered measuring cup with a hand chopper. Her mother hated gadgets.

Neither of her parents had ever lived in a city or a high rise, and so they were impressed with the efficiency of Kathleen's convertible studio 35 floors above Ohio Street. Her one large room could be divided into two using a brown, accordion-pleated divider that folded out of the wall, but mostly she used it as one room. Her double bed was discreetly nestled in one corner and her new, beige-tweed three-seater couch faced the southern exposure. Her mother couldn't quite get used to the idea that Kathleen's neighbors were, essentially, in the next room, and so she whispered her suggestion that since she wouldn't want people to see her bed—(she was surprised that Kathleen would want to use up so much space with a double when they would have been happy to give her the twin she'd had in her room in high school)—she could do a better job of hiding it. Her mother thought some bookcases could be used as a room divider, making the bed less, she said, obvious.

By the week before the Bar Exam, Kathleen was feeling relatively settled. Jill was still waiting on most of her custom purchases—to be delivered in October—so they studied together at Kathleen's.

Including both weekends, the Firm gave them two weeks off—10 days, starting Saturday, for study; Tuesday and Wednesday to take the test, and the third, long weekend to recover.

The first Saturday they studied at Kathleen's dining room table. Their plan was to take a 45 minute break for sandwiches on Kathleen's roof, where they could catch a little of the July sun at its height, and then an hour-and-a-half for dinner at a neighborhood restaurant. If they started at nine, and put in a little time after dinner, they could each get in 10 solid hours, at least in theory. That was how Kathleen liked to study, in large, uninterrupted chunks. It turned out that Jill had a more staccato style, and in the morning, she got up from Kathleen's dining table every 30 minutes, to get a drink of water, go to the bathroom, make an appointment for a manicure or stare out the window. Each time she got up, Kathleen bowed her head a little deeper over her yellow books. After lunch, Jill's attention span shortened, it seemed to Kathleen, and every 20 minutes she would mutter out loud, "No, that's stupid," and then Kathleen would have to say, "What?" and Jill would explain that none of the four multiple choice answers to a question on a practice test was correct. The first two times this happened, they probably squandered half an hour on each problem, struggling to remember second-year courses and to apply the rules of the outlines, convincing each other that the practice book indeed was wrong. Each answer was flawed. The third time, Kathleen remembered the assistant professor's advice.

"It's 'A,'" she said to Jill.

"No, I just told you why it can't be," Jill said, a little too vehemently.

"Doesn't matter, remember? If two answers are clearly wrong, and two are possible but not perfect, pick "A." That's the rule. Between "A" and "B," pick "A;" between "B" and "C," pick "B," *etcetera.*"

"That's not right! How can they give credit for a wrong answer?" Jill stood up. "That makes it just a guessing game that any fool can pass!"

Kathleen looked at Jill, waiting for her to get it. When Jill continued to stew, Kathleen said, "You *have* to pick *one* of the answers."

"'B' is a slightly better answer, though," Jill said. "So what does your precious rule say about that?"

Kathleen sighed. "If enough people pick an answer, they either give credit for it or throw the question out. So, I guess we're supposed to *play the fool.*"

Jill sat down. Twenty minutes later she was again up, getting a glass of water and sputtering to herself until Kathleen again felt compelled to say, "You know what? We're going to drive each other crazy. I'm still working on which two answers could possibly be right. If I get that far, I'm just going to play the game by their rules. Please don't take this personally, but tomorrow, I think we should study alone."

Jill sat down, pouted, and then stood up again. "Yeah. I know. I make people nervous. During law school exams my roommate actually hid from me. Can we take phone breaks?" Jill asked.

"Sure," she said. It was a comfort that Jill was just a short cab ride away. They could always be there for each other in an emergency, and she was grateful for that.

Two-and-a-half months later, the Bar Examiners of the State of Illinois announced that Kathleen Hannigan and all of the new recruits at Albright & Gill had passed the most important exam of their young lives. Fools or not, they were qualified in the eyes of the State to be lawyers. In the eyes of Albright & Gill, however, they were barely qualified to proofread. All would be assigned at first the most menial of legal tasks.

One of Kathleen's first assignments as a new lawyer was for the partner, Jay Greene, who had recruited her. Jay's client was an interior decorator who drove an old Bentley around town and parked it wherever he wanted. The Bentley had attracted parking tickets like magnets—136 of them. In two years' time. The city had finally caught up with him, and, since it had just acquired those yellow boots that made getting a ticket a much riskier proposition than before, the interior decorator had one last chance to make peace with the city. A summons had been issued, and Jay asked Kathleen to appear in traffic court on his client's behalf, plead not guilty and then see a city attorney named Tommy Mack to work out a settlement.

"What's the Bentley's defense?" Kathleen had asked, naively.

"Just tell Mack you're working for me," Jay had said, and Kathleen left his office uneasy about what they don't teach you at the Yale Law School.

At traffic court, she waited while at least 100 cases were called prior to hers. Had she known better, she would have gone up to the

COURTING KATHLEEN HANNIGAN

clerk, filed an appearance on a white half-sheet form, and been called at the top of the list, as a case represented by counsel. Towards the end of the long court call, she heard her client's name, and walked to the front, where the judge seemed impatient that it had taken her so long—30 seconds?—to arrive at the podium.

The assistant state's attorney said something so fast she couldn't hear it and the judge barked, "Plea?"

"Not guilty," she said and the judge said to see the clerk. She did, was given a court date, and then went to the building directory to look for the name Tommy Mack. The halls of traffic court were teeming like a bus stations with 17 different languages, polyester suits and worry. She found Tommy Mack's office and asked to see him—he didn't give appointments. She stood for half-an-hour in the crowded waiting room that served the six or so attorneys assigned to traffic cases, and was surprised when Tommy Mack turned out to be old enough to be Jay's father. He wore a short sleeved wash-and-wear yellow shirt and a brown tie, loosely knotted.

"Thank you for seeing me. I work with Jay Greene, and he asked me to talk to you about our client...."

"How long you been a lawyer?" Tommy Mack interrupted her.

Although at Albright & Gill one always wanted to appear more experienced, more knowledgeable, and more responsible than one's actual age, Kathleen's intuition told her to be humble. Sitting in the traffic courtroom, she had seen that the Albright & Gill name was a handicap in this arena. Its fees were bound to far exceed the fines, so hiring A&G was a sure sign of guilt. Prosecutors and judges would bend over backwards to prove that the law was blind as a bat to the money and power that could hire such a law firm.

"I graduated in June," Kathleen said brightly.

"My daughter has another year," he said. "She's been going at night. Her husband watches the kids."

"That's really tough," Kathleen said. "She must be very, very smart."

Tommy Mack beamed. The fact that Tommy Mack's daughter was very, very smart was a reflection on Tommy Mack. It gave purpose to the drudgery and disappointment of his daily work.

"I suppose your client could pay face value in full?" he asked. "He'd have gas money left for the Bentley?"

"I think that would be fair," Kathleen said, not certain if Jay expected a better settlement than forgiveness of the penalties and late charges, but believing in her own heart of hearts that it was more than fair. She hesitated, not knowing how to finalize the deal.

"Should we send a check...."

"To my attention, per our agreement," Tommy Mack said.

She thanked him for his time. "Best of luck to your daughter," she said.

"And to you, young lady," he said.

"Aw, fuck," Jay said when she told him.

"Mack wasn't very sympathetic," she began in self-defense.

"Lousy bureaucrat just wants to throw his weight around. Thanks," Jay said, without much gratitude.

He picked up the phone before she could turn to leave. Despite Jay's disappointment, Kathleen left with the sense that she was at last a lawyer. It hadn't required an elite legal education to get the job done, but it had required some finesse. She hadn't exactly flirted her way to success, but she hadn't been bullied either. Overall, she felt comfortable with the balance that had come naturally to her.

"**G**oddam it!" Brian was furiously paging through Kathleen's most significant piece of work in her first six months at the Firm. Having just delivered to him 10 copies of their Federal Trade Commission brief, Kathleen had sprawled in exaggerated exhaustion in one of his visitor's chairs, waiting to be told that she was finally finished with the project. She had written the second argument in the brief, and, after letting it sit on his desk for a month, Brian had fussed with it non-stop for more than two weeks. Finally, there was no choice but for it to go out. Tomorrow was the filing deadline.

"Goddam it!"

She sprung to her feet. She understood only that there was a crisis. It was her brief, and Brian's refusal to address her suggested that the crisis was somehow her fault. She couldn't believe anything was really wrong, or *that* wrong. She had learned in the past month that Brian cried professional wolf just to get himself up for the grind of a project this substantial. He thrived on false emergencies. Kathleen was, finally, sick of it. She was sick and tired of being edited by someone whose writing she did not admire, sick of being told to tell the word processing department to rush the whole 60 page document through again, sick of proofreading minor changes only to have Brian change his mind yet again. Between them, they'd already spent several hundred hours on this project. Six different drafts had gone to the client. Seven nights she had worked until 11:00. She had given up theater tickets to her secretary. The worst of it was, she couldn't see that all that effort had made all that much difference.

"Didn't you proofread this?" Brian was beet red.

"Yes," Kathleen said, defensively. "Well, this last go 'round, I spot checked the changes."

"This is all fucked up. Dammit! Holly!" He rushed to his door and called down the hall to his secretary. "Holly, don't leave!"

"Brian, what's up? What's wrong? What can I do?"

"You could have done your goddam job. Look at this, page 43." He shoved the page at her.

Page 43 trembled in her hand. It had a smudge between the words "patently" and "absurd."

"A goddam fly," Brian said. "Don't you check your goddam work?"

She wanted to laugh at the absurdity of Brian's outrage over a smashed fly. The page was legible, for godsakes. Brian had no right to castigate her as if she had done something truly wrong. This had nothing to do with lawyering. She straightened her back and shook her hair over her shoulder, chin up.

"I took it to photocopying, Brian. I presumed they checked their own goddam work."

"It's your job, dammit, to check their work."

"I didn't go to the Yale Law School to check whether the photocopying department's got flies on its pages!" She was surprised that she had raised her voice to Brian.

"I don't give a rat's ass where you went to law school, you're the junior associate and that's your job!"

Holly appeared, smiled crookedly at the image of the squashed fly on page 43, and signaled to Kathleen to follow her.

"Brian's a nice guy, but he gets nervous," Holly explained with maternal amusement. Taking charge, she told Kathleen to get her the original page 43, that there was lots of time to make the last pick up. She talked while she worked. "He's lucky he even found it—usually he's too rushed to proofread anything. Had it been a nit instead of a gnat, he never would have seen it!" Holly laughed at her own joke. Kathleen smiled, still fuming.

"Brian's being a pig," Holly said. "He wouldn't have yelled at one of the Turks over this. He would have covered for him, and they'd be upstairs right now, having a beer. I'd be sitting here alone fixing it by myself."

Kathleen released her spine and the tension in her shoulders eased. She was grateful that Holly knew the system and how to work it to get the document out on time, was willing to stay past five, and, more importantly, saw that Brian had been unfair. As Kathleen stood by, watching Holly rerun the page, a thought struck her. Some of the secretaries, middle aged and motherly, called the aggressive, unabashed, born-partner young male attorneys at the Firm "Turks." They aggravated the hell out of Kathleen: they took themselves too seriously, and jockeyed for position around whichever senior partner was the ranking member in any given room or situation, even in the elevator. Those same senior partners barely acknowledged Jill or Kathleen or any of the other women lawyers at the Firm. Now, something in the conspiratorial tone of Holly's remark made Kathleen realize that Holly expected her, as a woman, to stay with her, to show solidarity, to prove she was not one of the Turks—that she was even better than a Turk because she wouldn't pull rank and leave Holly there alone even though there was nothing else Kathleen could do to help. It was a double bind—Kathleen herself had been mistaken three times in the past month for a secretary.

Brian stuck his head in Holly's cubicle. "Just get it out, okay, Hol?" He yelled "thanks" over his shoulder as he rushed off to catch his train to the suburbs—the goddam suburbs. Kathleen's eyes stung.

What she really wanted was to burst into tears, but she set her jaw firmly against any wobble in her voice and said, "Thanks, Holly. I'll be in my office if you need me."

When her feet didn't move, she exploded in a defiant rush of self pity. "This is really unfair," she said to Holly. "I've been locked up here for two weeks straight while *your boss* has been worrying about *flies.* He should have cared so much about his goddam grammar!" She hated the sound of her own whine and immediately regretted breaking rank with Brian. "I'm sorry Holly, I must be tired."

Having thoroughly confused herself—she felt no particular loyalty to Brian and no particular solidarity with Holly either—she left Holly filling out the forms necessary to make 10 additional copies and headed straight for Jill's office. Holly was too competent to need her later, and besides, if Brian could go home, Kathleen didn't need to sit in her office like a dunce in a corner, waiting for permission to resume her life.

Jill's office was empty, and the light was turned off. Ned, however, was in his office, next door to Jill's. Harry, chewing his pipe, sat in one of Ned's two visitor's chairs, his feet on Ned's desk. Kathleen blurted out her story, peppering it with all of Brian's goddams.

The corners of Harry's lips turned up. "All of the work we do here is dog work, Kathleen. Get over it. Bill two fucking hours to leafing through each and every page of Brian's Philistine prose. Bill three, they're small," he said, and winked at Ned. "Those aren't."

Kathleen flushed when she realized Harry was staring at her breasts.

"Never mind," Harry continued smoothly. "You should see what I'm doing. I'm cutting and pasting the same damn brief I worked on as a summer associate. This is its third time through the grinder, on a supplemental motion they've already lost twice, and the argument still sucks. I could recite the thing backwards—it would make more sense." Harry sighed, and rested his gaze again on Kathleen's silk blouse. If he meant somehow to either intimidate her or to demean her concerns as flighty and female, she resolved not to dignify his move with a direct response.

Tears welled up. "I hate this," she said.

"Of course you do!" Ned said. She was learning that nothing fazed Ned, who seemed to take all things—good and bad—in one giant stride of fatalistic acceptance. Suddenly he jumped out of his chair and grabbed his trench coat from its hook behind his door. "The wife will kill me if I miss this train," he said, and rushed out the door.

Harry didn't move. "I'm bolting if you cry," he said.

"Thanks for your support," she said as sarcastically as she could muster. She should leave, she thought, before she showed Harry any other sign of weakness. She had never been alone with him before. She sank into the second chair in Ned's office, and together Harry and she stared at Ned's blank white wall.

"It was just a goddam fly" she said. "I didn't even swear like this before I went to that damn law school." In a parody of male aggression, she put her feet up on the desk next to Harry's, aware that her skirt was riding up her thigh. She stared at him, daring him to look. It was a pretty good leg, and she hoped it intimidated the hell out of him.

Harry chuckled.

After Christmas, Albright & Gill was beginning to feel to Kathleen like the right professional choice, but she had yet to settle into a social life. As it was, her personal life consisted primarily of Friday night splurges with other young, single lawyers at the Firm who had also failed to plan their weekends. These evenings started with a phone tree at four or so, spreading the word of the original gathering place. There were only a couple of suitable places near the office, and usually a dozen or so lawyers straggled in between 5:00 and 7:00. Around 7:00, the where-to-eat talk would begin, drink money would be thrown in a pile in the center of the table, and the delighted waitress would wish them a good night. By eight, they would be in line for dinner—pizza or Mexican or Chinese or one of those hamburger joints with hanging ferns—and at 10:00 they went dancing at a favorite disco. It was at the last bar that the group began to split up, lucky and not, and a hard core of three to five of them would collapse around midnight into a cab making several stops. If it got later than one, they went to breakfast to spare themselves having to wake up early. More often than not, Kathleen was part of the late-night pack. Ned, of course, went home to his wife after cocktails. Jill would leave before dinner. Harry rarely joined them.

On Saturday morning Kathleen slept until mid-morning, then "cleaned" her apartment, throwing out a brown edged head of lettuce and an occasional carton of separated cottage cheese. After tending to these modest domestic chores, she would call her mother to report that things were fine, and to listen to half-an-hour's worth of neighborhood news. Then, most often, she would head to the office. Sometimes, in the afternoon, she and Jill would play racquet ball, although neither one of them was particularly good at it. There was a health club on the third floor of Kathleen's apartment building, and discounted membership was a perk of residency. At 135 pounds on an average frame, Kathleen had a nice enough figure, although she thought her thighs were a bit flabby and her stomach could be flatter. While the health club was easily available to her and would have been the perfect antidote to the sedentary life of a young, library-bound lawyer, on many nights Kathleen simply didn't have the will or the incentive to get there.

Saturday nights tended to repeat Fridays, but with a smaller crowd. Rarely did she have a date, and none worth repeating. At 11:00 on Sunday mornings she met Jill at a pancake house in Jill's neighborhood. They had only two topics: career and men. Kathleen felt a bit like a traitor to the women's movement every time she voiced her grievances. She had, after all, chosen to put career first, and she could've chosen a less demanding place to work. She didn't need a man to make her life full, she would declare to Jill, and Jill, pulling on her earlobe, would say, "Hmm."

THREE

Louder, for the record.

At the beginning of her second year of practice, Chas asked Kathleen to help Brian and him to set up a national distribution system for a foreign car manufacturer. The client's General Counsel, George Fennel, a chubby faced and otherwise flabby bachelor in his 40s, was a Yale Law graduate, and apparently Chas thought that Kathleen's involvement would appeal to him on several levels. Chas was of a minimalist school of drafting that prided itself on what was left unsaid. This was not a very useful trait for a lawyer trying to bring a certain regimented order to a myriad of relationships, which had to mesh in their every detail to make the whole system work. George, in contrast, wanted to anticipate every potential misfire at every turn of the industrial wheel, and to write specific prose for every "what-if." Chas and George, who thoroughly enjoyed each other's arcane intelligence and ironic discourse over cocktails, were incompatible at the drafting table, and Kathleen was meant to bridge the gap between their styles. She didn't understand enough about warehouse financing, customs inspections and FOB charges to simplify as much as Chas might have, so George appeared satisfied. For his part, Chas liked her direct and simple, non-legal prose, and for the first time in what was now 12 months of practice, Kathleen felt that she was contributing something significant to the success of the project.

"This calls for a nice lunch," Chas announced as Kathleen delivered 15 bound copies of the final distribution, warehousing and cooperative advertising agreements to the conference room where the four lawyers had spent the week. "One o'clock. Let's go upstairs."

Chas, Brian, George and Kathleen took the elevator to the fifty-seventh floor, the Downtown Club. Although the Club topped a modern skyscraper, it replicated with excruciating exactitude an early twentieth-century gentlemen's club, all dark wood and leather and Oriental rugs. In fact, the Club was older than Albright & Gill itself, and more conservative—it had yet to admit women members.

The maitre d' greeted Chas. "Mr. Farnsworth, how nice to see you," he began. "Oh," he stammered when he saw Kathleen, "let's see." The gentlemen's gentleman lowered his voice and said something to Chas that Kathleen couldn't hear. Chas bit his lower lip.

"Joyce forgot to get a private dining room, Kathleen. I'm sorry. We'll meet you about 2:30 back in 40A?" His voice had a false cheer to it. He turned his attention to George. "Women are allowed, of course, but only in the private rooms, and they're all taken." Under raised eyebrows, Chas's eyes begged her not to make a fuss. Brian was paying no attention and was greedily scanning the dining room for familiar, and, if he were lucky, important faces.

She turned on her charm, and said with fake aplomb, "No problem. I'll see you all later." She wanted to add, "have a nice lunch," but stopped short. She waited for the elevator, not looking back. The lawyers would be heading for their table.

Alone in the elevator, she punched the "close door" button repeatedly. "Come on!" Her cheeks burned the way they had the day she'd first visited Yale. After the drive down from her college in Providence, she'd stopped a guy in the hall for directions to the ladies room. "There isn't one," he had said. Even if he'd meant it as a joke, his tone had been surprisingly hostile. Now, muttering to herself that women were allowed only if hidden in a private room, all she wanted was to get away from the Club as fast as possible, and she headed for Jill's office.

She closed Jill's door and sobbed.

"I can't believe Chas would let that happen," Jill said after hearing Kathleen's story. "I would've thought he'd refuse to stay. He just told you to get lost?"

"He didn't say, 'get lost.' I guess he didn't want to make a fuss in front of the client."

"I think he owes you and owes you big."

"What does that mean? He doesn't owe me, personally, anything! I could care less about the lunch, as lunch. It's a political question. Why does he belong to such a place?"

"Almost all the partners belong to the Downtown Club. You have to admit, it's convenient." Sometimes, Jill was too accepting for Kathleen's taste. Jill had grown up outside South Bend, Indiana, and her dad was on the engineering faculty at Notre Dame. Her mother raised a few chickens in their backyard. She wasn't sure why, but somehow those two factors seemed to explain Jill perfectly.

"You'd have to believe that if the Firm told the Club to change, they'd change the rules, right?" Kathleen said, with the sudden, cold realization that maybe the Firm *didn't* object to the Club's policy.

"Maybe it hasn't come up before," Jill said. But they both knew that there were two women partners and at least a few female associates who'd been at the Firm for a year or more longer than they—the issue must have come up before. It certainly should have.

They stared at each other, thinking their own thoughts. "Ever feel like we're not quite wanted here?" Kathleen said.

"Maybe it's just that we're kind of new, yet. You know, they haven't had that many women around before this," Jill said.

"Don't you feel that we're at a disadvantage, that we're not perceived as real lawyers?"

"Not if we do good work, Kitty." Jill said, slipping into her friend's nickname. "They don't make partners based on lunching."

"I'm not so sure," Kathleen said.

Later, after their afternoon session and the client had left, Chas came by Kathleen's office on his way home for the day. "Sorry about the lunch bit," he said. "I know it's Neanderthal."

"Don't worry about it. No problem, really. I'll know better next time."

It was, really, a problem, but she hadn't had the guts to say so to Chas's face. It occurred to her that she probably would have to become a partner at A&G in order to have any chance of changing a place like The Downtown Club. She called Harry to see if he wanted to get a drink. Harry's secretary said he was upstairs at the Club with Blake Mills, the Managing Partner.

"That's P-E-N-I-S." Sitting in a library carrel where the Firm kept its research computer, Kathleen was startled by the lips next to her ear. It was a precious fall Saturday—crisp, but sunny enough to shake the sailboats out of the harbors for a final tack along the lake front. She should've resented the assignment that had caused her to cancel all her weekend plans, including driving with her folks to Wisconsin to see the leaves on Sunday, but her mother was impressed that the Firm needed her daughter so badly. Her mother would not have been so understanding, Kathleen thought, if she knew the half of it.

Anthony, the famous music promoter, had been depicted in the nude in an illustration in a parody magazine. Anthony was outraged, and wanted his lawyer, Jimmy Logan, to sue the publishers for all they were worth.

Jimmy Logan was the only African-American partner in the law firm of Albright & Gill. He had been with the government for 20 years, and the Management Committee of Albright & Gill had recruited him to join their ranks because they wanted to be known as a progressive firm. Jimmy Logan, however, was more than a token. He attracted a celebrity client base that included prominent African-American athletes, music moguls, minority controlled banks and other business enterprises that the Firm had previously ignored. Although Jimmy was brilliant, he had spent most of his career with the Small Business Administration and therefore was totally inexperienced in the sports and entertainment law his clients needed. Chas' group of lawyers had been asked to assist Jimmy with those aspects of his clients' needs. Kathleen had already done one small project for Jimmy. She was thrilled to be doing another.

"Or you could try D-I-C-K or...."

"P-R-I-C-K," she turned around. "How did you know?"

"Many are called. Few are chosen," Harry said. "I was in Blake's office, talking about real legal issues pending before the FCC, when Jimmy called to report his little dick problem."

"Oh, defamation!" Kathleen said brightly. "I hadn't thought of that angle. Like maybe the picture shows it too little!" She laughed. "I'm not having a whole lot of luck."

"Fuck luck."

"Stop it!" Kathleen sometimes got tired of Harry's deliberate profanity, but she did adore him, for reasons she didn't exactly understand. Harry was almost 30 years old, had the beginnings of a paunch, and his goatee was beginning to gray. Slight bags under his hazel eyes gave him a sad look, the look of a disillusioned idealist disappointed to have found so early in life that this was, indeed, all there was to it. He worked with the drive of a perfectionist on matters he didn't give one whit about. He once told Kathleen that he had married hastily, out of the loneliness of being a graduate student in Britain. "It was existential panic," he'd said, " I didn't think anyone better—anyone at all—would come along. Poor thing, I'm sure she felt the same." His wife now traveled almost continually as a consultant, and they had been legally separated for six months. Harry said they were working on the divorce, which, ironically, required them to be together long enough to work out an agreement. He vacillated between the despair of his isolation and the exhilaration of it.

"How long are you going to be here?" Harry asked.

Kathleen stared at the screen containing the list of cases which contained the word "penis" or its equivalent. There weren't that many she had to read, once she eliminated the rape cases, and then what she had to do was to draft a credible complaint.

"My biggest problem is that I've never drafted a complaint. Or a memorandum in support of an injunction. I don't suppose that one brief you've filed 14 times would be useful to me?"

"No, but I could buy you dinner."

"I'm sure that would please your wife."

"Legally separated, remember? Besides, she's out of town. Again. I'm staying downtown for a couple of days. Eight at Le Titi?"

Kathleen could feel red, nervous splotches prickling the skin underneath her sweatshirt. "Good one! I'm not dressed for," she scrunched her nose to make her voice nasal, "Le Titi."

"Then get dressed. I'll be waiting."

A t 7:00 p.m., Kathleen was sitting in her office, furiously scribbling the first draft of her first complaint against those magazine publishers whose sense of humor was, in the words of her law suit, "depraved." She was writing all kinds of inflammatory prose about the publisher's lack of respect for personal privacy and the dignity of the human body, most of which she didn't believe. She was a fanatic advocate of freedom of expression and the First Amendment and, had he been her own personal client, she would have told Anthony that in the entertainment business, there's no such thing as bad press. She came to the last line, "Respectfully submitted," and wrote, "James Logan." She read it over and then added underneath, "Kathleen Hannigan." She left the document with a long note for the secretary who would be in at 9:00 a.m., left the office and hailed a cab.

Her high rise was a five minute cab ride from the office. It would be another five or 10 to Le Titi if she dared to show up. She immediately headed for the shower, letting the hot water knead her aching shoulders. What she should do tonight is sketch out the memorandum in support of the motion for an injunction. She should shower, order a pizza and at least write out the standards for when someone can get a court to order a defendant to stop doing whatever it is that someone finds so offensive. Harry—it must have been Harry—had left on her desk a copy of a brief in a totally unrelated case that set forth in sterile, usable language the applicable law in the Northern District of Illinois. It would be a good starting place, and she should start now. She stepped out of the shower.

She toweled off and drenched herself in Shalimar. She stood stark naked in the walk-in closet, which, in the style of city high rises catering to single folks, was larger than her kitchen. She hadn't had a real date since moving to Chicago almost a year-and-a-half ago, and she hadn't had sex in that long, either, with the exception of two weekend flings, both of which she'd met at the end of a Friday night group outing.

In truth, she hadn't dated all that much, at least not as much as she considered normal. Her mother had told her, back in high school, not to worry about it, that high school boys were just boys, and it would be different when she got to college. By the time she got to college, it was 1969, and dating was dead. She had a crush or two on men, one of whom had declared her his "best friend," and her mother had advised her, in their Sunday night phone call, to get her degree. There was plenty of time for men after college. In her senior year one of her buddy's girlfriends dropped him and he turned to her by default. She got a boyfriend, they had sex and Kathleen thought she was a normal person. She had gone off to Yale and he to Harvard and within months they were too busy to maintain a real relationship, but every couple of months they'd see each other for a weekend, with the bittersweet knowledge that they were drifting apart but needed each other's familiar and easy sexual comfort. Her "boyfriend" eventually found a Radcliffe undergraduate and they stopped seeing each other. She occasionally went out with a Yale medical student or a graduate student, and while she would sleep with them, they both knew it was more physical than romantic. It was the '70s.

Was this a date, if you worked with the guy, if you met him there, if he happened to ask you because you were both at work and he was lonely because his *wife*—from whom he was legally, but technically not yet separated—was out of town? She shouldn't treat it as a date. She should dress down. They were just friends. In law school, she had gotten in the habit of thinking of herself as a buddy—the men had been preoccupied with classes, they were next-door-neighbors in the dorm, they were fellow *Law Journal* editors, they were Moot Court competitors. As a student, she had been their equal. How equal would she be now if she couldn't have dinner with her friend and colleague, Harry Blomquist?

Shivering as she surveyed her closet, she said, "It's not like you have hundreds of choices, Kitty." She only talked to herself when she was nervous. Why should she be nervous? If it were a date, she would have told Jill, instead of "forgetting" to tell her when she had called earlier at the office to see if she wanted to get a pizza. She'd said no, she was just going to plug away at the brief. Of course, Jill had believed her.

It was 8:05 when Kathleen got out of the cab, in a long-sleeved black angora dress with a high cowl neck and A-line skirt.

"If this is a joke, Blomquist, I'll have to kill you," she muttered to herself.

The maitre d' assumed who she was. "Ms. Hannigan? Mr. Blomquist will be so pleased."

"Ravishing, my dear," Harry said, putting down his drink and standing when the captain swerved the table out so she could sit next to him in the high backed, curved booth. A single red rose lay on her service plate. They were in the furthest corner of the small restaurant.

"Chivas on the rocks for the lady," he said.

Kathleen was totally disarmed. No one had ever, ever, greeted her in such a manner. The waiter returned with two drinks, and whisked away Harry's first.

"A rose!" she started to say. He shushed her, urgently placing his forefinger on her lips, and then tracing her chin line to her ear. He gently pulled her towards him and then placed his lips on her forehead.

"Harry," she started to object, because she was supposed to object.

"Hush," he said. "I've been waiting for this evening for a long, long time." He raised his drink in toast to her. Kathleen was startled to see his eyes water.

"Harry, we can't…."

Harry took a goodly swallow. "Of course." He ordered another round, and the lobster bisque and the spinach salad and the veal chop and didn't ask her first. He conversed with the wine steward in self-effacing French.

Kathleen switched to her familiar role, the one she knew the best. It came easily to her to talk current cases and law firm politics and law school reminisces. During dessert—a splendid white chocolate mousse with raspberries—Kathleen felt Harry's hand under her skirt. He squeezed her thigh, and sighed. "I was afraid of that. No one wears garter belts these days."

"Harry, you are a nut case," Kathleen laughed nervously, without even wondering how many thighs he'd felt to find that out. "I don't think they even make them anymore. This *is* the twentieth century."

She'd had enough scotch to forget Harry's wife, and was both afraid that he was making fun of her and hoping that he was not.

"I'm not amused by political promulgations. Next time, my dear, wear your garters like a proper lady." At 11:00, Harry signed the check, rode Kathleen home in a cab and gave her a sad and longing look, as well as a kiss on her neck. "Next time," he said, "a black garter belt."

K athleen's carrel in the library was just as she had left it 12 hours before. The building guard looked at her a little funny when she signed in at the security desk just after seven, a bag of chocolate donut holes and a giant coffee in hand. She was wearing her favorite working clothes, jeans and an old, fraying fisherman's sweater over a flannel shirt, no bra. She hadn't slept well, and woke up once with the distinctly hot sensation of orgasm. She should be tired and hung-over but she was neither. She was both furious with Harry for toying with her emotions, and burning with reluctant desire. She wished she had time to find a real boyfriend.

At the moment, she had a brief to write. She took a fresh legal pad and wrote her three main arguments, one to a page. Then she sorted through the cases she had photocopied the day before, and put paper clips on the good quotes. Then she started to write, and every hour or so she would get up, stretch, walk down the hall to check on the overtime secretary's progress, and take a stroll down to Jill's office, begging her to be there.

When Jill hadn't shown up by noon, Kathleen called her at home, thinking maybe Jill was lucky enough not to have to come in that Sunday. Jill didn't answer. When she went by Jill's office at one, Jill still wasn't in, but Kathleen heard shouts in the big conference room. She stuck her nose in, and found half-a-dozen young male associates watching the Chicago Bears play Green Bay. Each of the guys had a document or a book or a legal pad. All but one had beers. Three huge pizzas were on the marble table. She grabbed a slice and stared at the screen for a few minutes.

"Seen Harry?" Ned asked. They were still junior enough to expect that they would all be working every day of every weekend.

"Yesterday. Why?"

"No reason. Just that since the wife is out of town, what else does he have to do? Unless of course, he got lucky last night."

Kathleen hoped Ned was just fooling around, that Harry hadn't been stupid enough to say anything to anybody about last night. Or had he? Was he the type who would cover his tracks with complete honesty? No, she decided, there hadn't been time.

"Blomquist?" John was suddenly interested in their conversation. Kathleen didn't like John Watkins, the fat prep school corporate lawyer who had quickly defined himself not only as a go-getter, but as the class gossip as well. John got under Kathleen's skin more than any of the Turks, and it stung a little when he said, "A girl would have to be pretty desperate for Blomquist to get lucky."

Ned laughed his good natured laugh.

"Got that right, John," Kathleen said.

J ill was the second lawyer to arrive Monday morning on the forty-seventh floor, but Kathleen didn't know that until, on her third trip back to her office from the coffee machines, she noticed Jill's door was closed. She knocked and it opened immediately. Ned was sitting in one of two visitor's chairs, crammed against the wall within easy reach of the doorknob.

He cleared his throat and appeared to continue his conversation. "Randy says we've got something unique here and I ought to switch to asset based financing instead of securities."

"Too early," Kathleen said. She meant too early for shop talk. Ned took her differently.

"Randy says that if you're going to change departments, you should do it early. Otherwise, he says, you lose too much time in your class."

"Well, yeah, that too," she said, curious that Randy Randolph, a tax lawyer from Harvard who was in their class, was being quoted by Ned as an authority on career. Ned had smarts and street sense and an easy, if vanilla, personality. Randy's smarts seemed rather pasted on to his shy West Virginia personality, and his perceived wisdom derived from his usual silence. Kathleen was sure that

Ned, Harry, and even John, the gossip, heeded Randy's advice because he so rarely gave it.

"So, Jill, we missed you yesterday. What's up?" Kathleen asked.

"Later," Ned said, in a sudden rush. "Gotta bill some hours."

"Don't forget to do a little work while you're at it," Kathleen said. Ned closed the door behind him, and Kathleen had the uneasy feeling that there was a secret she wasn't being told.

"Are you OK?"

Jill's hair was pulled back in a gold barrette, which meant she hadn't bothered with her heat rollers. She was wearing a little too much blush, and the bit of color in her pale foundation couldn't hide the dark circles under her eyes.

"I'm fine. Make sure Ned's not there," Jill said.

Kathleen stared at her. "I don't think he's eavesdropping, if that's what you mean."

"The worst thing happened," Jill began. "I can't tell you. Please don't tell anyone." Kathleen knew Jill was going to tell her, but apparently she hadn't told Ned.

"I had a date with Randy Saturday."

"He called you? When? Wow, I didn't think he had the guts, you know, wouldn't be good for his career," Kathleen blurted out her disbelief and immediately caught the essence of Jill's concern. "Not that anyone here would care, I don't think," she added, not sure if she thought they would or not.

"No, he didn't call me, and we didn't mean to...." Jill was struggling not to cry. Debbie, a friend at another firm, had called Jill on Saturday afternoon. Debbie had a new boyfriend, who had a friend, and Jill had agreed to have dinner with them. All Debbie had known about the guy was that he was a lawyer.

Jill had been shocked when she and Debbie arrived at the French country bistro on Clark Street and Debbie's boyfriend introduced his friend, Randy. She said the first thing that had popped into her head was that Randy would come back to the Firm and tell John, who would tell everyone, that she was so hard-up for a date that she'd accepted a Saturday afternoon fix-up. Or worse yet, that Randy would think that she had plotted with Debbie to be fixed up with him. Jill was not, definitely not, she said to Kathleen, interested in dating anyone she met at Albright & Gill. She couldn't help but feel that Randy had been disappointed, too, and that he'd not wanted to be seen with her.

"I don't know what happened." Jill buried her face in her hands, sucked in a breath and told her story. Kathleen found it a little hard to believe. Apparently, they had gone back to Debbie's apartment to watch *Saturday Night Live* and Arnie had casually lit a joint and passed it to Randy, who had taken a few drags and passed it to Jill. At this point, they'd already had two pitchers of Harvey Wallbangers and a bottle of French wine.

"God, I shouldn't drink!" she said.

"You didn't!"

Jill didn't answer.

"Oh my god," Kathleen said in a low and serious tone. No one had said the associates shouldn't date, but still, Kathleen and Jill had agreed that it would be better to keep one's personal life out of the office. Jill looked like she might throw up, and Kathleen rushed to put things in some kind of perspective, feeling herself flushed and breathless. She and Harry had only flirted, but deliberately. These two had just stumbled into bed, except it was on Debbie's floor.

"What if I'm pregnant?"

"Oh my god, I hadn't even thought of that." Kathleen sounded to herself adolescent in a way she'd never been adolescent. She was on the pill and had assumed Jill was, too. "Why didn't you call me yesterday?"

Jill didn't answer, looking at Kathleen as if she were a child who kept whining "why?" long after the mommy had made it clear there were no further explanations. "I wasn't home much," Jill said.

"Oh." Kathleen tried not to look alarmed.

"I got home around noon, and Randy came down here. I fell asleep until five, when Randy came over with all the fixin's for Southern Fried Chicken. He wanted to show me how to make it. He left early this morning. I wasn't even awake, really. I still don't know how to fix chicken."

Kathleen thought Jill's story wasn't all that bad. At least Randy was a peer, not a partner. It was a large firm. No one would have to know.

"What if it gets around…?" Jill moaned.

"Who's going to tell? Randy won't. Did you tell Ned?"

"No! And don't you, ever! That's the last thing I need!"

"So, if I were you, I'd just have a good time for a while."

"No! I have to break it off."

There was a knock on the door.

"Yes," Jill said. Randy stuck his head in and Kathleen immediately stood up to leave.

"Next!" she said lightly. He said good morning as she walked by him out the door, but he didn't look straight at her. When she was gone, he closed the door.

"And this is?" Leonard Stonehill, the legendary litigator, was flipping through the pages of her draft in the penis case. She and Jimmy had come to Leonard's outlandish office on the fiftieth floor. It was mirrored along one wall and the ceiling and anchored by a semicircular cream-colored soft leather couch so low to the ground that one could easily roll off into dense matching cream carpeting as thick and plush as a polar bear. "Post-modern bordello," Harry once had called it. This was who a young associate could aspire to be when he or she grew up. It was who you were if you were bigger than Albright & Gill and could be whoever you wanted—that's how much business Leonard Stonehill brought to the Firm, and presumably, could take *from* the Firm if his fellows on the Management Committee didn't like his office décor.

"This is the lady who wrote this for me." Jimmy rather innocently always gave the credit for other people's work to other people. "She's my expert!"

Kathleen smiled at Jimmy's use of the word "lady," but didn't know how to correct him. She was more worried about being called an expert when all she knew she'd learned over the weekend.

"Hmmm." With a flourish, Leonard circled something on the brief. He peered over wire rimmed half-glasses that Kathleen thought looked more like a fashion statement than a medical one. "We can work with this," he said. "Have Marshall clean it up, file it and we'll get ready to go. This afternoon."

They left without Leonard knowing Kathleen's name. "Who's Marshall?" Jimmy asked.

"I think he means Marshall Long, the senior associate in his group."

"Okay. You do whatever it takes. I'm calling Anthony. We'll get those bastards."

Kathleen didn't know what Leonard wanted "cleaned up," but she sought out Marshall.

"Damn," Marshall said. "I hope this doesn't stink." He didn't say "stink" in a mean way, but a hopeful one. Mostly he sounded tired and not interested in fixing anything.

Tall and lean, Marshall looked to Kathleen a little less corporate and a little more academic than most of the Firm's trial lawyers. He was plenty starched, however, and his white shirt nearly crackled as he took the brief from her and dropped it in the center of his desk. It was his hair, tousled in a way that looked fresh off a sailboat that marked him as outside the smooth, unruffled Albright & Gill mold. He would be her type, she thought, but for the gold wedding band on his left hand.

There were file boxes against the walls of his window-window office, and several precise piles of papers on his credenza—what might be called a moderately, but not compulsively, neat office. Two etchings framed in bronze were his sole wall decorations, both old-English legal prints of wigged barristers, the kind of thing proud parents give their sons to acknowledge their admission to the bar. They were in good, if old-fashioned taste, and, Kathleen thought, they revealed nothing about the son other than that he was dutiful enough, or indifferent enough, to display them. It didn't occur to her that he might have chosen the etchings himself.

"I'll take it from here," Marshall said.

At two, Leonard and Marshall led the way to courtroom 204 at the Federal Courthouse. Jimmy and Kathleen had to hurry to keep up with the litigators' long, confident strides. The courtroom was jammed with reporters, who were disappointed that Anthony, the star, was not with his lawyers. A couple of white reporters recognized Leonard and sidled up to him, notepads closed by their sides, as if to hide their desire for a private quotable quote. Leonard chatted confidentially with them while Jimmy nodded to an African-American reporter at the far end of the courtroom. Jimmy gave Kathleen a little push as they worked their way to the counsel's table.

There were three chairs. Kathleen opened her briefcase and took out a stack of cases she had copied and highlighted in yellow. She felt a little of the Moot Court rush she had enjoyed in law school and wished that it was her case to argue. She was, after all, the one who had spent her weekend—most of it anyway—preparing. She was well into her fantasy, *May it please the court*, when Marshall put his briefcase on the table and said bluntly, "Sit there," pointing to the first row of spectator seats behind the lawyer's table.

"But I have the cases," she started to protest, when the clerk said, "All rise." She was steamed. Marshall Long knew the least about the case of any of them. She looked at the defendant's table and saw six men, two at least as young as she, crowded around their table. Perhaps Marshall was only being strategic. Maybe Albright & Gill did not want to publicly admit that a woman had worked on such a sensitive case. Well, at least her name was on the brief. She flipped to the last page of the "as filed" copy that Jimmy had given her on the way over. *"Respectfully submitted, Leonard Stonehill, James Logan and Marshall Long."*

She fumed all through the hearing, her neck flushed red with anger. Who had decided to take her name off? Everybody knew that the last name, the junior name, was always the name of the person who had done the real work, the person who had lost a weekend to research and writing and photocopying. Was this Marshall's way of stealing credit for something he didn't do? She'd seen briefs with four or even five names before. Would they have taken a man's name off?

In what seemed like only minutes, the judge ruled, and outside the courtroom, Leonard said a few self-congratulatory words to the television cameras, this time standing next to a smiling Jimmy Logan. They trudged the few blocks to Albright & Gill, and Leonard regaled Jimmy with stories of past victories. Marshall followed a step behind the two partners but in front of Kathleen. Equality in the workplace apparently prevented Marshall from offering to carry her oversized trial case. She understood that the less you carried into court, the higher your status, but she thought that by giving up her weekend, she had at least earned the right not only to have her name on the brief, but also to sit at that counsel's table. On the way back to the office, the trial case felt heavier than before, and she stopped to switch it from her left arm to her right. The lawyers in front of her hurried on.

She caught up with them as they waited for the elevator, and Jimmy said, "Here, let me take that for you."

The offer was ludicrous, but her shoulders were sore. "Thanks, Jimmy, but Marshall here asked first." She handed the trial case to a startled Marshall, and stepped out of the elevator ahead of them, forcing the three lawyers to remember another part of their upbringing. Part of her wanted to confront Marshall directly about the brief, but part feared that if she complained, he and Jimmy would cut her out of future cases for Anthony. And Anthony's cases were more interesting to her than automobile distribution systems. In Jimmy's office, Kathleen felt a tinge of pleasure when Jimmy and Leonard couldn't get Anthony directly on the phone. He was "not available," and his administrative assistant said she would pass on the word of their victory.

FOUR

Q: *What is your occupation?*

All the time she was growing up, Kathleen had been waiting for a time when she would feel normal. Normal people got normal grades in school and got into normal amounts of trouble. They went out with boys and went to proms and worried their parents when they stayed out past curfews. Her mother was fond of saying that Kathleen had never given her a lick of trouble.

"I can't imagine your wanting to move so far away from us," her mother was saying on the phone. The penis victory was a couple of months behind her and Kathleen was facing a second holiday season without a boyfriend. She needed a shock to the routine of her life. She floated the idea of a move while she talked to her mother on the phone for the second time that week, her father's bowling night. East or West, she said, she wasn't particularly fussy, as long as there was a big body of water.

"Of course, you should do what is best for your career," her mother said. "Maybe it would be easier some place else."

Her mother said "easier" as if it was something to be ashamed of. Kathleen had not said there was anything wrong with her career or that there was any need for things to be "easier." Her mother had made up that part, knowing exactly how to get her to do what she wanted her to do without having to ask her directly.

This was the place in their frequent conversations where Kathleen could cradle the phone against one ear and load her dishwasher, scour the kitchen sink, wipe a heel mark off the kitchen floor. Reminding Kathleen that she was an adult and old enough to make her own decisions, her mother would reminisce at length about how beautiful she had been as a baby. To hear her mother tell it, as an infant she had never even cried—just slept, ate and smiled. She had golden curls and blue eyes and the sweetest personality, and hadn't been at all jealous when her baby brother was born, the same month that she turned five.

Of course, her mother would say, Michael had been a good baby, too, sleeping though the night, not fussing when Kathleen had picked him up or tried to play with him. Her mother would say that much, and then switch the subject, as if Michael's death was none of Kathleen's concern.

Kathleen did not remember that much about baby Michael, although in retrospect she saw more and more clearly how his death, when she was only six, had changed the tone of her family even more than his birth. To her five-year-old eyes, Michael Daniel was a squirmy little thing whose arrival had made her "daddy's big girl," and he had looked a lot like the baby brothers and sisters her friends had. They only had the baby for a year, and when it was gone, she had delighted in her daddy's seemingly undivided attention. Every night that first summer, her father would pitch balls at Kathleen in the backyard, first for catch, and then baseball, and then tennis. They would play until it was too dark to see the balls, her father coaching, instructing her with each pitch or toss. He had a quick eye and could tell her precisely what she had done wrong each time.

The next summer he put up a basketball hoop over the garage door. This she could practice by herself, and because the hoop was stationary and the ball large, Kathleen thought she should be able to make a free throw every time, if, as her father told her, she put her mind to it. She would practice alone for an hour after supper, and then she would call him to watch. She knew it would please him if she could make five shots in a row. He always seemed to her, like her mother, so disappointed.

Now, Kathleen promised her mother that she wouldn't leave Chicago without discussing it with her first.

Which is why it made her doubly angry the next day, when she stopped by Jill's office and found her packing brown file boxes.

"I had a few talks with Sally, and I think I'll like their practice better. It's more personal. Less political. I can do my work and not have to worry so much about partnership. It's a smaller group, so they watch out better for their associates." Jill didn't look up.

Kathleen didn't know what to say. Something about Jill's move to the Probate and Estate Department didn't feel right. What could possibly be so fascinating about a bunch of old people trying to control their children's lives from the grave? Wouldn't it be more exciting to be the first woman partner in the A&G's Corporate Department? Did Jill want to do something easier? What made Kathleen think estate planning would be easier? The fact that the only women partners in the Firm were in this group? Damn! That was just the kind of thinking that made the prestige of a practice area dependent on how few women were in it! Kathleen didn't like herself when she thought this way, but she was annoyed with Jill for not toughing it out, for not having the drive to want to set a Firm precedent.

It hurt Kathleen's feelings that Jill had made the decision to leave the Corporate Department without consulting with her. For the past year and a half of their friendship, Kathleen thought they had told each other everything—except, of course, about that evening with Harry.

Jill flipped through a black binder and then put it in a box marked storage. She studied the next binder on her bookshelf. Once or twice before, Kathleen had seen her friend retreat like this into a protective shell of intense concentration on some trivia. The first time, Kathleen had battered away at it, trying to cheer Jill out of whatever sadness was preoccupying her that day. That was a while ago, and Kathleen had forgotten why Jill was upset. Probably Jill had, too, but at the time, Jill had shouted at her, "leave me alone."

Later, Jill told her that she would have liked for her to stay with her, but she didn't want Kathleen to insist on trying to cajole her out of her bad mood. "When that happens, just let me be," Jill had advised.

"You don't feel like bashing the corporate stereotype?" she risked asking, although she didn't want to alienate her best friend.

"We're not all as competitive as you," Jill said.

"I'm not competitive!"

"You sure are! Listen to yourself some Friday when you and Harry get into it!" Jill and Kathleen locked eyes.

"You'd rather I took his crap?" Kathleen blushed. The truth was, she loved Harry's crap, and their arguments were all sport, all affection.

"I'd rather you admit you're competitive."

"So why are you picking on me? It's not my fault the corporate group is hard on women." Kathleen looked away.

Jill let the silence continue to sting, and then relented. "Because," Jill said, stretching out her arms, "you're close by." They hugged.

"Want to practice your estate planning on me?" Kathleen said, by way of apology.

"Are you planning to die?" Jill said.

"Eventually," Kathleen said, although, like most people under thirty, she didn't believe it.

"Rich?" Jill asked.

"Filthy," Kathleen said. She couldn't quite imagine having that much money, but that was the direction they were headed, if they stayed at A&G. And staying was the game. Those who left before partnership were the weak, culled from the back of the pack by the very fittest of Darwin's survivors. Yes, staying would be the key. Kathleen looked at Jill's packed boxes and, once again, felt just a bit superior. Her parents took such pride in the sacrifices they had made—the middle-class, foregone European vacation sort of sacrifices—in order that she could go East and get an education, that Kathleen could not imagine disappointing them. She had their pride to uphold. No, *she* wouldn't leave her department for an easier practice.

A few days before Kathleen's second Christmas at the Firm, she got a call from Sally Streeter, the younger of the two women partners in Jill's new department, inviting her to lunch. When she went by her office to pick Sally up, Kathleen was impressed that Sally had progressed to window-window-window and had a lovely northern view. She noticed, however, that nothing in the office suggested that it was occupied by a woman. There were two art prints on the largest wall, both abstract, and an Ansel Adams photograph on the other. The volumes on her bookcase were neatly arranged, and apparently all of her active files were hidden in the credenza drawers. It was a neatness Kathleen had come to associate with the offices of people who were either not very busy, like people on vacation, or extremely anal, like tax lawyers.

"I envy you girls—young women—coming up now," Sally said over her special garden salad. "I see you in the library and in the elevators, and you all seem so sure of yourselves. You fit right in with the men. You, especially, Kathleen. I've been at the Firm now 17 years, and, outside of the Probate and Estates bar, I don't have the kind of relationships with my peers that you seem to. Oh, when Mr. Taylor was around, I think they felt that they had to accept me, but I guess I never developed those ties because, well, I didn't have to. Parsons was the only other woman, and in the same boat I was, except she didn't seem to care. Now, I don't know how. I thought you might be able to help me."

Kathleen was astounded. No one at Albright & Gill admitted such a weakness. No man admitted that he had feelings about A&G at all, except of course, feelings of pride and fidelity. She searched her chef's salad for the right words. How do you tell someone else how to fit in? Fitting in—being one of the guys—came naturally to Kathleen, too naturally, judging by the state of her social life.

"Well, do you have lunch with them?" Kathleen asked, even though she wasn't sure who "them" was.

"You mean, do they ask me? No! They don't! That's the problem!"

Kathleen rested her fork in her salad bowl. "I think it would be okay if you asked them." She pictured herself as a high school senior doing her calculus at the kitchen table during the weeks before the prom. Her father was shouting that she didn't understand the area under a curve because she didn't want to, and while she denied it in a loud voice, she knew he was right. All she had really wanted was for the phone to ring and for it to be for her. It had never occurred to her that she could have made the call herself, that she could have asked a boy to take her. Apparently, Sally still believed that the man should make the first move, even when the lunch was strictly professional and they were both partners.

It was hard for Kathleen to take Sally seriously. She had a soft and tentative manner, a breathy, almost sexy voice that was a little difficult to hear amidst the clatter of the busy restaurant. Kathleen wondered how Sally had ever found her way to Yale and to being one of the very first women partners at a place like A&G. To switch the subject, she asked her.

"My father," Sally said, as if that explained everything. "And you?"

She had not expected the question to be turned back so quickly. Sally had stolen her own one-line answer. Yes, it had been her dad who had trained her in logic and toughened her up in discipline and determination, but she wanted to give some credit—if credit were to be given—to her mother.

"When I was a little girl, my mother said I could be anything I wanted to be when I grew up," Kathleen said. Kathleen's mother was a nurse. She even had a master's degree, and before she'd had children, had been a head nurse at the community hospital. She worked only part-time after Kathleen was born, but Kathleen had always perceived her mother as someone who went to work, just like her daddy. Kathleen had always believed her mother: once the doors of opportunity were open to women, all they had to do was walk through them.

Kathleen laughed. "I didn't know any better, so I believed her."

On the way back from lunch, Sally repeated to Kathleen how helpful she had been, and asked if she could call her again.

Kathleen bit her lip. She truly felt sorry for Sally, who'd been so sheltered that she needed to be coached by a second-year associate. Although it wasn't a hundred percent true, she told Sally that having lunch again would be "great." She hoped that being too friendly with Sally wouldn't brand her as "soft."

When she got back from lunch, there was a memo on her desk to all lawyers from Blake Mills concerning the Holiday party. The party was a dinner for the lawyers, just the lawyers, not spouses or guests. Up until a few years before Kathleen and Jill had arrived, it had been an event for the male lawyers of the Firm. The two women partners, Parsons and Streeter, had been given $50 each and told to take their husbands to a nice restaurant. (Parsons didn't have a husband, and reportedly gave her $50 to the YWCA.) The Holiday Dinner traditionally had been held at the Commercial Club, but since the Club refused to relax its rules to allow women to attend, even for the Firm's private party, the Firm had moved the affair to a ballroom at the Palmer House Hotel.

Blake's memo announced that the evening's speaker would be George Fennel, the automobile company's General Counsel. The memo said there would be a short break after dinner and before his speech so that those who found it necessary to leave early would be able to do so without interrupting his presentation, which the Management Committee was sure all would find to be a fascinating look at the decision-making process within an international automotive company's legal department. The lawyers understood the memo to mean that the speech would be a crashing bore and old men who could not hold their liquor should not walk in front of the speaker's podium to visit the facilities.

Kathleen envisioned hordes of men marching to the men's room, like the daily 10:00 a.m. rush hour on the forty-eighth floor of Albright & Gill, when the Turks hoped to join Blake at the urinals. Was there a line? Did they glance over at each other, or stare straight ahead at their own images? Did all urinals face mirrors? There was a lot Kathleen didn't know about men, not having had a brother to whom these questions could be put, even if she had dared to ask. It had to be that if there were a mirror, and if Blake and the other senior partners looked in it slightly to their left and right, they would see only themselves, eager and unabashed. In that same mirror, the young men would see that they were made of the same stuff as the managing partners and company presidents and congressmen, and, but for the color of their skin, Jimmy Logan's athletes—the clients of Albright & Gill. Was there etiquette of unzipping, relieving, zipping, speaking, nodding? Kathleen tossed Blake's memo. It didn't pertain to her.

D uring their third year at Albright & Gill, the Class of 1976 graduated to single-window offices. Kathleen began to feel a sense of belonging to Albright & Gill. She felt, too, that she had the trust of Chas and Brian, the two busiest partners in her department. The other two rarely asked an associate for help. The senior associate in her group was technically entitled to give her work, but he kept his door closed. He'd not been promoted to window-window, and Kathleen surmised that he wasn't on track towards partnership. As a result, she worked directly with Chas and Brian without the intermediary of a senior associate, and found herself doing projects that rightly should have gone to someone more senior.

She spent about a third of her time on celebrity licensing and entertainment matters for Jimmy, which made her job sound glamorous. The Hiring Committee always asked her to interview law students so that they would understand how "fun" a place A&G was to work. She enjoyed her mild fame, but resented the Hiring Committee's implications. Even her supposed friends, including Ned and their gossipy classmate, John Watkins, suggested—and not so subtly—that her practice was "soft." John was actually heard to say that the deals he and Ned worked on involved tens, even hundreds, of millions of dollars, and required a precision in drafting which was not demanded when Anthony licensed his face to a bag of corn chips. By her third scotch, Kathleen wanted on such evenings to pummel John into a pool of his own vile spittle, and their exchanges would get mean.

"You think that the number of zeros makes your work more important?" she would demand.

"More complex."

"So, I couldn't handle it? Is that what you're saying?"

"No, Kathleen, I'm just saying it demands a certain rigor."

If Ned had left for his train to the suburbs, then it was usually Randy, the tax lawyer from West Virginia, who would silence John. "We all do different things. Sometimes we use one skill and sometimes another. None of what we do really matters. What matters here is that we do whatever we are supposed to do, given the assignment from the client."

"Doo-doo," Jill would chime in, her pun funny only because Jill rarely made a joke and rarely drank—it was a sure sign she was well into her second Margarita. Everyone (especially Randy) knew she couldn't hold her liquor.

John would be offended. "How can you say it doesn't matter, Randy? What we do facilitates commerce! Isn't our economy the greatest in the world?"

"So is our crime rate," Randy said one night. "We have this huge disparity between the haves and the have-nots. All we do here is protect the Great Divide."

"If that were true, poor boys from West Virginia wouldn't have Harvard law degrees," John countered. Kathleen shot him a look.

"Of course I was the beneficiary of tokenism," Randy said evenly. "Like Jimmy Logan. Or, I dare say, our friends Kathleen and Jill."

"Yeah, well, some of us tokens have to be twice as good to make it in this white, male world," Kathleen said, her eyes wide. "It isn't a level playing field!" She felt at once very sorry for herself.

"I know," Randy said.

As Kathleen continued to work closely with Brian and Chas, she was taken into their confidences, and sensed for the first time a certain tension between the two men. Post partnership, Brian had a new bravado, like an 18-year-old boy in the summer between high school and college, heady with success and unprecedented freedom. He was full of *nouveau* ambition and an oedipal energy that Chas, in his mid-forties, couldn't match. Chas had been born rich and lazy. Brian had been born poor and with a scholarship in his outstretched hand. Partnership had fueled his ambition. He moved swiftly to make himself into a business-getter, his senior partners' formidable competitor. He had astounded himself with his own initial success, and made friends with the chief executive officer of the third largest advertising agency in town. The agency had good, interesting work, and Brian couldn't possibly handle the account by himself. Kathleen became Brian's most important lieutenant.

Unfortunately for Kathleen, Brian's professional ambitions outstripped his organizational skills, which had always been weak. He relied heavily, and always at the last minute, on the associates to meet his unrealistic promises to the client and to draft the numerous speeches and articles that bore his name. Resentfully, Kathleen would waste a weekend researching a topic he knew almost nothing about, but on which he had represented himself to be an expert. He never gave her so much as a footnote in acknowledgment.

Kathleen had her window office, but she did not feel free to tell Brian that she would not write his articles and speeches. Because he was the partner and she the associate, she saw her career as dependent on furthering his career. That was how the system had worked for generations of lawyers at Albright & Gill: the seniors lived off the juniors, brought them along, left their legacies to their sons. Now that there were daughters, Kathleen assumed it would work the same way for her.

A nthony, the legendary rock promoter, was in town to write more of his own legend. Jimmy Logan asked Kathleen to handle the copyright and entertainment law aspects of his most recent project, and together they accompanied Anthony to a series of meetings with potential sponsors for his next music promotion, which was to be a three-night festival at Soldier Field in 1983, a mega-event with pay-per-view coverage on HBO. Because of the newness of pay-per-view, Anthony was almost a full year ahead of himself. After two long days of stifling negotiations in one of Albright & Gill's conference rooms—Anthony had kept complaining that it was too chilly—he took his entourage to his favorite steak house, Gene & Georgetti's, to celebrate their success. A sponsor had kicked in an unprecedented $5.6 million to have its name in the title of Anthony's concert.

Jimmy was downright giddy. "We did it, old boy! We did it! This is it!" He poured down his first Jack Daniels on the rocks and called immediately to the surprised waiter, who scurried off to get him another.

Sometimes, when Jimmy and Kathleen were on the plane back from New York, someplace over Cleveland, the first-class booze would saturate Jimmy's senses and he would whisper in Kathleen's ear the name of a company that Anthony swore couldn't lose. She would lean away, only to have Jimmy grab her arm and pull her closer.

"Did you hear me? I'm gonna make you rich! I'll make you a partner, if that's what you want, but that's not where the action is, baby! Not the action I'm talking about! You stay with me." It was the liquor talking, Kathleen knew. Jimmy had absolutely no tolerance, none to match his appetite.

"Gimme a kiss, baby."

"Jimmy!"

"Just a little kiss, baby."

"Jimmy, stop it!" She would roughly shove Jimmy's hands off her.

The first time this happened, Kathleen attributed it to a prolonged weather delay at the bar at LaGuardia. They had each had several drinks by the time they had settled into first class. The next time they flew together, Kathleen limited herself to two drinks, the first to calm herself and the second to steel herself against Jimmy's possible onslaught. It didn't save her. She still had to tell him to stop.

"White bitch!" he would shout. Well into his second drink, he would accuse her of leading him on, and whine, "I don't get any at home." She tried to ignore it. If she was lucky, the stewardess would come by and ask if she could get them some coffee, and Kathleen would smile, embarrassed for them but grateful for the interference. Afraid of Jimmy's flailings, she would take a glass of club soda. Occasionally a stewardess didn't get it, and stuck religiously to the ritual of offering first class passengers both wine and cordials, and Jimmy would bless her and try to give her a pat on the rump. More often than not, the attendant would slip by, leaving Jimmy swatting at thin air.

Because the first sexual harassment suits were just being brought, and because Jimmy hadn't been sober, it never occurred to Kathleen that she might have a legal cause of action against Jimmy or the Firm. She was a professional, and Jimmy didn't have any actual power to give or withhold partnership. He never actually demanded anything, and he never remembered anything he did or said the night before. She liked doing Anthony's work and she saw it as her ticket to partnership. Her worst fear was that Blake or other members of the

Management Committee would think that she got good reviews from Jimmy or Chas or any of them because of sexual favors granted or promised. The only person Kathleen told about Jimmy's behavior was Jill, and Jill, horrified, agreed that there was no good way out of her predicament. If Kathleen tattled on Jimmy, the partners would close their male ranks in solidarity: *she* must be teasing him, inviting his advances—didn't she have a few drinks herself on the plane?

Anthony saw to it that Jimmy quieted down during dinner. A big man, Anthony could hold his liquor, and he could control Jimmy with a stern look. The two men were friends, and Kathleen understood that men like Anthony had few friends. None, anyway, that could be trusted the way Jimmy could be trusted. During working hours, Jimmy was as astute, articulate and as Albright & Gill as any of them.

The three of them left the restaurant, and Anthony insisted that they share a cab. They were to drop Anthony at his hotel, and then Jimmy at his apartment a few blocks east and Kathleen just a few more south. Kathleen sat in the middle, between the two men. When Anthony got out, Kathleen started to slide her purse and briefcase off her lap to the space between Jimmy and her, but he pushed them out of the way.

"Kiss it," he said.

It was dark in the back of the cab. She dared not look at Jimmy. She hoped she hadn't heard him right. In a high, giddy voice, Jimmy repeated, "Kiss it!"

"Driver," Kathleen said sternly, but before he could respond, Jimmy's face was on hers. He smelled of stale bourbon. She struggled and shook her head away, but Jimmy was surprisingly strong, his left arm around her neck, pinching it until she squealed in twisted pain. "Stop!" She pushed him away, and he fell back against the door, momentarily jolted to attention, as if awakened from a bad dream. The driver jerked to a stop. They were in the driveway of Jimmy's apartment and his doorman immediately opened the cab door.

"Get out!" she snarled.

Surprised, Jimmy leaned over as if to give her a friendly peck on the cheek, as if nothing had happened. She pushed him away and into the extended arms of the doorman, who remained unflustered by the string of epithets Jimmy flung randomly at the white bitch, the damn driver, the son-of-a-bitch doorman who should mind his own damn business.

"I'm sorry, ma'am." The doorman gently closed the cab door. Jimmy staggered into the revolving door, his shirttail sticking out of his open fly.

Kathleen sucked in a deep breath, straightened out her clothes, and closed her eyes. The cabbie startled her when he asked where she wanted to go.

"Home," she said.

K athleen was frightened. Jimmy had never gone so far, or been so physically forceful. She knew Jimmy well enough to know he had no specific intent to harm her, no specific desire, even, for her. Yet she knew she would, by circumstance, continue to be the primary target of his bourbon-induced deliriums.

The next day, she called Sally for lunch. Kathleen and Sally had lunched three or four times a year since Kathleen had been a first-year, and since they weren't quite due, Sally sounded especially enthusiastic on the phone. They met under the lobby clock on the building's ground floor. Sally's hair had a little more gray now than when they had first met there, some of it professionally added to her new, shorter style. Sally's transformation was remarkable, as if someone who had taken all her fashion cues from *Good Housekeeping* now bought nothing that wasn't featured in *Vogue*. Sally's clothes, though not flashy, screamed rich, important, accomplished. They seemed to give Sally a new sense of self. She was happier than ever, she said, and thanked Kathleen for—and here it was hard to say what, if anything, Kathleen had to do with Sally's discovery of clothes and self—for *everything*.

Kathleen herself had changed her look from extended student to young professional. She had shortened her hair to just above shoulder level, and routinely used heat rollers to smooth out its natural curl. Today, as they ordered Cobb salads, her concerns far exceeded the pettiness of appearances, and she wondered how she could ask Sally's advice without being told to do something she didn't really want to do. Sally probably hadn't ever experienced the likes of Jimmy, and she would no doubt tell her to talk to Blake. She couldn't imagine having to look into Blake's cold gray eyes and tell him she was bothered by a drunk old man's ravings. Nothing, after all, had actually happened in the back of the taxi, and Jimmy had only asked. Well, yes, more than just asked, but she had been able to fend him off easily enough, hadn't she?

"Sally, I've got to ask you something, as a friend, not a partner."

She told Sally the story of the night before, imitating Jimmy, "Kiss it! Kiss it!" Sally's face showed no alarm, and Kathleen couldn't tell if Sally understood or not. "So, what should I do?" she asked.

Sally sat in silence, her eyes appearing to study Kathleen's face but betraying by their very stillness that she was deep in thought, only some of which had to do with Kathleen's dilemma.

"I'm not sure I've had any directly relevant experience," Sally began. Her look was so far away, Kathleen was certain that Sally did have something relevant to say—even if not "directly." But Sally was not a brave soul, and Kathleen could only guess. Perhaps on a business trip the elderly Mr. Taylor, Sally's protector, had made a dignified but still indecent proposal when he had walked her to her hotel room. Kathleen almost smiled at the idea. He must have known that even if such a thing had happened, Sally would never have told anyone—what would anyone have done? That would have been 20 years ago now, and anyone would have concluded that those were the problems one could expect when women were allowed in a law firm.

"I'm going to assume you don't want to bring charges," Sally sounded, now, more like an attorney analyzing potential litigation than a sympathetic friend. "You could, I suppose, accuse him of assault, sexual assault, even battery, if he grabbed you. I suppose you might sue him for sexual harassment, but that might implicate the Firm. It's messy. It's not my place to say, but you know, they would go after your…," Sally searched for the right words, "your prior experience. So let's assume we can resolve this within the family, so to speak. Normally that would mean having a discussion with Blake but," again Sally hesitated, and Kathleen realized she had been naïve. Of course, Sally would not trouble Blake with something so *personal*.

"I don't think so," Kathleen finished Sally's sentence.

"Honestly? I don't either," Sally said, seemingly relieved. "Although, as your friend, I have to say it's an option. As someone who wants to be your partner some day, I don't recommend it."

Kathleen laughed a nervous, knowing laugh. It felt good to confide this to someone like Sally, who had such an idealized vision of Kathleen that she would never suggest to her that she had herself done something to provoke Jimmy's behavior. Sally seemed to assume that "they" would close ranks around their partner Jimmy and the girl associate seated across the table from her would not become a girl partner if she blew the whistle. Sally just assumed certain historical things about the Firm. She had made her career out of fitting in rather than trying to change it.

For the next year, Kathleen teetered nervously, expectantly, on the verge of partnership. She was on track and had received consistently good reviews from the partners in her department, and from Jimmy. Chas said not to worry, but as she got older, Kathleen knew that he had to say that, in a way. She was his responsibility. After her fifth year, for her not to make partner would be widely interpreted as a Management Committee slap at Chas. At partnership time, more so than at any other, the senior associates were pawns in the hands of the department heads. The chess masters of the Management Committee could trade one-for-one, sacrifice a pawn here or there to send a signal, check-mate a department head, or indenture him with the favor of a promoted senior associate. There were a couple of shoo-ins and a couple of embarrassing why-are-they-still-heres—someone had lacked the guts to do what, for the good of both sides, needed to be done. Everyone else—in Kathleen's class in Chicago, about 15 of them— was like so many numbered ping pong balls in a state lottery, but no one knew if it was a pick-four or a pick-five game.

In her pre-partnership waiting period, there was little she could do that would nail it. The trick was not to muck it up, now that she had come this far. Perhaps for the first time in her life, Kathleen understood that doing everything right was not a guarantee of results.

She shared this insight with Jill over a Sunday morning breakfast at their favorite 24-hour restaurant.

Jill glared at her.

"Don't look at me like that. I'm just the messenger here," she said.

"It's not news," Jill said. She recounted the little failures that were not her fault—like choosing the Corporate department in the first place and then waiting too long to move to Probate & Estates. "Doing everything right is impossible. Don't you think I tried?"

"You did fine. I'm sorry."

"No, you're not. You think *you* have done everything right. That I haven't. That if *you* don't make partner, it will be a travesty of justice, but if *I* don't, it will be deserved."

"How does that follow? All I was saying was that this whole decision is out of our hands."

"It is. We don't even know what it would mean to do everything right, so I'd appreciate it if you wouldn't act like there's some cause and effect here. If it depended on how hard you studied or how hard you worked, we'd both be right in there." Jill's nose got red the way it did when she was about to cry.

Kathleen looked at her plate. She hated it when she and Jill got into it. But who else did they have? Everybody needs someone to shout at. Her folks wanted to be supportive of her, but they had never worked in a situation like this. Hospitals and engineering companies had hierarchies and corporate reporting structures. There were slots to fit into, and her parents were the kind of people who knew where they belonged.

Kathleen picked up the thin link sausage on her plate and pointed it at Jill. Both of them were understandably nervous about partnership and pissed off that they were spending another Sunday morning with each other.

She waved the phallic sausage at her friend. "The most important thing," she said, "we'll never get right."

I n the fall, Kathleen's apartment building went condo. She had lived there since coming back to Chicago after law school, moving up after two years from her convertible to a one-bedroom on a lower floor. Now, existing tenants of the building were being offered 20 percent discounts from the listing prices. At breakfast another Sunday, Jill took out a napkin and convinced Kathleen that not only could she afford to buy, but that she couldn't afford not to. Even with the monthly assessment for maintenance and operations, it wouldn't cost her that much more to begin to own rather than rent. Jill knew something about this because her building, further north, had gone condo three years before, and even though she could barely afford it then, she had purchased a two-bedroom which already had gone up fifteen thousand dollars in value.

"Can you imagine?" Kathleen said to Jill. "The same address my entire life?"

"It's not your entire life. It's your first condo."

After breakfast, she and Jill returned to Kathleen's building. James, the doorman, white handkerchief in hand, opened the door and said, "It's a pleasure." They got in the elevator and pushed 40. There was a new little plastic sign that said "models and sales office." The "sales hostess" took Jill and Kathleen to see a model two-bedroom with a southern exposure. The unit on the thirty-eighth floor was available. It had newly painted off-white walls, off-white kitchen cabinetry and countertops, gray carpeting and brown-black venetian blinds. With Jill's encouragement, Kathleen said she'd take it.

E ffective July 1, 1983, the Class of 1976, which, when recruited, had been promised partnership in six years, in fact became partners of the Firm. The announcement was made at 4:00 p.m. on May 1 by simultaneous distribution of a memo to "All Personnel"— the most egalitarian type of memo the Firm sent, reserved primarily for deaths and partnerships. It presented the names of 12 individuals, eight of whom were, according to the memo and with no pun intended, "resident" in the Chicago office. Kathleen's pleasure at seeing her name there, along with Randy Randolph's and John Watkins' and Harry Blomquist's (resident in the D.C. office), was awkward. Jill's name wasn't on the list, but within minutes after receipt of the memo, she was in Kathleen's office with a dozen long stem yellow roses in a florist's vase.

"I'm so happy for you," she said, and Kathleen's eyes watered.

"I'm so sorry," Kathleen said.

"Ned sends his congratulations, too."

"You talked to him?" Kathleen knew immediately that Jill was far more upset than she was letting on. Ned had left the Firm two years ago, at the urging of his wife, who wanted to have children and to raise them in a smaller town. They had sacrificed Ned's career to Champaign, Illinois. Kathleen knew Jill missed him terribly. Next to Kathleen, he was Jill's best friend.

"Well, yeah. The only shoulder I have to cry on."

Kathleen got up and hugged Jill tightly. "You've got mine, too," she said.

"Well, *you* should be celebrating," Jill said. "They said I have a good chance next year. Don't forget, I did switch groups, so I guess that's one excuse."

"Well, how about dinner tonight? On me? I hear part of the tradition is treating 'the little lady' to a fabulous dinner someplace really nice."

With just the right touch of irony, Jill said, "I can play 'little lady' if you can play 'partner.'"

FIVE

A: *I am a partner in the law firm of Albright & Gill.*

O ne morning a few days after the announcement
memorandum had been circulated and tossed by all but the
named new partners, Ernie Gordon, a senior member of the
Management Committee, stopped by Kathleen's office, papers in hand.
He placed a sheet in front of her on which there were 20 lines in
two columns. Twelve of the lines had names typed beneath them.

"I don't suppose the partners recommend reading an agreement
before you sign it," she said, hoping he would understand the joke.

"It hasn't been read in years. My guess is you wouldn't understand
it even if you did read it. I never have myself. Understood it, that is."

"So, it's not subject to negotiation?"

"Well, there are two choices," he played along. Ernie was
himself still a little more Iowa than blue-stocking, and appreciated
the irony of asking his hand-picked partners to do something they
would be disbarred for recommending to a client—signing the
Partnership Agreement without an inkling of what it said.

The Class of 1976 signed. They hosted the requisite party at
Maxine's, just like all the classes before them. At an organizational
meeting to discuss the inevitable, Kathleen had recommended that
the cost of the party be donated instead to a *pro bono* legal aid
clinic. The Class voted not to fool with tradition.

In keeping with what Kathleen and Jill had come to expect as
the natural rhythm of their lives, while the initial pass-over put her
career on hold, Jill's social life blossomed. Having decided to
change the things she had at least some control over, Jill had
shamelessly called nearly everyone she knew—college friends she
hadn't seen in years, trust officers at banks, lawyers she met on bar
association committees—and asked them to fix her up. After several
months of manic dating, including a dolphin trainer who met her
on horseback in a city park, her cleaning lady came through. She
had a client who was a partner in one of the other big law firms in

town, divorced for five years and only encumbered every other weekend with three teenage children, 14, 16 and 17.

Steve Anderson was 10 years older than Jill, well-settled in his career, and, despite child support, rich. He'd had the college sweetheart-wife, from whom he'd grown up and apart, and the trophy 20-something girlfriend, who, eventually, had tired him with the urgency of her youth. In his early forties, Steve now apparently was looking for what a how-to book might call a "life partner." He loved the fact that Jill was a fellow Michigan alum and soon-to-be partner at Albright & Gill. She was delighted by Steve's maturity, his temperate expectations, his understanding of the demands of her profession. When she needed to work late, which happened a lot less frequently knowing that she had something better to do, he would let himself into her apartment, put two chicken breasts and two potatoes in the oven, and insist, when she got home at nine or so at night, that they light the candles and have dinner together. Jill only had time to see Kathleen, without Steve, if Steve was out of town on business, which was once or twice a month. Often, Jill was inclined to work through lunch so that she could leave the office as early as possible. Kathleen missed her company, but tried not to blame either the Firm or Steve. The truth was, Jill seemed so happy and relaxed these days that Kathleen began to think Jill's consolation prize was better than the jackpot itself. Partnership, after the initial glow of congratulations, was turning out to be a fizzle. Not much changed in the daily life of senior associates once they became junior partners.

As a partner, Kathleen was still responsible for helping Jimmy with Anthony, who was enjoying phenomenal success. He was offered large advances for his endorsements and personal appearances, and demanded a contract rider of niceties that included first class air transportation for 12 (including a seat for Kathleen), three 24-hour limousines, a block of rooms to include four suites, and full meal privileges—with wine list—for his entourage. In Kathleen's view, these amenities did not make up for the rigors of traveling with Anthony. He was always "on." He was always working something, and his work wasn't the sort that she could easily pass off to an associate. Kathleen was Anthony's advisor, his negotiator, and often, despite her seniority, his scribe. There was no way to justify adding an associate to the team to write the first draft while she twirled her thumbs or drank with Anthony, Jimmy, or the business folks from the other side. Occasionally, though, she and Jimmy required the expertise of another partner, such as a tax lawyer, and so, every few months, she and Randy Randolph would find themselves together for a week in New York or New Orleans or wherever Anthony wanted them to be. As the sole shareholder of a business that produced intangible services like concerts and career management for aspiring musicians, Anthony had some interesting tax issues, and apparently the IRS thought so, too.

Kathleen welcomed Randy's company on her trips with Jimmy. In First Class, they were coupled off, Anthony and Jimmy in front, and the two junior partners behind them. If First Class was full, Kathleen and Randy were paired in coach. Randy would pump her for inside information on Anthony, and Kathleen would give what little she had. Randy said he was feeling like an outsider, and she assured him that Anthony liked him, it was just that tax lawyers, in Anthony's view, ranked right down there with divorce attorneys. The best course, she said, was to be patient while Anthony learned to trust him.

Randy took her advice to heart, and half the time, would decline Anthony's reluctant invitation for dinner, saying he wanted to go over some numbers or Code provisions. That left Kathleen to fend for herself, flanked by Anthony and Jimmy and whoever else Anthony had rounded up for the night. Unlike Randy, Kathleen was part of the inner sanctum, and didn't feel free to decline these dinners, which Anthony offered up as a perk for those privileged to work for him. Thus, her representation of Anthony consumed more of her time than she could, in good conscience, bill. But it helped her to explain to herself why her social life was so dismal.

Once in a while, if Anthony had, for his own reasons—usually a woman—dismissed his entourage early, she would say good night to Jimmy and head down to the hotel bar to have a quiet drink by herself. One night in New York, she was surprised to find Randy alone at the bar. When she took the stool next to his, he changed color.

"Gee, I've never seen anyone do that!" she laughed. "Do you know you do that? Like a lizard!"

"It's uncontrollable," Randy said through his flush. "Long night with the man?"

"Short, actually. So I thought I'd see what was going on. I'm glad you're here. I don't usually like to sit in hotel bars by myself—too much of a hassle."

"Well, from what I've seen with Jimmy, you've had more than a little self-defense training."

She ignored Randy's remark and ordered a scotch.

"How do you stand it?" Randy asked. Kathleen scanned her memory. She had never said anything to anyone except Jill and Sally about Jimmy's behavior, and she was confident neither of them—unless maybe Jill—had mentioned it to Randy.

"What do you mean?" she said as indifferently as she could manage.

"I've seen him pat stewardesses on the rump, hold hands with cocktail waitresses, that sort of thing. When he gets a few drinks in him, he's unpredictable. I know the type. Jill told me that he pawed you over Cleveland once."

Kathleen felt her own complexion turn. "Jill was wrong," she said a bit more harshly than she intended. Randy held her gaze with the tenacity of an IRS agent. Kathleen wished Jill hadn't told him, but now it was out. "Not once. Always, when he's got liquor in him."

"You shouldn't protect him, you know." Randy's color had calmed down, but he was tapping his fingers on the side of his beer glass.

"Easy for you to say. It's *me* they would question, not him. *I'm* the one they would leer at, wondering how far he got. I don't want my partners picturing Jimmy and me in any hot embraces."

Randy stopped tapping. "You don't think they would support you?" He seemed genuinely surprised, and then angry. "I wouldn't want that leech near any of my sisters," he said in a particularly country accent which Kathleen found endearing. "I have to believe the Firm would can him—immediately. He's a walking time-bomb, and someday, some secretary is going to blow the whistle and it'll cost the Firm a bundle."

Randy pointed his finger two inches from her nose. His drawl gave a slow weight to his words. "I thought you were a feminist! But you are putting your personal comfort and ambition ahead of the interests of all the women who have to come in contact with him."

Shocked that Randy would criticize her, let alone her devotion to feminism, she imitated his drawl. "Well, honey, then I'm just plain screwed, ain't I?" It was clear to her, if not to him, that she couldn't both blow the whistle on one of her partners and expect to be respected and trusted as a full and loyal partner by the others. Partners stuck together, didn't they? Wasn't she blazing the way for other women, so that eventually they would outnumber Neanderthals like Jimmy?

He didn't answer. She ordered another scotch. "On the gentleman's tab," she said, still playing the belle. She sighed, and in a resigned voice, told him, "It takes more strength to go public than to just fight him off, one drink at a time. I hear what you're saying, Randy, and I appreciate your support, but I really wonder what any of you guys would do if you were in my shoes."

"Randy!" a voice behind her prevented him from responding.

"Robert!" Randy was off his stool and shaking Robert's hand, his left on Robert's shoulder. "Good to see you!" Randy motioned to Kathleen. "This is my partner, Kathleen Hannigan, Anthony's lawyer. Kathleen, meet Robert Gardener, my law school buddy."

Robert was well over six feet tall. His sandy-colored hair had been brushed back, blown-dry, and with every strand neatly in place, possibly sprayed. His after-shave smelled fresh, with an edge to it, like newly cut wood chips. He wore an expensive gray wool suit, a thin gold ID bracelet, and a club tie. His high cheekbones gave him the appearance of a model, but the focus of his right eye was slightly to the right side. A good photographer could work around that, Kathleen thought.

Robert said hello, still shaking Randy's hand. He smiled broadly, the kind of greeting one gave to someone else's law partner—the passing, introductory kind of smile used in a long receiving line, where "nice to meet you" was political, not personal. At first sight, Kathleen had felt a tingle of excitement, that little charge of electricity that escapes plush carpeting on cold days, always unexpected, a mild surprise. She noticed Robert was not wearing a wedding ring.

"Well," Randy said, withdrawing his right hand while slapping Robert's back. "What can I get you?"

Robert ordered a Bombay on the rocks, but didn't offer Kathleen a refill. He wasn't necessarily being rude, perhaps he just hadn't noticed hers was empty. At the same time, he hadn't shown a flicker of interest in her sticking around, either. Jill always accused Kathleen of being overly sensitive to even the most inadvertent of dismissals, but in Kathleen's view, this wasn't even a close call. Robert had acted "taken"—definitely not "eligible" or even remotely "interested."

Robert was standing between them and there were no empty stools nearby. Kathleen looked at her watch. Randy was red again.

"Why don't I let you two catch up? I'm calling it a night. Randy, should we meet for breakfast?"

"Thanks, no," Randy said quickly. "I'll get room service. How about if I meet you at Anthony's? Nine-thirty?"

Kathleen agreed, although it registered as a bit odd that they wouldn't meet at the hotel and walk the few blocks to Anthony's office together. That's what they usually did. He said something about his having kept her waiting on their last couple of trips together, which was true, but the hesitation in Randy's voice made it sound like a lame excuse.

"Be careful out there," she said, and turned to leave. It may have been the flicker of amusement she noticed in Randy's eye that almost caused her to stop dead in her tracks when she was halfway out of the bar. How could she have been so stupid, so blind?

They flew back to Chicago early the next evening. In First Class, Jimmy nearly shoved Randy into the seat across the aisle. Leaving Kathleen no choice but to sit next to Jimmy. Jimmy ordered a bourbon and water before take-off, and Randy fell asleep as the plane taxied to the runway. She must have nodded off herself, because she woke with a start when Jimmy grabbed her hand. They were someplace over Cleveland, and she immediately turned towards Randy. His head was back, his mouth open.

"Oh, Jimmy, there's something I wanted to show you," she said, and started to grab her briefcase from under the seat in front of her.

"Later, baby. Just a little kiss."

"No, Jimmy," she said firmly, and turned again towards Randy, who was still asleep.

"Let the boy sleep," Jimmy said meanly. "Just a little kiss." The flight attendant came by, and Kathleen asked for a glass of water. Jimmy shoved his glass in the air, like a power fist raised in revolution.

"Bourbon, sir?"

"Yes, yes!" he said, eagerly.

"Make it light," Kathleen said quietly, digging her eyes into the young man. Then, deciding to enlist Randy's help, she called his name. He squirmed.

"Help me," she whispered between gritted teeth, but Randy was out cold.

The stewardess brought Jimmy's bourbon, and that distracted him until they were on the approach to O'Hare. Kathleen prayed they wouldn't circle.

Randy woke up just as the plane touched the runway, and stretched. In the cab line, Kathleen told Randy to guide Jimmy, who was unsteady on his feet, into the front seat, next to the cabbie, where hopefully he would fall asleep.

When she heard Jimmy snore, she turned to Randy. "So, say I take your advice and tell Blake about my issues with travel," she said, her voice challenging. "Can I count on your testimony?"

"I'm sorry, Kitty. I was so tired on the plane. I know I was no help. But if you go to Blake, I'll back you up."

"Blake will want an eye-witness," she snarled, still angry about his criticism of her feminism.

"I've seen enough to know," he said. "I believe you."

"*Inferences!* I can hear Blake now!"

"Next time, wake me up. Do whatever you have to do. But wake me up!"

"That would be like taking my life in my hands," she relented. "You sure were dragging all day. What did you guys do last night, anyway?" She figured the question would not embarrass him, but give him instead a chance to cover his tracks. His answer was vague enough to sound true.

"Robert wanted to show me a couple of clubs. New York, New York! I'd die if I had to live there. I'm too old!" Randy laughed.

"You're not even 35!" she protested. "How does Robert do it?"

"Drugs!" Randy laughed as if the answer were preposterous. "Just kidding. Maybe there you just have to keep going to survive. You forget, I'm just a poor country boy from West Virginia. Anthony's more than I can handle. Hell, Chicago's more than I can handle."

Kathleen agreed that Anthony made all of their travel a lot more—tiring, fattening, stressful, noisy—than it needed to be. "He thinks he's doing me some great favor including me in all these evenings on the town, and to tell you the truth, Randy, it gets very, very old, very, very fast."

"Yes ma'am," Randy said, exaggerating his drawl.

"Oooooh, ma'am," Jimmy said in the front seat as the cab stopped in front of Kathleen's apartment building.

"Gentlemen," she said with a mock formality, relieved to be the first one home.

In the fall of the next year, right before Jill was to become a partner, she married Steve. Even though she begged every day for six weeks, Kathleen was not invited to the wedding. Neither was Ned.

"It's not fair," Ned complained to Kathleen on the phone. "We've nursed her through all those blind dates and all the worrying, and now we're not even invited?" It amused her that Ned sounded so much like a girlfriend. In many ways, Kathleen thought Ned was a better girlfriend to Jill than she was. Jill and she had the kind of relationship that was emotionally close because of the circumstances of their lives, but which lacked the intimacy it could have had if either of them had allowed herself to be vulnerable to the other. Like a large family of over-achievers, A&G did not encourage showing that kind of weakness. In some ways, they were competitive, although Kathleen would have denied it. Jill, if she were being honest, would have accused Kathleen of having a superiority complex and not respecting her. Yet, until Steve came along, they were each other's most constant source of support.

Kathleen agreed. It wasn't fair. Only Jill's family was invited. It would be a late afternoon wedding and then a dinner in a private room at the Drake.

As consolation, Jill asked Kathleen, a month before the wedding, to go with her to find a dress. Not a wedding dress, but something elegant, and something she could wear again.

"You seem pretty cool about this," Kathleen said as they sorted through the cream silk suits at Marshall Field's.

"I guess it's not that big of a deal," Jill said.

"How can that be? Isn't this what we both said was missing?"

"It's no longer missing," Jill said. "It feels like Steve and I have always been together and getting married is just a formality."

"Maybe if you were having a *real* wedding," Kathleen ventured.

"Then it would be a hassle. It would be hard to keep it manageable."

"Well, Ned thinks that he and I should have been invited, at least."

"I know. But then my mother would want her best friend, and then there would be cousins, and then it becomes a big complicated affair. I don't have time for all that. It's not even my style."

Kathleen knew Jill was right. She admired her friend's ability to know what she wanted, go after it, and then withstand the social pressures to have the big wedding that would let the world know she'd gotten it.

F all was also recruiting season, when the Firm chose its new associates from the ranks of third-year law students. The students were first interviewed on their campuses and then were invited to spend a day meeting one-on-one with a number of A&G attorneys. Kathleen was frequently called upon to interview students, especially women. One day, after yet another half-hour conversation with a recruit from the University of Chicago, Kathleen was walking the student to her next interview, at 11:00, with a commercial lawyer on the fifty-second floor. A young woman with short brown hair stood over one of the secretarial stations half-way down the hall towards where Kathleen and the recruit were headed.

"Can't you read?" the woman was shouting at an African-American secretary who looked to be in her early twenties. "It says eight copies, not three! By 10:30! I promised this draft would *be there* by 11:00."

"You shouldn't make promises like that. You can't say for sure like that!"

"Don't talk back to me, dammit! I make whatever promises I need to, and it's your job to get the fucking job done!"

"It's just a draft, it can go out now." The secretary's tone was low and even.

The shouting woman didn't turn her head as Kathleen and her student passed. *Damn right it will go out now!*

"I don't know what's going on," Kathleen said to the recruit, "but I can assure you that that is *not* how we treat secretaries around here. We don't even treat *associates* that way," she said, and winked.

Kathleen introduced the recruit to the next interviewer and walked back down the hall, past the secretary, who was blowing her nose.

"I'm sorry," she said. "It's none of my business, except that I was just with a recruit, and whatever just happened here was embarrassing to the Firm. Who *was* that woman?"

The secretary sucked in a deep breath. "That bitch," she said, "is Miss Ann Rose."

By insulting an underdog, Miss Rose—whoever she was—had tripped one of Kathleen's wires. Without introducing herself, or getting the secretary's full name, Kathleen turned down the hall, reading the names on the bronze nameplates as she went. She hadn't yet come to "Ms. Rose," when she heard herself paged to Brian's number. It would have been easy to ignore, but because she had been given an excuse for avoiding conflict—and perhaps because she really didn't know the full story—she ducked into the "house phones" alcove mid-way down the hall, and dialed Brian's extension. He had a client in his office who just wanted to say hello to her. Could she stop by for a social visit? Through the one-way glass of the phone booth, Kathleen saw the Rose woman striding to her secretary's desk, and told Brian she'd be right there.

Although the Firm paid top salary and claimed to give new lawyers an opportunity to associate themselves with the finest traditions in Chicago's legal community, every summer, when the student interns arrived, the Firm suffered an inferiority complex of costly proportions. It was as if the collective persona of the Firm looked in the mirror and realized that it looked like hell—gray skin, gray hair, gray suits, grayed. Anyone with any sparkle at all was appointed to the Summer Committee and charged with the task of remaking the Firm into the place where the very best of the very best would want to work. The future of the Firm, the Management Committee was fond of saying, was in the quality of its youngest lawyers. However, the Management Committee, the grayest of the gray, itself did not wish to interact with its future. Skittish as a tongue-tied bachelor great uncle with a 10-year-old nephew, it delegated that job to the Summer Committee. It was inevitable that as a young, single woman partner with that "fun" practice to talk about, Kathleen would be appointed to that Committee.

That summer, the Committee dutifully showed off the Firm's departments, its clout and the better side of its personality with parties and free lunches and tours of the city. The Firm rented a cruise boat for the Fourth of July and treated the law students and their guests to one of Chicago's proudest public moments, a spectacular off-shore fireworks display accompanied by the William Tell Overture broadcast on the radio live from the Grant Park band shell. Even after the fireworks faded, the view of the brightly lit city from a perspective two miles off shore was breathtaking. Many Chicago natives, even though they flocked to the beaches by day, never had the opportunity to see their own city from that vantage point. Kathleen thought it worth every hour on the Summer Committee just for that one evening.

The Summer Committee also organized field trips to court hearings and trials and client meetings, where the interns could admire A&G in action. At the end of the summer, the Summer Committee would evaluate whatever work the summer associate had been able to squeeze in and recommend to the Hiring Committee that he or she receive an offer of permanent employment. The Management Committee instructed the Summer Committee not to make an offer to anyone at the end of the summer whom they were not confident would one day be a partner.

By Kathleen's third tour of duty in the summer of 1987, almost half of the summer class were women. Yet historically, no class of incoming lawyers ever approached 50 percent women. This summer, she wanted to make a difference in the acceptance rate— most of the women would get offers of permanent employment, and she wanted to make sure they accepted. She decided to invite all the women in the Firm to a get-together after work at her apartment. She expected some of the guys to rib her, but she was honestly surprised when some of the women objected.

Jill said, "I think it sends a bad message, Kathleen. How would you feel if they had a male-only get together?"

"That would be wrong."

"And the difference is?" Jill had a nasty habit of beginning her most devastating questions with "and."

The Chairman of the Summer Committee, just a year or two older than Kathleen, waffled. "The Firm's not paying. It's not a Firm function," was his official position, but at a Committee meeting, he asked her, "Will there be a panty raid, too?"

"Only if you organize it," she said. "You can follow the smoke to the burning bras."

Why was everyone so threatened? Kathleen called Sally. Over drinks a week-and-a-half before the "women's party," as it was being called, Kathleen asked Sally what she thought.

Sally was tickled to be asked for advice. "I'm ashamed I didn't think of it myself," she said.

"Will the Management Committee resent it?" It was a little late to be worrying about the Management Committee, and it was a bit like asking your mother on your wedding day how you look, but she held her breath waiting for Sally's answer.

"They might," Sally said. "But who cares? How many times have they met—all men? Every meeting of the Management Committee itself is all male!"

Kathleen beamed with a mother's pride at Sally's last argument. "I don't mean it as an affront to the Firm. It's just that I know—I assume, anyway—that these women belong to women's groups on campus, and might have special concerns about joining a place like A&G. I don't see how it hurts us to say that we are attentive, anyway, to the needs of women. Even if we aren't, or even if we don't know what those needs truly are." She was calming her own nerves. Although she was a partner, she still felt the new immigrant's reluctance to rock the professional boat.

A t the party, the young women had questions, lots of them. They were looking for the tenderness behind the bravado of the Albright & Gill they were dating that summer: how many hours at the office, really? how many weekends? how much travel? what about babies? how much vacation? It didn't seem likely that the truth would increase the acceptance rate among the women, and, if the truth be told, Kathleen was a little disappointed that as a group they seemed considerably less concerned with their careers and professional ambitions than the Class of 1976.

Despite the bits of truth which eked out, the party was turning out to be a grand success, and Kathleen was the enthusiastic center of it. She hadn't consciously thought of it, but by planning and hosting the party, she had set herself up as the woman leader of the Firm.

When the party had been in full swing for about an hour, Kathleen saw Ann Rose arrive. Although Ann had been at the Firm five years, Kathleen didn't know her except in passing, and she harbored a very poor impression from the time she'd heard her shouting at her secretary. Kathleen knew Ann did regulatory and commercial lending work for one of the Firms' largest bank clients and had a reputation as a superstar. Since Ann rarely attended Firm functions and never showed up in Conference Room A for Saturday or Sunday televised sports, it was curious that she had come to this controversial gathering.

It was the middle of the summer, but Ann was wearing dark gray trousers, zippered but slightly pleated in front, and a stiff white long-sleeved shirt, without embroidery or pearl buttons or other designer details. Her hair was dark, cut short, and brushed back off her face, no bangs. Overall, it was a very crisp, clean look, and Kathleen could have liked it if it had been set off with dramatic, long red fingernails or a chunky gold bracelet or a fascinating silver and jade necklace, but as it was, Ann's look was not just "strictly business," but no-risk, slightly boring, slow-and-steady-growth business at that.

Ann marched straight for Kathleen. She said hello, apologized half-heartedly for being late, and immediately asked to use the phone. Kathleen directed her towards her bedroom. Ann did not emerge for at least half an hour.

Career wise, it was said that Ann Rose had been on track towards partnership since her first days at the Firm. It was rumored that when she had attended a get-together at her department head's home the summer she joined the Firm, Jules Steinberg had answered his doorbell and asked her, "Do I know you?"

"You should," she was said to have replied. "I'm a second-year associate in your group." Jules was so embarrassed that the next Monday he brought her in on a deal he normally would have assigned to a fifth-year associate, as if by humbling her he could re-establish his own authority. Her performance reportedly had been so superb that her work from then on was thought to be beyond even the mildest criticism.

In truth, she *had* been a new associate. She bore the second-year label because she had clerked for the Indiana Supreme Court for a year, and she had only been at the Firm for three days. Now, going into her sixth year, Ann had avoided any major errors along the way, routinely billed 2300 hours—about 400 above average—and had just recently purchased her own fax machine so that she wouldn't have to wait for documents to be delivered from the bank of machines on 39 to her office on 52.

Kathleen happened to catch Ann's eye when she emerged from her phone call. Ann stood awkwardly for a moment at the entrance to the living room, where most of the women were divided up in to small groups. In her role as hostess, Kathleen made her way to Ann's side, and immediately two perky blond summer associates joined them. Kathleen introduced Ann as the senior woman in commercial lending.

Ann stiffened. "I'm the senior *associate*."

Kathleen had heard that the Firm was making a new client presentation to First Credit Corp., so, hoping the summer associates would see that women were involved in the business of the Firm, she asked Ann if she were involved in the pitch.

"They hired me," Ann said without a smile.

"*Us*," Kathleen corrected, half tongue-in-cheek. "Blake always says we have *Firm* clients, not personal ones." Kathleen repeated the party line: that over the Firm's long history, it had been highly successful in breeding generations of lawyers to successively grow and stay with a client, so that, for instance, a large client with maybe 30 or 40 lawyers working on different aspects of its business would think of itself as a client of the Firm rather than of one individual lawyer. The party line, Kathleen knew, was a lie. In the billing books that separated one partner from another at the time of compensation reviews and elections to the Management Committee, one partner in fact received personal billing credit for those 30 or 40 lawyers and their work on the Firm's "institutional" client, like a quarterback getting credit for a team's entire season.

"Blake's wrong," Ann said.

"Wrong?" One of the perky summer associates repeated. "What do you mean?"

"It means she's looking for other employment," Kathleen laughed nervously. Partners at Albright & Gill never said—never publicly anyway—that Blake was wrong. While Kathleen found the unfailing Blake worship at the Firm annoying, she understood two things as being true: that Blake could demand a much larger cash draw than he took each year from the Firm, and that if an economic decision was good for the largest stake-holder in the Firm, it was probably good for her, too.

"Clients hire lawyers, not law firms," Ann said, factually, evenly, without further embellishment. She looked directly at Kathleen, who admired, with the fascination of a polar opposite, Ann's stripped sentences, her lack of sentimentality or common emotion.

Kathleen wanted to say that sometimes clients hire lawyers just to have the power of the Albright & Gill letterhead behind them, and sometimes, clients throw some business to a friend, regardless of his skills, just to stay in good graces at the country club, avoid the awkward silences in the men's sauna, give the brother-in-law a break. Sometimes sophisticated clients want to create a conflict of interest, so they give some business to a firm in order to prevent it from representing a competitor. Kathleen wanted to say that clients hire lawyers for all kinds of reasons.

Nonetheless, even if Ann was claiming the First Credit Corp. business as her own, she was in some ways claiming a victory for all the women of the Firm. "Congratulations, Ann!" Kathleen said. "That's a big engagement. Terrific for the Firm!"

"It is," Ann said.

The phone rang. One of the guests answered it, and called out for Ann Rose. With no more than a nod to her hostess, she left the little group and headed back to Kathleen's bedroom. Kathleen, who could spiral into a wailing hole of insecurity at the slightest criticism, felt herself chastised. The associate Ann Rose, the big business-getter, had an important phone call while she, the minor partner, entertained the silly girl lawyers over wine and cheese. Kathleen saw Ann emerge 10 minutes later, briefcase in hand, and slip out the door.

The party ended around 11:00, the last two summer associates hugging her and saying, almost in unison, that when they grew up, they wanted to be just like her. Kathleen laughed a flattered laugh and thought to herself that of course they'd rather be like her than like Ann Rose. She poured herself a scotch and sat amidst the clutter of the party. Notwithstanding Ann Rose, she had felt so comfortable, so "empowered"—the word was Sally's, and too self-help-y for Kathleen's taste, but nonetheless, the right one for the evening—by the sight of so many intelligent, articulate women with all of their career decisions and so many choices ahead of them. It had been such a contrast to the partnership meetings held in the

Firm's largest conference room, every second or third row of its theater-style seating containing the odd woman out.

Sitting alone on her couch, Kathleen envied the choices the younger women seemed to think they had. No, not choices, she thought. They seemed to think they could have it all, without choices, that there were no trade-offs, no consequences, no limits. Were there? Was she, herself, where she wanted to be? Well, sort of. What more could she want?

She thought of Jill, who had skipped the party, offering Kathleen several different excuses, from meeting with a client to having dinner with Steve. Kathleen knew, however, that Jill didn't believe in the party, and so she would not have wasted her time attending, especially when she could have been with her husband instead. She pictured Jill having dinner with Steve at a neighborhood restaurant, walking home, lying next to him in bed, holding his hand as they fell asleep. Jill wanted nothing more than to be with Steve. At 36, if Kathleen admitted that *that* was the "more" that she wanted, she would have despaired. She had dated so few men in the past 10 years—perhaps by choice, who could say?—that she couldn't even picture a Steve in her future. She knew she didn't want a Steve enough to suffer the number of blind dates it had taken Jill to find hers, but she wanted something in her life that was important enough to make up for the absence.

Management Committee. The thought had been in the back of Kathleen's head for some time. If she were on the Management Committee, perhaps then she could make a difference. If not her, then who? Sally didn't get it and Jill didn't want it. There were a couple of other women partners a few years younger than they, but they were, in Kathleen's view, bland. They had not yet participated in the Firm's Committees, and, if Kathleen's instincts were right, none of them had the drive. Two of them had small children at home. It was sexist of her to think it, but she doubted the younger women had staying power.

Ann Rose was, Kathleen thought, the Management Committee's type, a clone among clones hand-picked for the job. If Ann were on the Management Committee, she would assume no special responsibility for women. She was *not* the kind of woman Kathleen would want to hold up as a role model, and the first woman appointed to the Management Committee would certainly be touted as one by the Firm, the business press, the women's magazines. Besides, Ann wasn't a partner yet, and by the time she was by all rights eligible, there *should* be a woman on the Committee. It was almost the '90s. Kathleen would come of age first. She would, by her own estimation, be the perfect candidate, a role model for the other women. She wasn't married, but she was not, like Ann, defeminized, either.

The only real obstacle was Brian. Her department was only a dozen lawyers, and the Firm would never choose two Management Committee members from so small a group. Brian, with the most billings, would be the obvious choice. But Kathleen was hopeful. Brian would self-destruct under the weight of his own ambition, and would, sooner or later, step on the wrong toes. It would eat him alive if the Management Committee chose her instead of him, but the Committee could explain that they wanted women to be represented and she was the natural choice. She finished her scotch, toasting to her successes, the night's and the future's.

SIX

Q: *Do you know the plaintiff in this case, Ann Rose?*

"**U**h, uh, ummm."

Kathleen waited. She recognized the voice, of course, but it aggravated her to no end, and she saw no particular reason to let Brian off the hook of his own inattention.

"Oh, Kathleen? Good. Come down."

She slammed the phone down. Would he ever, ever learn to respect other people? Would it kill him to ask "would it be convenient?" or "do you have time?" It was, in truth, not convenient, nor did she have a lot of free time. Here she was, going on 12 years of practice, and Brian acted as if she had nothing to do but serve *his* clients. Why did she still run when Brian beckoned?

She was not smiling when she walked into Brian's office, but she stopped short when she saw Ann Rose sitting in one of his visitor's chairs. She must have been sitting there when Brian had called Kathleen, expecting her to drop everything and come. Like a concubine to the king.

"A crisis?" She wanted Ann to know Brian's summons was an aberration, not the usual way in which she, a partner, should be treated. With a forced casualness she smiled a business-like smile at Ann, who nodded.

"Do you know each other?" Brian asked.

"Really, Brian, you should get out more," Kathleen said.

Not waiting for the answer, Brian hurried on. "We have a chance to represent Gloria Elkington Golf."

"Gloria Ellens?" Kathleen said. She made it a point to read the sports pages. She knew Gloria Ellens was one of the most important women in professional golf.

"Brian, my client is First Credit," Ann said. She explained that First Credit was financing a Swedish company's buy-out of a 51 percent interest in a company that manufactured ladies' golf

91

equipment. The primary assets of the golf company were its patented putter technology and the licensing deals it had with various LPGA players.

"Ann wants me to look at the IP issues. We've got a bunch of personal service contracts here, and we're worried about assignability and registrations, that sort of thing; specific performance and morals clauses and whether any of the key players can block the deal. Take a look, see what you think."

Kathleen's head was throbbing, and she felt a prickly heat on her upper chest. She looked at Brian and at Ann. Her eyes stung. She wished she could imitate Ann's impassive stare. Her pupils bulged with anger, eating up the blue of her irises. Ann was blessed with dark brown irises that camouflaged such involuntary emotion. Ann had the cold, inscrutable look that Kathleen envied.

"Won't do any good for me to take a look if what Ann wants is for *you* to do the deal." She clicked her ball point closed.

Brian flashed her a look that screamed "Traitor!" He took a quick ninety-degree look out the window, where the grayness of November had settled.

He jerked his head back. "These are complex issues, Kathleen. You've got some experience with Jimmy. We need you."

Brian was the kind of slime who knew how to beg, appealing at once to Kathleen's confidence in her superior intelligence and her need to be needed. But his compliments were double-edged. *Some* experience, indeed! Kathleen had more experience in this particular area than anyone in the Firm, as much as the very best sports lawyers in the country, actually. Brian himself didn't have the expertise to declare her qualified or not, and his pretense upset her as much as his condescension.

"Ann knows where to find me. I'm in the book," Kathleen said between clenched teeth.

"I can't do it all myself," Brian said.

The truth was, he couldn't do it *at all* without her. He didn't have even the slightest idea *what* to do.

"I need you."

Kathleen paused, biting her lower lip on the right side to keep it from twitching. "But, Brian, *I don't need you.*"

They were ignoring Ann now, each of them refusing to blink first. Whoever spoke next would lose ground, and they each had their territory to defend. Kathleen raised her chin in a little circular motion and involuntarily arched her eyebrows in an unintended question.

"Whew!" Ann got up. "I don't know what's going on here, but work it out." She left. Neither Brian nor Kathleen acknowledged her leaving, their eyes still locked.

"Fine," Brian said hastily.

Kathleen nodded.

"Just make sure I'm in the loop so they know who I am. It would be a good client for us. Just our kind of work."

Kathleen had to decide, quickly, whether it was worth yet another go-round with Brian. First Credit was the immediate client. Gloria Ellens was in the future. Their battle wasn't over doing the work. It would have fallen to Kathleen in any event. It was solely about the recognition of which of the two partners was in charge. Already, they had ceded some of their authority to Ann, six years Kathleen's junior.

Ann was the one who was the traitor here. The women's party had only been three months ago. This was a woman's company. There was a woman lawyer on the credit side of the transaction. What was Ann thinking, calling Brian? Sucking up?

Ann could have called Kathleen, woman to woman. Wasn't that what the woman's party was supposed to be about? Geez, if even women like Ann refused to buck the system in favor of women, how would the system ever change? Or did Ann actually think Brian the better lawyer? Kathleen felt twisted in the same double bind she so often had felt with Brian. If she didn't save him from his own incompetencies, the Firm might think that the entire IP group wasn't up to its standards. If she did help him, he got the credit without doing the work.

"I'll get with Ann," Kathleen said, by way of conciliation.

By the time she was at Brian's door, however, he was on the phone. Kathleen shook her head and laughed out loud. You could say anything at all to Brian, anything at all. Nothing stuck. His recognition of being in the wrong, of being grabby, or disorganized or difficult to work with was momentary—no matter how valid her complaint and sincere his apology, the resolution was brief. Like a child's confession of sin, a contrite and fear-induced promise never to pinch your sister again as long as you live, so help you God, Brian swore, repeatedly, to change. He would thank Kathleen after one of these skirmishes—he hadn't realized, he hadn't thought. She appreciated that there weren't many partners at Albright & Gill who would thank you for telling them to go to hell, but it still didn't mean that Brian would ever be anything other than Brian.

It took Kathleen and a junior associate a few days to acquaint themselves with the content of 15 file boxes, each 14 inches wide and 18 inches long: thousands of pages of present and past trademark licenses, celebrity endorsement contracts and patent and technology agreements. No wonder Brian had been so panicked when he had called her, admitting in front of Ann Rose, as she saw it now, that he needed her. He panicked whenever a single document—let alone a roomful—exceeded more than four single-spaced pages. Kathleen called Ann.

"Yes." Ann's tone did not invite Kathleen's usual warm-up banter, so she skipped it. "I need to talk to Gloria's lawyers and the bank's lawyers about the use of her name as a trademark going forward, and her personal services to the new company."

"Tell me."

Kathleen explained that Gloria Ellens' name was a trademark and had market potential in all classes of goods, not just in the golf equipment and clothing classes for which it was already registered. The new company, she said, would have to have discretion on how the name was used, but Gloria would need to maintain some approval rights, for technical legal reasons. Kathleen wanted to talk directly to First Credit's and to Gloria Ellens' lawyers.

"Send me a memo, I'll talk to them," Ann said.

"I can write it up for you Ann, but you're not a trademark lawyer. I think it would be better if we spoke to them together."

"I don't. And it's *my* client."

"Well, technically, Ann, it's the Firms' client, and, as a partner of the Firm, I'd like to be in on the call." This was an odd situation. An associate was claiming to control access to the Firm's clients, at least, to control Kathleen's access—she didn't know the names of the lawyers she needed to work with at either First Credit or Gloria Ellens—and Ann was a time-locked safe.

"I'll call you if that becomes necessary," Ann said with a dismissiveness that made the possibility seem as remote as Kathleen's following Sally Ride into space.

"I hope…." Kathleen began before she heard the click.

G loria Ellens' people were gracious enough, and understood the lawyers' disappointment when the legend herself did not attend the closing. They distributed a sleeve of Gloria Ellens golf balls (machine autographed), a powder blue, white embroidered golf towel, and a matching powder blue visor to each of the 23 lawyers who had taken part in the transaction. Brian, without explaining his presence, had shown up in Conference Room A, the Firm's largest, and had asked for a second set for his wife, who, he had to admit in the chatter that followed his impolite request, didn't actually play golf but was thinking of taking it up.

Gloria Ellens was run by five white, clean-cut, five-foot-eight men with light brown to dusty blond hair, healthy tans and apparently perfect vision. All had worn monogrammed white double knit golf shirts with a blue tulip where the polo rider should have been, and powder blue jackets meant to convey "A Man's Power in a Woman's Soul," the original slogan of Gloria Ellens Golf, which had been chosen by Gloria Ellens herself over the objections of five male marketing executives, who didn't like the Soul word but had no doubt that a Man's Power was a good thing indeed. As a group, the five were quiet, easy-going good old boys from Georgia who wintered in Florida and whose idea of running a company was manning the hospitality tents on the LPGA Tour. With Gloria sliding past her prime, there would be fewer shrimp on toothpicks in their future and a little more hustle required to reach target. The Swedes, a taller, blonder matching set of five, were to bring the new marketing energy and money to Gloria Ellens Golf, and Brian huddled with them while the good old boys signed their names, over and over, on bills of sale and security interests and lease assignments and trademark licenses and all the pieces of paper which constitute a multi-million dollar company. In the crowded conference room, Kathleen had gotten jammed in the corner with the coffee pot. Across from her, she heard Brian describe his work for Anthony.

Brian's work for Anthony? Brian didn't work, Kathleen thought bitterly, and certainly not for Anthony! How many of her evenings, even her weekends, had she given up to work for Anthony, and how much had she suffered with Jimmy, only to have Brian now stealing her stories, her credentials, her experience?

"Brian," Kathleen approached them, "you're stealing my best stories!" She reintroduced herself to the boys. "I've spent a good part of the past 10 years traveling around with Anthony," she said gamely. "Brian doesn't know the half of it!" She could smile at them and at the same time shoot poison darts with her eyes at Brian. "I think the best Anthony story was when he and I were in New Orleans…"

Kathleen didn't get to her punch line. Ann's voice was calling for order.

"Good afternoon, gentlemen. I'm Ann Rose, of Albright & Gill, representing First Credit. Jules Steinberg of our Firm sends his regards to you all. He could not be here today, but I have the pleasure of announcing that, with the backing of First Credit, Gloria Ellens Golf and Womansport have just completed the documentation of their strategic partnership. Now John Hays, President of Gloria Ellens Golf, has something he would like to say."

Congratulatory words were said, and plans made for the closing dinner that evening.

The dinner was held in a private dining room at The Everest Room, one of Chicago's most expensive restaurants. Brian positioned himself in the center of the long table where he could entertain both to his left and to his right. The Chief Financial Officer of the Swedish company presided at one end of the table. The other end was left empty, in reverence to Gloria Ellens, who, the good old boys said again, was hoping to make it up from Atlanta in time. Ann sat as far from Brian as possible, on his right, and Kathleen sat opposite her, where she could keep an eye on Brian. A woman lawyer from First Credit's in-house staff sat at the other end with the Swedish CFO. Three among 20. Kathleen ordered a scotch, the good old boys had bourbons, and Ann ordered a kir. Brian, who didn't really drink, ordered a glass of red wine and downed it like water in two gulps. There was what Kathleen would have called an awkward silence at her end of the table while they studied their menus a few minutes longer than necessary.

"The food is good here," Ann said, confidentially, to the good old boy seated next to her.

"So I've heard," he replied.

At the center of the table, Brian was talking with his mouth full, strewing crumbs from the crusty roll on himself and on the guests to his left and right, but they were laughing gratefully—as long as Brian talked, there was enough noise in the room to give it an almost festive air.

The pretense that this was a party brought out the tap dancer in Kathleen. She knew how to please a crowd, how to earn their attention and, she hoped, their admiration. She wasn't best friends with men for nothing. In her opinion, this party needed a quick infusion of party atmosphere. She wanted to shake things up a little, maybe ask what the "L" stood for in LPGA. Instead, she asked where the LPGA was being played this year.

"Same as last year, Kings Island," one of the good old boys said, and then added, "Ohio." At least then they had a location for travel talk, which, given the location, was quickly exhausted. Travel suggested sports suggested Anthony.

Celebrity being their main commodity, the good old boys were interested in Anthony and in promoting events and careers, and Kathleen got a good 15 minutes of conversation in about her representation of the greatest promoter of them all.

Ann excused herself as soon as she had finished her swordfish, before dessert, before the after-dinner coffees and cognacs. She said she was expecting a fax. If she had intended to demonstrate her importance, that she was needed back at the office at 10:30 at night, it seemed to Kathleen that her move had backfired. The good old boys stood briefly, shook her hand, thanked her for her help in getting the deal done, but did not encourage her to stay. First Credit's counsel took Ann's cue and asked also to be excused. Her baby-sitter would be wanting relief. Kathleen had no excuse for leaving early, and no intention of leaving Brian alone to pitch new trademark business from the reconstituted management of Gloria Ellens Golf.

The good old boys settled back into their chairs as if the real work of the evening could now begin. The vice-president of marketing passed a box of cigars. He offered the open box to Kathleen and said he was an "equal opportunity smoker." She declined with a polite smile.

The good old boys talked a little shop. Kathleen warmed her cognac and listened. About an hour later, standing outside The Everest Room, the equal opportunity smoker helped Kathleen with her coat. He leaned over and spoke into her ear, "Would you like to get a nightcap with me at the Ritz?"

"Thanks, but it's late," she said.

"Can't fault a guy for asking," he said, not at all rebuked.

"Oh," Kathleen said, surprised both that she had missed his implication and that she hadn't seen it coming. "Much too late." She smiled, shrugged her shoulders, and, getting into the first cab that stopped at the restaurant's flashing yellow light, waved good night to the good old boys.

At home, she kicked off her shoes and stretched out on her bed, fully clothed. She was mentally drained, as if the whole of the evening, the whole deal, for that matter, had rested on her shoulders. In some ways, it had, at her end of the table, anyway. She sensed that as always, Brian had upheld his. But Ann had been no help, a complete fizzle on the dance floor of small talk. By her silence, by her refusal to pick up a verbal ball, Ann made Kathleen feel silly and flirtatious. Yet, if Kathleen hadn't talked, and told that story about Anthony, and asked the accountant about his daughter's soccer league, then only Brian's self-absorbed monologues would have broken their monastic silence. Yes, she thought, her mother would have been proud she had raised her daughter to be so nice.

A lbright & Gill was unusually quiet when Kathleen arrived around 10:00 the next morning. It took her the entire walk to her office in the middle of the hall to recognize the unfamiliar stillness as the absence of sound. As if in a library, a sneeze behind a secretarial cubicle almost echoed. There was a page on the intercom system, which suggested that the phones were working, and when she listened for them, she could hear phones ringing up and down the hall. She stopped at her secretary's desk and delivered her usual box of Friday morning doughnuts.

"Thank God it's Friday," she said with false good cheer.

"Oh my God," Carol said. "You don't know!"

"Know what?"

"Randy's dead! Ann Rose found him at his desk, last night! Dead!" Carol was crying. Kathleen didn't think she'd heard Carol correctly.

"Did you hear me? Randy Randolph's dead!"

"Tell me...." Kathleen's throat was tight.

Carol reported what she'd heard. Ann had come back to the Firm after the closing dinner and had walked past Randy's office. His lights were on, and the radio was playing a country music station louder than Randy usually played the classical station he favored during the day. Ann, in what was for her an unusual show of camaraderie, had stuck her head in Randy's doorway, to commiserate that they were the only two apparently burning the midnight oil. His head was face down on his desk, resting on his crossed arms. Ann had raised her voice and then had gone all the way in.

Ann called 911. The paramedics got there almost immediately. They must have been the ones to call the police. Two Chicago police officers and two detectives in plain clothes had photographed the scene, cordoned it off with yellow plastic and bagged a bottle of aspirin from Randy's top drawer. Then the paramedics put the body on a stretcher and took it away.

According to Stewart Lydon's secretary, Ann had called Blake Mills at home, and Blake had told her to call Stewart because he was the head of the tax group. Stewart told his secretary that he hadn't known what to do, but that Ann had said she would be okay, that she was going to finish up her work and then go home.

Carol said that Randy's secretary had been moved to an empty desk for the day, and had been given a script for answering Randy's calls:

> We are sorry to inform you that Randy Randolph was found dead last night, apparently of natural causes. Funeral arrangements are pending and will appear in the *Chicago Tribune*. The Firm will reassign his matters in due course after consultation with clients.

Carol said she thought the secretary should have been given the day off—it wasn't every day your boss committed suicide. Kathleen was appalled that Carol would use that word, but Carol said she knew it was suicide because that's what everybody said, and the security guard had told the mail room clerk, who had told the receptionist on 41, who had told another receptionist, who had told the secretarial administrator, who had told Carol not to tell people, if they asked, that it was—almost certainly—suicide.

Kathleen went up to Ann's office and knocked on the closed door. When there was no answer, she opened it, thinking to leave a note on Ann's desk, and was mildly surprised that Ann was there. "Didn't hear you, Ann. Just wanted to make sure you're okay."

"Fine," Ann said curtly. Her answer made Kathleen's question sound ridiculous, when she was just trying to give Ann a chance to say whatever it was she might want to say, if only to repeat her horror to someone who would listen long enough for her to begin to get the image out of her head.

"How terrible for you," Kathleen tried again.

"I'm okay," Ann said with a ring of finality. She didn't say, "Thanks for asking," or "I'll let you know," or any of the "nice" things she might have said to make Kathleen feel a little better.

"I know there's nothing...."

"Right. Look, Kathleen. I found a body. Period. It's not the end of the world. When someone is that unhappy, there's nothing you can do. Randy made his choice."

Kathleen glared at Ann. She wanted to shake her, physically shake her out of her business self. Kathleen wanted Ann to let her do something she knew how to do—to comfort, to console, to be strong for someone more vulnerable than herself.

"We all make choices, Ann," she said quietly. "Some conscious, some not. There are lots of ways to run, to hide, to kill ourselves. If you ever want to talk, call me."

Kathleen left, although she herself still wanted to talk. She called Jill, and together they called Ned, who sounded like he was crying down there in Champaign. They hung up and she thought of calling Harry, but didn't want to hear him make cynical jokes. She called Jill back, and Jill said they weren't getting anything done and they might as well take an early lunch. Kathleen didn't feel like eating.

"Let's get out of here anyway," Jill said.

It was only 11:30 and the nice Italian restaurant across the street gave them a table in the back even though they didn't have reservations. Kathleen ordered a Chianti and a side of garlic bread. Jill had the macaroni and cheese, but she only picked at it. They ate in relative silence. There was nothing to be said, unless Jill wanted to say something about their date so many years ago, and she wasn't saying anything. Neither of them had ever slept with someone who had died. It was, to Kathleen, anyway, a rather curious phenomenon, to have come close to conceiving a life with someone no longer living. She ordered a second Chianti, and might have ordered a third, but Jill said she didn't have time.

"Before we go, tell me, did you know?" Jill asked.

"I suspected, after this one trip to New York, but we never talked about it. When did you find out?" It occurred to Kathleen that Jill had known and had never told her. All this time each had thought she was keeping Randy's secret, each had had an unspoken pact with him.

"When I didn't make partner the first time, he took me to dinner. To cheer me up. He said he felt badly about that night—you know—and he knew the Firm thing had probably sounded like an excuse, and it was, but not the excuse I thought. He said he wasn't ready to be public about it. Then, he hadn't even told his family. That was four years ago." Jill dug a hole in her macaroni and cheese.

"You know, he gave me hell in New York for not going public about Jimmy, and I told him that he didn't know what it was like...." Kathleen's voice trailed off in a whisper.

Randy had accused her, then, of not doing her duty to other women, of not blowing a whistle on Jimmy when she could have saved other women the assaults she had suffered. What disservice had Randy done to young men and women of the gay community by keeping his secret for so long? A successful attorney at a major firm certainly could have used that platform to dispel some localized homophobia, but hadn't he weighed his personal comfort and ambition just as she had? Or was his suicide the service—the object lesson being that denial of one's true self leads to death, figuratively and sometimes even literally? But there had been no official ruling of suicide. Kathleen judged herself guilty of drawing unjustified inferences, based solely on stereotypes and her own sense of the melodramatic.

When they returned to the office about 1:30, the morning's pall had lifted. The Firm seemed alive again, noisy with keyboards and printers, people in the halls, and an occasional laugh from behind a secretarial cubicle.

"Randy's partner was here!" Carol announced to Kathleen, handing her two pink message slips. "I never knew he was gay. You should see the guy! Tall and gorgeous. Like a model. An incredible head of hair, reddish blond. Kind of wavy. They'd known each other since law school! Isn't it wild how someone can keep something like that secret? Who would have thought?"

"What was his name?" Kathleen asked.

"Bobby something," Carol said.

Perhaps, Kathleen thought, Bobby had taken the Firm off the hook and restored its noise level. She could hear them. It wasn't us, after all! We would have stuck by him the way we did with Leonard when he dumped his wife of 20 years and took up with that law student. Even found the law student another job.

Kathleen went into her office, closed the door and let the Chianti cry. Around 3:00, the official memo came out, to "All Personnel":

We regret to inform you of the death of our Partner, Randolph A. Randolph. Funeral services will be held in West Virginia on Monday and will be private. In lieu of flowers, the family requests donations to the Legal Aid Society. We will host a memorial service on the following Friday at 3:00 p.m. in the Main Dining Room of the Downtown Club for Randy's clients and friends.

Kathleen was sobbing when the phone rang. The voice did not identify himself and it took her a full minute to understand.

"At the memorial service, we'd like you to say a few words on behalf of the partners in your class. The other speakers will be Stewart, Leonard and myself."

"Thank you. I'd be honored," was all she could muster.

"Miss Bryce will be in touch." Miss Bryce was Blake Mills' assistant.

She put the phone down quietly. It had never occurred to her that she would outlive one of her classmates. In fact, she had never thought about dying with these people, and yet what was the alternative? Jill, Harry, even John…. They had all made partner and were all on the path to die together, to attend one another's funerals and say nice things about each other, about the privilege of practicing law together, oh my, these many years. Yet they hardly knew each other! She sniffed back another round of tears, these as much for her own loneliness as for Randy's.

The next day the police took down the yellow plastic. It wasn't homicide, and without a note they were reluctant to call it suicide.

His heart had stopped, a natural cause of death. The day after that a paralegal began to sort through Randy's files and inventory them for reassignment. Randy could have been away on a business trip, or on vacation, or at a new firm. It was all the same, and the multi-million dollar business of Albright & Gill went on, as it had for years. Although they had never been the kind of friends who talked on a daily basis, Kathleen had the urge to call Randy, now that he wasn't there.

On Saturday morning, Kathleen called Jill. "I know it sounds shallow, but you've got to help me find the right dress for Friday." It gnawed a little that Randy was dead and that she, too, had become a grave robber, seizing the opportunity to show off her best stuff to the Management Committee, which, out of duty, would, of course, attend its own Memorial Service.

Jill, who completely understood that in front of clients, staff, lawyers, and the Management Committee, appearances mattered, threw herself into the hunt. Jill dragged Kathleen up North Michigan Avenue, rejecting navy suits because they obviously were avoiding black, gray pinstripe pantsuits because they lacked style, chocolate brown dresses because of the potential static cling. Kathleen was grateful for Jill's expertise. On Sunday afternoon, they found a black ultra suede suit with ornate gold buttons and a black silk blouse with gold braid at the neckline. It was twice what Kathleen usually spent on her very best outfits, but it was the right, festive kind of black, and, she felt, necessary.

In the evenings during the week before the memorial service, Kathleen focused on what to say. Monday night did not go well. She prepared herself with a new legal pad and a fresh scotch on the rocks, but no words came. At her kitchen table, she started writing out of desperation, then crossed out all the high school graduation speech prose that spewed out of her. She slept only because the scotch let her. Tuesday night was no better. By Wednesday night, she was panicked. She wanted to write something out, have Thursday night to learn it, and by Friday know it well enough not to have to read it, to be able to make it sound spontaneous, from the heart. How was she going to be spontaneous if she didn't get something down on paper now? She pictured herself at the podium. She liked the suit Jill had helped her find. She looked out at her audience and there were all those men, not thinking of Randy, but looking at her—a woman— as the one closest to Randy. Which probably wasn't even true—Jill and he had actually talked about it. Why hadn't Blake asked Jill? Or why hadn't he asked a man to speak, John, say, or Harry?

She started to write, almost illegibly, about difference. Randy must have felt different, no matter how much he endeavored to— and did—look like and act like the others. Something in Kathleen wanted to blame the Firm, the oppression of its holy reputation, the silent rules of its hierarchy. It was the unspoken that would kill them. The best and the brightest couldn't tolerate difference, couldn't bear any deviation from their cultural code. She came to a stop in her thoughts and felt too alone. She cracked open a window in her living room, just to connect to the street noise below. An angry driver leaned on his horn. For once, Kathleen understood the logic of leaning on it. She smiled. We're all different and we're all angry about it.

Randy probably didn't feel different! He had a work life and a love life and probably saw no incompatibility whatsoever. *She* was the one making his death into some kind of a cause because *she* needed to make some sense of it. There had been no ruling, she reminded herself. She was projecting. She scratched everything she'd written and then crumpled both pages.

She reversed herself again: of course Randy felt different! We all do! We *want* to be different. We *need* to be different. Even if in just the littlest ways, different enough to tell ourselves apart from one another. That's how all these egos got formed in the first place, trying to deviate in some defining way that would make one stand out from—above or below—the crowd. A Harvard man from West Virginia stands out both places. A gay partner at a blue-stocking law firm, likewise. Part of the problem was that Albright & Gill permitted such a narrow range of difference.

That narrow range of difference obscured their most important sameness, the sameness that the partners of Albright & Gill would not admit. That they were each afraid that they weren't good enough for the life they had chosen. That their reputations far exceeded their worth. That they were worried—financially, sexually, and interpersonally. That they were only human and afraid of being found out.

If you scratched the surface of any of them too deeply, would they bleed the blue blood of an unlived life? Did they know in their capillaries that Albright & Gill was not as important as they—the elusive, collective they—thought it was? She was writing the eulogy for her own youth, her own soul, not for Randy. She tore off the page and started again.

K athleen stood in silence with Blake, Stewart, Leonard and a young Catholic priest in the lobby of the Downtown Club, outside the room where the memorial would take place, waiting to be told what to do. They were 15 minutes early. There was no music to fill the terrible silence, and, under the circumstances, no appropriate small talk. Had the deceased been retired, the lawyers could have greeted each other, "glorious career," "good life," "a blessing." As it was, the guests seemed to arrive all at once, at the last minute, like at a Mass in a resort town, and they filled the theater-style rows of chairs with a silent nod to the few already seated. The Firm had only invited clients and the Firm's personnel, effectively excluding Robert.

At exactly 3:00—because Blake was as punctual as a punch-clock—the priest led them by twos, Kathleen and Leonard, Blake and Stewart, up a makeshift aisle. The priest opened with a reading of "The Lord Is My Shepherd." Blake said a few expected words about the sadness of the occasion and of a young man taken as he was rising to the apex of his career, groomed for leadership at Albright & Gill and indeed the tax bar of the entire nation. Stewart read a tribute to Randy's keen mind, his work ethic, and his loyalty. Nice, general words. No specifics. Not, Kathleen thought, how it should be done. There should be something unique, something honest, to say about Randy. It was her turn. She smiled the slightest smile.

"This is indeed a sad occasion, and it reminds me how much we will miss Randy's sense of humor and his wonderful sense of proportion about life. When I first met him, he promised never to call, 'Here, Kitty!' if I promised never to ask him about his name. You have to wonder what kind of parents name their child Randolph A. Randolph."

The audience seemed grateful for the relief of the relentless tension of the past 15 minutes. They laughed a little louder than her gentle story was funny. She continued.

"And you have to wonder what kind of child overcomes such a name. You knew Randy, so you know the kind of person he was—the first in his family to go to college. And then, to go on to the Harvard Law School. He dedicated himself to becoming a partner at Albright & Gill, and, as Stewart said, he was one of its best team players. I could mention all the deals Randy ushered through, his special work with Anthony, all the times he took extra time to walk a young associate through the Code or explain a simple tax issue to a senior partner,"—here there was more laughter—"but that wasn't the best part of Randy. The Randy I loved and admired, the Randy I liked to spend time with,"—and here, she was exaggerating the amount of time they had spent together in the past couple of years—"was the Randy who volunteered with Big Brothers Mentoring Program, tutoring a youngster named Julian. The Randy who always had a new biography with him, and not enough free time to finish it. The Randy who cooked some of the best fried chicken you've ever tasted. The Randy who settled our arguments over drinks on Friday nights with a simple, 'It really doesn't matter all that much, in the grander scheme of things. You're gonna be dead for a really long time.' That Randy, I'm afraid, none of us knew well enough. I would like to think that he wants us all to remember him and the importance of things—the importance of the things other than those which bring us together at Albright & Gill, the little things that make a life. A lot of people profess to understand the Tax Code, but it's the special ones who also make time to reach out to Julian and to fry chicken for their friends.

Albright & Gill takes great pride in its culture and traditions, so much so that we sometimes don't give each other much latitude. We deny or hide our differences rather than own and celebrate them. Randy believed we all need to be free to be different, to be ourselves no matter what pressure we might feel to conform. We, as a Firm and as a community, need people who are uniquely themselves, not carved out of a pre-existing mold, and who are comfortable with their uniqueness. When such people are gone, it is a great loss to us all. We will sorely miss Randolph A. Randolph."

Kathleen sat down. She was afraid she was splotched and that Blake would see the trembling of her right hand. Her voice had remained steady. She had spoken in her most professional voice, low and slow. She hadn't stumbled, even though she hadn't used a text, and she had used the mike well. She felt selfish evaluating her own performance, while Randy, her friend, was dead, but she couldn't help herself.

Leonard spoke in summation, another dry rendition that startled Kathleen back to attention. He read a few short sentences quickly and without emotion, in a get-it-over, this-is-the-necessary-business-part-of-the-meeting tone. She knew he could have been passionate. In fact, he had shown all kinds of outrage that time he argued to save Anthony from his distress over that nude illustration. She recognized the false rationality of Leonard's tone, though. It masked a deliberate refusal to acknowledge the discomfort of his feelings, and was tinged with a bit of resentment at the inconvenience of it all.

She was glad when they opened the bar. The partners spilled out of their rows and into the reception area, anxious to put this episode behind them. At the back of the room, Blake shook hands with the Catholic priest and Stewart and Leonard. He nodded at Kathleen, silently, and she held his gaze until he turned back to the priest and guided him to the bar. She waited for Jill, who had managed to be one of the last out of the rows.

"That was good, Kitty. Real good. Never in a million years could I have done it. It was just right. Just right."

"Thanks. I think it sounded okay, don't you? I'm sure no one was really listening to the words. I wasn't as clear as I wanted to be. All I really wanted to say was that this place doesn't define us, but— you know what, it does! It's in the first line in his obit, 'Randy Randolph, a partner in the prestigious law firm of Albright & Gill.' That's it. There's nothing else to say." She sucked in a breath, and her voice cracked. "What if this *is* it? What if all there is for us is Albright & Gill?"

SEVEN

Q: *Were you a friend of hers?*

The summer after her women's party and the Gloria Ellens deal and Randy's death, Kathleen was moved from the Summer Committee to the committee that graded associates and recommended their salary and bonus levels. The Evaluation Committee was chaired by Marshall Long, whom Kathleen had not fully forgiven for shoving her aside during Anthony's case more than 10 years before, even though they had worked together quite peaceably since. Marshall was one of the most respected of the younger partners, and Kathleen was quite proud to be in his company, even if it did mean giving up an entire Friday and Saturday to the Committee's work. The 11 attorneys on the Committee met in a private room at the Downtown Club. There were 198 associates to be evaluated. They started with the first-years because they were the easiest and could be dispensed with in an hour. All of the reviews were versions of "too soon to tell," and the three associates who had clerked for the Supreme Court were given an extra $500 in their salaries. The two associates who had very low billable hours—less than 1600—were given $500 less than the average raise. The rest received a $3000 bump, and the Evaluation Committee moved on to the next Class.

As a new member of the Committee, Kathleen listened to the banter of her fellow partners and wondered how she'd ever made it through the process. As an associate, she, too, had been known to miss a typo, miss a case, miss a fly. She'd never billed 2200 hours, not even close. She'd never, as an associate, brought in a client worth more than $20,000 in fees, not even enough to cover her own starting salary. Judged by the standards the Committee professed to be imposing as the Classes got closer to partnership, Kathleen felt woefully inadequate.

As the Committee entered the second day and considered the oldest three classes, the self-righteousness of her partners—all, like herself, in their late 30s or early 40s—reached fever pitch. Some pontificated: the future of Albright & Gill would be left in the hands of those judged by this Committee to be worthy of "A" ratings and thus most likely to make partner. It was an awesome responsibility. And what an *average* lot they were!

"What do you expect, with this kind of growth?" one member asked. "We've needed the bodies. But that doesn't mean we owe them partnership! Look at the starting salary!"

"Ridiculous," a couple of members agreed.

Names and evaluations bounced around the room like pinballs, but with a surprising degree of order. A name would be read and then a partner would summarize the evaluations in the folder and make a recommendation for a "grade." Then the members would chime in, saying that the associate was no better than someone they had just given a "B," and that the evaluation of the partner should be discounted because he was notoriously "easy." The evaluators would get distracted by their analysis of why the easy partner was a partner in the first place and how they wished they could evaluate him right out of the Firm. Kathleen was shocked by their candor, and while she may have herself agreed with the bottom line, their conversation preyed on her worst fears. What had been said about her when the Committee had read her evaluations?

"Ann Rose," John Watkins began. "I'd say she gets an 'A' as an associate. She comes up for partner this year. Jules Steinberg, of course, thinks she's the best associate he's ever seen. Gives her credit for bringing in the Gloria Ellens deal. He says First Credit loves her. Billed 2357 hours last year. That's an 'A+' in my book."

For the first time that day, there was complete silence in the room. One member of the committee cleared his throat, and then another. Kathleen unintentionally sneezed.

Marshall asked, "Any disagreement?"

Kathleen was curious. "Any reviews besides Steinberg's?"

"Yours, Kathleen, and four others."

"Also raving?" another partner asked.

"I'll read them," John said.

"Kathleen Hannigan," he began. "Contact: Worked with her on the Gloria Ellens deal. Categories: Not marked. Under Comments, Hannigan says, 'I'm not in a position to evaluate Ann's performance on the credit aspects of the deal (I was responsible for IP issues only), but I have some concern about Ann's ability to play 'team,' and her demeanor with clients. She refused to let me talk directly to the other IP lawyers, and at the closing dinner, she made no effort to be sociable, i.e., engage the client in conversation, social or otherwise. I think Ann could be more effective if she developed her social skills to match her legal ones.'"

John did not stop to comment on her comments. "Peter Banks, of the corporate group, also said that he had limited contact—one deal for First Credit—and he gave her all 'As' on the performance criteria. His comment is, 'A real macho lawyer. Should tone down profanity in front of clients and staff.' Here's one from Gregory Bleecher, again all 'As,' but he comments, 'Certainly has a different personality. Could use a course at charm school. I worry that her considerable legal ability is overshadowed by her overly aggressive personality, her trouble working with others, and her somewhat masculine style.'"

John shrugged. "There's one more, from Mr. Whitestone. We probably should discount this one, given that he is of the old school—geez, what is he now, 68? Anyway, he gave her 'Bs' all the way and added this juicy comment, 'Someone ought to tell this young lady to act and talk more femininely, maybe wear more jewelry and make-up. Not be so mannish.'"

"Oh great," Marshall said. "What should we do, tell her to dye her hair blond? Wear shorter skirts? Someone ought to tell Stanley this is 1988!"

A member of the Committee asked, "What do we do if someone is clearly excelling as an associate, but we don't want them to become partner? If we give an "A," we're just paving the way, at this stage. I can't stand her personally, but I don't have to deal with her. I'm asking because I don't know. What's our duty here?"

Marshall shook his head. "We evaluate associates. The Management Committee makes partners."

"Well, she's clearly an 'A+' associate," Kathleen said. She hadn't meant to betray Ann. She'd only been curious about what others would say about a woman superstar. She was surprised that her partners had drawn so dramatic a distinction between their evaluations of Ann's legal ability and her interpersonal skills. Kathleen saw that if it were up to the members of this committee, they wouldn't put Ann on the A&G team. In contrast, Kathleen knew that people liked her. Did that mean she should worry that she herself had been chosen for her personality rather than her playing ability?

"Well, I'm not totally comfortable with it, but what the fuck," a partner said. Kathleen chuckled at the irony of his profanity, but the others hadn't heard it.

At the end of the day, Marshall gave each member of the Committee the names of about 15 associates with whom they were to have a one-on-one interview. For the youngest associates and those who got "As," this was a relatively cursory "everything's fine" conversation. For those who had "issues," the interview could be a painful process.

Kathleen found criticism as difficult to give as to receive. She was the kind of person who'd never even sent back a meal in a restaurant, and the thought of delivering "bad news" to an associate gnawed on her generally good spirits. She had one "C" and two "B" messages to deliver, and she had the further bad luck to have been assigned Ann Rose.

To her surprise, the "C" went well. The associate—in the labor group—knew he was in the wrong place and told Kathleen that he knew he could do better work, that he just wasn't inspired by A&G's clients or his assignments. He had already interviewed at two different places and expected to be gone by the end of the year, happy to be out of the place.

Kathleen was honestly shocked. She had been so focused on her own career within the Firm that it never occurred to her that people left because they actually wanted to—she thought that was the positive face the rejected put on to make their exits graceful. In her family, you finished what you started and you aimed as high as possible.

The "Bs" were less sanguine, but both associates were third-year and willing to believe that they had enough time in front of them to "turn things around." They each quizzed her on what, specifically, they could do to improve. She gave each a one word answer—"organization" in one case and "writing" in the other—but she secretly wondered if even "A+s" in those categories would save their careers from the initial, less-than-stellar images. "A+s" might not even save Ann's career, so who was to say what anyone's chances of partnership were?

After 14 "practice" interviews, she couldn't put Ann Rose off any longer. Not that Ann Rose gave a damn. Kathleen had gotten calls from a few anxious associates who wanted her to know—just in case—that they would be out of town, in depositions, or otherwise unavailable at the end of the week. Could she possibly work them in earlier? When Kathleen called the star associate to ask if it would be convenient for Kathleen to stop down and talk, she was told no, and given an appointment to meet with Ann the next day.

Kathleen awoke that day cranky from a fitful sleep and resentful that her subject had probably slept as soundly as ever, unconcerned about whatever news the Evaluation Committee had for her. Kathleen fretted over the message implicit in the Committee's discussion. There was no easy one-liner for Ann the way there had been for the "Bs." Kathleen wasn't even convinced that it was a matter so much of Ann's personality as it was of image. The image, of course, was in the eyes of the beholder, and most of the beholders at Albright & Gill were men.

There'd been no similar conversations about the personalities of the men reviewed by the Evaluation Committee, and so Kathleen puzzled over the words the Firm used for "we don't like you." She knew the Firm's other euphemisms, like "your future is not indefinite," which meant, "find a new job," and "we wish him well in his new endeavor," which implied that the Firm didn't approve of the new endeavor and didn't itself expect to profit from it. If the Evaluation Committee had a message for Ann Rose, it seemed to Kathleen to boil down to "you're a little too bitchy" and that was a close relative of "we're jealous," which was next-of-kin to "we're threatened."

Ann's office was uncluttered. One art print, a mass of orange and brown abstraction, occupied one wall. The credenza was completely clear and the bookshelves above it three-quarters full, the books held in place by rectangular beige marble bookends. No manila folders lined the floor, no stray papers obscured the fine wood of her desk, no little yellow stickers clung to the phone or her blotter. Except for the small dictaphone to one side of the desk, Kathleen would have guessed the occupant of the office was on a six-month sabbatical. It did not look to her like a working office, yet it was the office of the star associate who just this week had impressed the Evaluation Committee with her productivity.

"Wow! I don't know how you do it!" Kathleen said as she sat down.

Ann raised her eyebrows, as if Kathleen had started in the middle of a private thought.

"This is the cleanest office I've ever seen," Kathleen explained, "and I've seen quite a few in the past couple of weeks." Ann raised her chin, her shoulders falling ever so slightly. Kathleen sat up a little straighter and urged herself to cut the small talk, get to her business and get out. Whatever she had to say was obviously not of particular interest to Ann, and already Ann seemed to Kathleen to have the upper hand.

"As you know, I sit on the Evaluation Committee." Kathleen paused momentarily to let the importance of that sink in. "I'm happy to report that," she stopped herself from saying, "of course." She didn't want to give away so soon even an inch of her authority. "That all of the reports the Committee received…." (A good way to put it, Kathleen thought, reserving as it did the possibility that others, who didn't report, might feel differently.) "Were excellent. 'As' and a few 'A+s.'"

Ann didn't move, but she wasn't stiff, either. Kathleen finished her speech, "and, having said that, your raise will be the top one given to your class."

"Thank you," Ann said peremptorily, and started to get up, signaling that the interview was, from her point of view, over.

"Oh, Ann," Kathleen said in a mixture of whine and disgust. "Sit down. You're not making this easy, but there's more we should talk about. I'm concerned. I'm truly concerned for you." Kathleen momentarily lost her courage, and asked, tentatively, "Are you happy?"

It was Ann's turn to look disgusted. "Am I supposed to be? Does the Evaluation Committee give grades for happiness now?"

Kathleen shrugged. She was angry with Ann for not being curious—had she been in Ann's shoes, she herself would've been begging the reviewer for her maternal, heart-to-heart advice. She lowered her voice and spoke slowly, "It has some concern about your interpersonal skills."

Inexplicably, Ann smiled broadly. It was the first time Kathleen could remember seeing Ann smile a smile with teeth. "Kathleen, if the Evaluation Committee wants me to play cheerleader like Kathleen Hannigan—who doesn't know Professional from Prom Queen—tell them, in whatever interpersonal way you find appropriate, to fuck themselves."

Kathleen seethed at Prom Queen, but was determined not to be distracted by the *ad hominum*. "Exactly! Listen to yourself, Ann! One partner said you ought to stop using profanity in front of clients. It's not feminine."

Ann threw her head back in a false laugh.

"They don't pay me to be feminine, Kathleen. They pay me to practice law."

"My fear, Ann, is that they will tell you to practice elsewhere when it comes time to make partner. The Evaluation Committee doesn't decide those things, but your file is filled with people's perceptions that you are too aggressive, too bitchy, too harsh. One guy even went so far as to say you ought to wear make-up and act more femininely, that you're too mannish. You know as well as I do that this place runs on perceptions, true and false, and that there's a certain culture here. You either fit in to the partnership or you don't. Why shoot yourself in the foot? You're such an excellent lawyer, but it might not matter. The only thing holding you back is your attitude—the perception of your attitude. Why not be a little softer, if that's what it takes? There aren't that many women partners here. We need you to join our ranks, but sometimes I think you're deliberately making it harder for us, like they'll think we all are as…as hard as you."

Ann stood up. "I am who I am, Kathleen. I'll take my chances."

Kathleen shook her head, defeated, and left. She'd said what she'd come to say.

Just a few months later, Kathleen sat in Jill's office. Even though they tried to at least say hello to each other every day, their professional paths rarely crossed. This time, however, Kathleen had convinced Anthony to let Jill plan his estate, and Kathleen was describing for her Anthony's various income-producing intellectual property rights and interests and some of the planned beneficiaries.

Kathleen didn't understand why Jill enjoyed her practice. She avoided contemplation of death and found discussions of who-gets-what-when-I'm-gone unsettling. The idea that families challenged each other over antiques and dinner rings was appalling enough, but she instinctively didn't care for the kind of people who tried to control their money—and the people they gave it to—from the grave. She thought—when she thought about it—that money was wasted on most rich people, who seemed to her to be overly concerned with hoarding it and completely dumbfounded when it came to truly enjoying it.

"You know, Anthony will change his mind six times in the next two years," Kathleen said.

"It's not expensive," Jill answered. "There's some work, but our fees just barely cover it. Probating the estate, that's where the fees rack up."

"So planning to die is the cheap part?" Kathleen said. "You make your real money after? When the client can't complain? What a deal!"

"*Our* money. You make it sound like blood money."

"Sorry." Kathleen smiled. "OK, I'll try to get you a schedule of Anthony's intellectual property assets, and what else? What else do you need?"

Jill took a deep breath and then blurted it out. "Time," she said. "I don't know how else to tell you. I should have told you all along, but...I wasn't sure. I'm leaving the Firm."

Kathleen couldn't move. Everything in Jill's office came into too-sharp focus: a collection of paperweights on Jill's desk, including the brass "Yes/No/Maybe" decision-maker Kathleen had given her as a joke a couple of years back; the old casebooks won as prizes when she'd been a student; the toy truck of the magnate whose foundation Jill had set up; the manila files neatly stacked against the wall like heirs in line for their money; the sterling-silver framed picture of Steve. It seemed to Kathleen that Jill, coolly composed and freshly manicured, had become everything Albright & Gill wanted its women lawyers to be. She'd never been a trouble-maker, had never demanded special favors or attention, had settled into a practice that "women were naturally good at," had played by all the rules. Now, she wouldn't be pressing the Firm for further advancement.

Kathleen was furious that her supposed best friend had made a second major professional decision without her input or advice.

"If I'd told you earlier, before I decided, you would've made it too hard. You would've said that I had to stay, for women and all. But I can't. Maybe it's wrong of me, but I don't want to. I'm tired of it."

Kathleen was about to tell her that if she were tired, she could take some time off, but Jill held up her hand. "I want to have a baby."

Kathleen opened her mouth to say, "At your age?" but again Jill didn't give her time. "I'm almost forty—so are you, by the way—and I know it's not going to be easy. The doctor says I can do it. That I should reduce the stress. So, I'm going to be teaching at John Marshall. Not a tenure-track appointment, but just to see, to get some teaching experience, and to see."

"Done deal?"

"June first."

"What about Steve? He's had three kids."

"But *I* haven't had kids. *We* haven't had kids. He's pretty young for being almost 50. He said I should go for it, if that's what I want." She laughed devilishly. "It's the 'going-for-it' part he likes!"

Kathleen slumped in her chair. She felt a little tremble in her lower lip.

Jill's voice was wistful. "Don't you ever wonder what life would have been like if we'd been born even five years earlier? Or just gotten married right out of college? Or hadn't gone to law school in the first place? Don't you ever get the urge—I don't know how else to say this— just to be more of a woman? Biological imperatives and all that?"

Kathleen's eyes filled. Over the years, they'd talked about wanting boyfriends, steady relationships, perhaps, even, husbands. Not children. Between themselves, they simply had avoided that issue, that complicating and perhaps inevitable issue. It was one thing for Kathleen to have to admit to herself that she still, and sorely, wanted a man in her life. But never would she have confessed a desire for children, and she tightened at the thought of Jill handing her an infant to cuddle. Kathleen squeezed her eyes to dam her tears. She'd never, that she could remember, cradled an infant in her arms. She'd been too young to hold her baby brother, Michael, and when she was a teen her mother had refused to let her babysit, for fear something would happen. There was something wrong with her, she thought—she had a fear of babies.

"The truth is, Kitty, I really want a child."

Kathleen nodded. She could not imagine what that would be like.

EIGHT

Q: *Were you what one might call*
a role model for Ms. Rose?

A nn Rose was not elected to partnership at the expected time.
In the summer of 1989, the Firm sent its clients its usual
discreet card, resembling an engraved wedding announcement,
informing them of the 20 associates who had joined their ranks.
Rumor had it—and this one probably started with the secretary
who took notes for the Management Committee—that the Firm
wanted Ann Rose to mature a little before partnership, but she
needn't worry. She did outstanding work that was appreciated by
the Firm.

Kathleen and Brian met by chance at Holly's desk. "Did you
hear?" Holly asked. "The associates are circulating a petition for
Ann Rose."

Brian looked puzzled. "What's she running for?"

Kathleen laughed. Brian's sole interest in Firm politics—perhaps
in people—was that which affected him directly. Ann Rose did not.

"So, who's organizing this?" Kathleen asked.

"No one who wants to be identified," Holly said. Kathleen had the
feeling that Holly wanted her to think she knew, when she probably
didn't. It would be very easy for petitions to circulate in brown
interoffice envelopes without someone in particular taking charge.
Holly had also heard there was a meeting at 4:00; the true leader
probably would not emerge until then. It could even be that Ann
Rose herself was the ringleader, although Kathleen thought that
was not Ann's style. Still, the prospect of the associates circulating a
petition secretly pleased her. Hadn't she always said that things
would change as more women joined the Firm and became
partners? The catch was that while the young lawyers' politics were
in the right feminist place, Kathleen herself intensely disliked the
woman who would benefit most directly from their activism.
Kathleen thought a man in Ann Rose's position might also have

been told to grow up, and that would not have merited a petition. It would be interesting to see what would happen.

Kathleen and Brian went into his office. The floor around his desk was strewn with papers.

"You've got to do something about this place," Kathleen said, in a friendly, big-sister sort of way.

"I'm working on it," Brian said, a little hurt. "I think it's better, don't you?" He hurried to straighten out the papers on his left while Kathleen's eyes bulged in exaggerated disbelief. The phone rang.

"Don't," Kathleen began, too late. No one was quicker on the phone trigger than Brian, and lately Kathleen had been amusing herself by trying to get him to focus on one thing at a time—for instance, not answering the phone while giving an assignment to an associate or while talking to her.

"Yes." Brian handed her the phone, his face grave. "It's Blake. For you."

"Kathleen Hannigan," Kathleen said out of habit, stretching across Brian's desk and then walking around to avoid dragging his phone out of its socket. Brian got up and offered her the chair behind his desk. She sat down and he hovered.

"Yes," Kathleen said and hung up. Brian furrowed his brow and turned his chin a little to the left. Part of Kathleen would've loved to have left Brian twisting by the noose of his curiosity over what could possibly have been so important that Blake would track her down in Brian's office. But she didn't know yet herself.

"In his office, now, was all I got," she said. "You clean up yours and I'll bring Blake down for inspection later."

Brian followed her to the elevators. "Do you think it's about me?" he said to her.

She burst out laughing. "I doubt it, Brian."

"Well, if it's an IP issue, he would have called me, wouldn't he?"

Kathleen heard the whine of "mommy likes me better" and shook her head. "Brian!"

"I'll be here when you get back," he said as the elevator doors closed.

Two other members of the Management Committee, and Marshall Long, the head of the Evaluation Committee, were in Blake's office. The two seniors half-stood out of their chairs and Marshall stood up fully. Blake remained seated behind his old style, leather inlay library table which he used as a desk. It was spotless. Three thin files were in the center. He nodded towards an empty side chair.

"Apparently some of the associates feel aggrieved that Ms. Rose was not named to partnership this year," Blake began. No one in the room moved a muscle. Marshall, his head slightly bowed, looked like he was barely breathing. The others fixed their gaze on Blake, who may have been staring at the bookcase on the wall 15 feet behind her. Blake had a majestic corner office. For some reason, which probably had to do with a power Kathleen didn't understand, his back was to his magnificent view of Lake Michigan. The glare from the windows washed out his facial features and any trace of expression.

"I believe that they will be meeting in Conference Room 48G at 4:00 this afternoon."

Kathleen stopped herself from nodding that he was correct. She understood that she was in powerful company. She wanted to belong. She could not appear complicit with the associates.

He looked at her. "I want you to handle the situation."

Kathleen's mind raced through a decision tree of responses: If I say this, then…but if I say this, then…. She couldn't fill in the blanks quickly enough to get her lips to move.

"Why me?" she wanted to ask, but didn't. She had been flattered, in an odd way, when Randy had died and Blake had reached out to her. This, however, was high risk. Perhaps Blake had called on her because she was on the Evaluation Committee, but maybe, just maybe, his calling her meant that he perceived her as the woman leader of the Firm.

"I can meet with the associates, Blake," she tried to keep her voice even and disinterested, as if she called him "Blake" every day. "But what is the Management Committee's formal position?" He looked mildly annoyed, as if she should know the answer. Although she probably did, she thought it better to be able to quote him rather than to guess.

"My position is that partnership at Albright & Gill is a privilege, not a right. Excellent lawyers become partners when they are ready."

She squeezed one hand over the other. "Do you expect that Ms. Rose will be ready the next time such decisions are made?"

"She will be given due consideration as will all eligible associates at such time as the partnership next desires to admit new partners. Thank you, Ms. Hannigan." Blake's eyes brushed hers and then rested on his phone. He buzzed his secretary and turned his attention to the top file.

The four lawyers filed out of Blake's office, Kathleen repeating to herself Blake's words.

"Any suggestions?" she said to Marshall when they were out of earshot of Blake and his two secretaries.

"Be careful what you say." Marshall smiled benignly. "Lunch?"

At a 24-hour restaurant not far from the office, Marshall and Kathleen reminded each other that interpersonal skills were an important qualification for partnership. Waiting for their meals, she said, "The problem is, Marshall, that there are partners here with interpersonal skills no better than hers. Perhaps worse."

"Right, and some of them wouldn't make partner by today's standards, but the truth is, Kathleen, and this is not for publication, we expect less from them as far as personality goes. Everybody knows Bob is gruff and Jerry a bit rude. It's just different."

Despite his words, Marshall's manner was calming.

As they returned to the office, Marshall surprised her by volunteering. "Do this," he said. "Go. Listen. Let them vent. State the Firm's position—you heard it. Say what an excellent lawyer Ann is and how decisions are based on a variety of factors, and how everyone makes partner when he's ready, and I guarantee you, this will blow over. *No one* is going to stick his own neck out for Ann Rose."

At 4:00, Conference Room 48G was empty. Kathleen walked by, a legal pad in hand, and could see through the glass panel that the room, which could hold 200 if the chairs were arranged theater style, had not been rearranged since its last use, and there were three long tables, each accommodating 16 people, and a stack of extra chairs against the wall. She strolled around the corner to an enclave with a phone for visitors. She picked it up and dialed her own number, keeping an eye on the double doors to Conference Room G.

A small group of young associates arrived, but she saw them only from behind. Then another group, and another. At six minutes after four, Kathleen estimated that there were 36 associates gathered, and she slipped in behind a group of five. She took a seat at one of the tables, close to the door. She watched the attorney sitting across from her draw loopy daisies in the margin of a blank legal pad. The room was as quiet as a church before a funeral.

She remembered her own rabble rousing days as friendly and festive. Then, they had worn buttons, and carried placards, and burst into songs and chants with the fervor of their causes—anti-war, anti-Nixon, anti-establishment. In contrast, this group sighed and yawned and cleared its throat as if it were uncertain, as yet, whether or not it had a cause. It certainly did not appear to have a leader.

She did not recognize many of the faces at the table, which surprised her because she'd prided herself, from years on the Summer Committee, on keeping up with the waves of new legal talent that each year washed up on the shores of Albright & Gill. It was clear to her that most of the associates present didn't recognize her either, although they must have noticed she was older than what might have been considered "normal." Yet, a lot of women in law school these days were "returning" students, so Kathleen, without a strand of gray, didn't stick out as obviously as she'd feared she might.

At ten after four, a very thin, very young looking woman stood up. She had mousy brown hair, cut short, and large, horn-rimmed glasses. She wore a plain gray suit and a stiff white shirt, buttoned at the neck. She did not look like a leader colorful enough to be noticed, let alone followed.

"Thanks for coming. I'm Rachelle Fineberg, and I'm a first-year associate in the Commercial Law Group. As you know, the senior woman associate in my group, Ann Rose, was passed over for partnership this week, and I believe that the Firm owes us an explanation. When I was recruited to come to Albright, I met Ann, and I was told by my recruiter that she would become a partner with the next class. I clerked for the U.S. Supreme Court and I had a lot of choices. I specifically chose to come to this Firm—and I could have gone to Sidley or Kirkland or Mayer Brown or Winston or Jenner or Skadden or Sonnenschein or Schiff...." Her list of all the top firms in the city both gave her credibility and ran the risk of alienating those who didn't have the same number of choices, but she continued, "and I chose A&G for the opportunity to work with women like Ann Rose. Ann Rose last year billed more billable hours than any other associate, was responsible for bringing in at least $250,000 of her own business—more than any of the others—and has terrific relationships with the Firm's existing clients. I asked Ann Rose what reason she was given for being passed over and she said it was her personality, that she was too aggressive and not feminine enough. I say that is sex discrimination, and that we associates must not tolerate it."

There was a mild sprinkling of applause.

"We have 55 names on our petition, so far, and I'm sure we'll get more. The petition reads, 'We, the undersigned, hereby state that, based on our personal experiences with Ann Rose and/or our understanding of the criteria for partnership at Albright & Gill, we believe that Ann Rose meets the highest standards for partnership and should immediately be elected to partnership.' So, if you haven't signed yet, please do. The last thing is, we need to decide what action we are willing to take if our petition is not accepted."

Kathleen stood up. She thought that use of the word "partnership" three times in one declarative sentence was an antique style of legal drafting not up to current partnership standards. To say so would be a partner-type comment, procedurally picky and substantively meaningless, so she kept it to herself, but it amused her and diffused her nervousness. She took a deep breath.

"For those of you who don't know me, I'm Kathleen Hannigan, a partner in the IP group, and I serve on the Evaluation Committee. Mr. Mills asked me to crash your meeting here today"—she realized as she said it that "crash" dated her—"and to convey to you the Firm's respect for Ann Rose as a lawyer. Partnership decisions are extremely complicated—none of us can say for sure why one is chosen and another not—but certainly the Firm, as a partnership, has a right to assess a person's qualifications as a totality when it decides to whom it will extend the privilege of partnership. Different people are ready at different times, and there are many partners of the Firm today who perhaps did not make partner the first time they were up. Mr. Mills sends his assurances that Ann Rose will be considered again at such time as the Firm next makes partners. So, I think you will want to consider that as you deliberate your possible courses of action. Let me also say that I am not here as a spy or to report back to the Management Committee, but to answer any questions you may have."

"You are a disgrace to feminism." Rachelle, perhaps feeling the protective armor of her Supreme Court clerkship, raised her voice. She no longer looked mousy. "Women will get nowhere if we have to be like you to become partners at firms like A&G. You, Sally, the rest of you, you all care more about fashion than you do about law. Ann Rose doesn't fit your frothy definition of femininity so she gets passed over. And you support the male partnership in their sexism!"

Kathleen raised her chin and looked around the room, trying to make eye contact with as many of the associates as possible. She knew that how she handled this situation would be dramatized, criticized, and reported back to those not in attendance. Kathleen didn't know Rachelle at all, but she intuitively liked her spunk. Had it been Ann Rose speaking, venom would have spewed, unconsidered, from Kathleen's mouth, but because Rachelle was an underdog here, a mere first-year associate and not a threat to Kathleen's advancement at the Firm, Kathleen could see some of her collegiate, feisty self in Rachelle. The difference was that Rachelle could express it. Now that there were more women at the Firm, and women partners like herself, first-years like Rachelle could feel freer to stand up the way Rachelle was standing up, knowing she probably would not be punished for it.

"There are many brands of feminism, Ms. Fineberg."

"Your brand hurts women."

"This is not about me or my feminist politics, Ms. Fineberg. I was a feminist before you were born,"—Kathleen wasn't quite that old—"and without people like me, it is doubtful that your class at Albright & Gill would be half women. As to the partnership's right to determine who it will make partner, that rule predates us both. The partnership does not discriminate on the basis of race, sex or religion, or"—and here she remembered Randy—"sexual orientation,"—saying so made her feel more liberal, even, than Ms. Fineberg—"and the Firm wants you to know that it will consider Ms. Rose for partnership when the time comes."

A young African-American male associate named Howard raised his hand and began to speak. "I think we've just been told that our petition is worthless unless we are ready to take action. What action are we ready to take?"

"How about an exposé in *The American Lawyer*?" one woman suggested.

"That would take a month or more, and the Firm doesn't care what a newspaper says about them," another said.

"The only effective option is one which has an economic impact," Howard said quietly, studying his fellow associates while the grave implications sunk in.

"A strike?" a young man said.

"I have a brief due," a couple of lawyers said simultaneously, and Kathleen nearly laughed out loud at how quickly and thoroughly A&G had inculcated its values.

"So you get the brief done early, and then we strike for a day. At least, we plan the strike, and see if the Firm will reconsider in the meantime," Rachelle said.

"Are we prepared to actually strike if we don't get satisfaction?" Howard asked.

Kathleen sat quietly. To intervene further struck her as heavy handed, ineffective, and, ultimately, likely to backfire. She had been at Albright & Gill long enough to know that the official position was not to care, at least openly, what the associates thought. Like youthful experiments in hair—color, length or style—the minor discontents of associates would pass and be forgiven. Soon enough, they would learn their place. Soon enough, they would have mortgages and kids, financial commitments in excess of their ability to earn elsewhere. Soon enough, they would see that Albright & Gill acted only in their best interests.

"A strike could be misinterpreted as our just wanting a day off," Rachelle said. She was flushed, and the blood gave her pale face a rosy glow. Despite herself, she smiled widely and shared her brainstorm, just as it was coming to her. "Here's an idea. On the appointed strike day, we'll do something like dress in jeans and work shirts, and we'll come to work, but we'll bill all our time to *pro bono* matters. For women's groups, or other minorities. We could invite a feminist law professor to talk to us at lunch, or something like that!"

The room brightened with the genius of Rachelle's plan. They would present their petitions to the Firm with a cover letter setting forth the ultimatum. A couple of the women would see about making rose-colored arm bands for everyone to wear. They would let the other offices know about their plans, but there wasn't time to make a concerted effort to encourage them to participate. Howard would gather a list of relevant *pro bono* matters that could be assigned, and would coordinate the work. If someone knew someone at *The American Lawyer*, that would be good, too.

Kathleen watched them leave the conference room. Rachelle and Howard were the last to leave.

"Nice work," Kathleen said to them. They hesitated and then hurried out. The beauty of the plan was obvious—how could the Firm criticize a day of *pro bono* work? How could Blake have expected her to derail it?

"Thank you, Ms. Hannigan."

Blake had listened to Kathleen's report with a gentle amusement. He had asked the name of the associate who had proposed the plan, and had nodded when Kathleen said her name. She suspected, based on a slight upturning of the right side of his mouth, that Blake had some respect for that Rachelle Fineberg. Kathleen didn't know that Fineberg's father was the CFO of one of the Firm's top 50 clients, a light manufacturing concern.

"Get me Nathan Fineberg," she heard Blake say to his secretary as she left. Whatever Blake's countermove would be, he didn't share it with Kathleen, nor did he give her a clue as to what he might have expected from her.

That night, she called her mother to say hello, and to solicit her comfort. "You did your best," her mom said, but Kathleen knew that her mother could not appreciate fully the implications for her career. Her mother knew nothing about the culture of law firms. Kathleen was beginning to wonder how much she herself understood. She accepted her mother's soothing, as effective as a kiss on an "owie." She couldn't insist she was a failure—she loved her mother too much. Her mother wouldn't believe her, anyway.

On the morning of the day before the strike, the associates were, as a group, agitated. As far as anyone knew, there'd never been an associates' strike at a major law firm, certainly never at Albright & Gill. More than one cup of coffee spilled in the coffee room. The copy machine, spitting out rumpled copies, got a few extra kicks. Several secretaries swore as they took perfectly typed letters back to their computers to center perfectly, this time, the writer's direct dial telephone number under the pre-printed place on Albright & Gill's letterhead. The associates consoled one another in quick meetings in the hallways that their strength was indeed in numbers. If everyone participated, then the Firm could hardly fire them all. Albright & Gill would be like a plantation without slaves, an airline without pilots.

The petitions had been delivered to Blake in a new, unused, inter-office envelope so that no prior history of routing would give away the identity of an organizer. Blake reportedly was in D.C. for three days, but the associates told each other that didn't mean anything. Arm bands cut from cheap rose-colored cotton were anonymously delivered to every associate.

Kathleen thought it interesting that no effort was made to involve the younger partners in the strike. If anyone had a right to feel aggrieved, it was those partners who felt strongly about Ann and yet had no power, in their own firm, to admit such a capable lawyer and business-getter to partnership. There were such partners, of course, but the associates apparently assumed—and perhaps rightly—that they would be unwilling to put their own partnerships on the line for someone else's. Besides, the associates might have reasoned, most of them were men, and the women— like Kathleen—had been co-opted. Kathleen was amuck in her own split loyalties. She'd come to truly dislike Ann Rose, but she was afraid the associates were right. Kathleen also disliked other of her partners, whose personalities were no less foul than Ann's. Would there be a need for a strike if Ann were male?

On that afternoon, the associates' mood turned glum. The halls were unusually empty, the coffee pot sat full. At 3:00 p.m., the mail staff delivered a memo to each lawyer in the Firm.

As many of you are aware, the American Bar Association and the Rules of Conduct strongly suggest that each lawyer give at least 50 hours of *pro bono* service to the community each year. In furtherance of that goal, the Management Committee urges each lawyer to utilize his or her time on Friday on *pro bono* activities, subject to client needs. Additional secretarial support will be made available over the weekend to fulfill client responsibilities without overtime charges.

In addition, Senior Judge Thomas R. McMillen, U.S. District Court for the Northern District of Illinois, will lead a discussion of public service at 4:30 p.m. in conference Room G, with a short reception to follow.

Kathleen clasped her hands, prayer style, against her lips. For at least five minutes, she had no active thoughts. The rebellion had been kicked out of her and she was in a coma of non-feeling. "Utter bullshit," she said out loud. Then she noticed Rachelle at her door.

"I brought you this," Rachelle said, handing her a rose-colored arm band.

Kathleen gestured to her chair. She propped her face in her right hand, her elbow braced against her desk.

"What are you going to do?" she asked Rachelle.

"We're going to make sure everyone wears an arm band, to show this was our idea, not theirs, and we're going to tell *The American Lawyer* the truth."

"Have you talked to Ann? Does she want all this?"

"Ann has other remedies," Rachelle said. "This is a statement about what lawyers at this Firm will tolerate in terms of gender and racial stereotyping."

Kathleen nodded to say she understood. It might also have conveyed that she agreed. She let the ambiguity stand.

"Are you going to wear it, or will it clash—I'm sorry, that's just rhetoric. Actually, I came here to work with Ann Rose, but I have to tell you that you're the one I've come to admire."

Kathleen laughed, not to ridicule Rachelle, but out of the discomfort she felt whenever she was labeled a role model. The intended compliment didn't make up for the scintilla of truth in Rachelle's remark about clothes. Yes, she had become very conscious of her clothes. At a place as large as Albright & Gill, clothes were a billboard. The only perception many of her partners would have of her skill as a lawyer would be the passing impression her clothes might make.

"I didn't know a thing about clothes until Jill Alton taught me. She was the first person I met here in my class. June 4, 1976, to be exact." Rachelle looked at her blankly, and Kathleen realized Jill had left before Rachelle had arrived. "She was a partner until a year ago, but she decided..." Kathleen was going to say, "she couldn't take it any more," but instead she said, "to teach."

"I don't mean clothes. I just mean that you seem to have it all together. You've succeeded here, and kept your, your..." Kathleen expected Rachelle wanted to say, "femininity," but had seen the problem in that. "Your self."

Kathleen felt tears forming. "I'm not sure what I've kept," Kathleen said.

"It would be great if you would wear the arm band tomorrow."

COURTING KATHLEEN HANNIGAN

"I just might," she said.

Rachelle thanked her and left. For a long time, Kathleen stared out her window, without particular interest.

In the kind of daze that could collapse in either tears or deep sleep, she called Harry in the D.C. office, where it was an hour later and even the hardest working of associates would have been justified in going home. "Don't you have a life?" she demanded.

"The law is a jealous mistress. Like you, my chick-a-dee."

"I haven't talked to you in a year."

"But you're counting, that's good. I have been buried here. I haven't set foot in Chicago in longer than that."

"You could attend the All-Partners' meeting you know."

"You know I'd rather resuscitate a wart hog than that."

Kathleen roared, the first sincere laugh she'd had all day. "So, what's your take on this Ann Rose brouhaha?"

"Uppity women sing the same old sexist song, and still can't hit the high note." She heard Harry take a sip of something.

"Come on. I need a real answer, Harry. Blake appointed me to 'handle the situation' and the proletariat here handed me my head. You know about the strike, right? 'Power to the *publico* day' at Albright & Gill? Which Blake just usurped as the Firm's idea? I'm screwed, no matter what."

"I do see, my dear, that your ambition has met the moguls of fate." Harry was into his *faux intelligentsia* act, which would have been mildly entertaining but for her distress.

"Do you think Blake would absolutely crucify me if I wore an arm band tomorrow?"

"Rumor has it he will be in D.C. tomorrow." Harry paused. "Truth is, my little honey-bee, I don't think he gives a damn one way or the other what you or the snotty-assed associates do. But I have to say, if you will let me, that you need to find a man, or at least a good fuck. You need some purpose in life other than the petty politics of Albright & Gill."

She tried to imitate Harry's mock formality. "You know, Harold Blomquist, you are one selfish son of a bitch." She heard him snicker. "I need you to be a friend, help me out, give me some real answers."

"I gave you real answers, my pet. You didn't like them."

Kathleen knew he was right, even if he had been drinking out of his bottom drawer.

That evening, she found the key to her apartment building's storage locker (in the junk drawer, by the sink) and found the pine box she'd bought at the end of her freshman year in college in which to store her things over the summer in the dormitory basement. She had last opened it in 1981 for a '60s party. She found a short brown suede vest, fringed with orange and blue beads. It had been her favorite, most expensive piece of hippy clothing, and it had cost her probably $25. Underneath it was an embroidered work shirt she could wear on Friday, in solidarity. The friend who had done the needlework was now a pediatrician up in Canada, married, with two children of her own.

She took the embroidered work shirt to the kitchen sink and rinsed it out, then threw it in the drier. She thought she'd wear it with a navy skirt and a leather belt with a heavy gold buckle.

S trike day was gray, from the ground up. In her memory, such days were cloudless, crisp October days, warm enough for just a light sweater tied loosely around the hips. Strikes and demonstrations were like festivals, filled with the energy of youth marching in solidarity, taking the future into their own hands, and requiring the world to bend to their will. Powerful, heady stuff, those days—when individual action would give peace a chance and the college town police wouldn't dare arrest a promising young career. The Ivy League students put what they had on the line, knowing in their heart of hearts that it wasn't much, just all they had. Indeed, for many, there was a safety net of family support and money and connections that would break their fall. Of course, what they'd had on the block was the illusion of their own power, and, in the end, they'd been successful.

She was one of the first to arrive on the forty-seventh floor on strike day. It was 8:00, and it amused her that the associates' free legal work for the poor was apparently less urgent than billable work for paying clients. ARMBAND—the Ann Rose March Against

Bias and Neo-Discrimination (it was the best Kathleen could come up with so early in the morning)—would get off to no particular start. No organizing banners or bullhorns would work the crowd into a frenzy of rectitude. Slowly, associates would drift in, arms wrapped in rose-colored strips or not, and protest, silently. When it was over, they would look at their to-do lists of documents to be produced, research to be done, memoranda to be written, and reserve some of that secretarial time over the weekend. The *pro bono* clients would be helped, the paying clients postponed a day, the secretaries time-and-a-half richer, and Ann Rose, still, officially, an associate at the law firm of Albright & Gill.

She was working on a paper on freedom of expression. It wasn't exactly *pro bono* work, but it wasn't billable, either, so she wasn't sure she was entitled to wear the rose arm band, even if she decided to put it on. It was almost 9:00, and she still didn't know. Maybe she could wear it in her office, but not in the halls? She took it out of her purse and started to tie it around her left upper arm, putting one end in her mouth to try to make a knot. She was thinking that this was the real reason it takes two to make a movement, when just then Rachelle appeared at her door.

"Oh, let me help you," she said. "This is great, Kathleen! It really feels like we are taking some control of our lives!"

"You should have gone into community organizing," Kathleen said.

"I might still!" Rachelle said.

"What makes you so brave about this?" Kathleen asked, genuinely puzzled.

"I don't give a damn! I really don't think my future is here. You know, my dad's a client. Or did you know? So I've seen both sides of this Firm, and frankly, I can't see myself grubbing for partnership."

"Then why the big deal about Ann Rose's partnership? Shouldn't this be her business, not yours? What makes *her* your pet cause?"

"*She* is not my cause. She's not the poster child I would pick for a pet cause, either. But she does stand for my pet cause today because I don't want to give up anything. I hate them telling me what I'm supposed to be like as a woman. I just know they are imposing different standards on Ann Rose, than they would on Dan Rose. If there were a Dan Rose, he could be the most aggressive, hard-hearted, asshole there is and they would say he was a tough lawyer. Or he could be catatonic, and they would think he was the strong-and-silent type. They wouldn't say he needed charm school."

"You really don't care about partnership?" Kathleen herself had never considered not making partner. Even now, she realized, her indecision about wearing an armband was about her wanting to be perceived as a partner, and as a senior partner. It was a large Firm, and perceptions mattered. She wanted to stand out, but not like that. Besides, women like herself, who met her standards, did in fact make partner at Albright & Gill. Surely she was not required to support the bitchy ones in order to prove herself an adequate feminist. The associates couldn't expect her to risk any of her own partnership prestige over Ann Rose, who in any event would make partner next year, after she'd learned her lesson. If some would see this as Kathleen Hannigan's personal ambition stripping her of the courage of her convictions, then so be it. They didn't know how hard it had been, how much personal insult she had suffered through, to get to where she was, to get the Firm to a place where someone like Ann Rose even had a chance.

"Only on *my* terms. You know, I'll have a family some day, and they'll come first, not Albright & Gill, and I want to do community service, and keep in shape and go to the symphony once in a while, and I don't see Albright & Gill giving me the time to do it all. Maybe it works for you, but you're not married!"

It was an off-hand remark, but it left a stinging red blotch on Kathleen's face. She wasn't married. Harry had said as much the night before, in his own crude terms. Now, the strike was putting her marriage to Albright & Gill on the rocks. She felt like a woman whose husband was in love with someone else and she didn't have the heart—yet—to admit it and let him go. Or to admit that for her part, she didn't love him anymore either, and perhaps she herself should be the one to go. What Rachelle seemed to be saying, whether she understood it or not, was that both parties could be very right, and at the same time be very wrong for each other.

"Listen, I have a little more organizing of the community to do," Rachelle said with just the right touch of self-deprecation. "I'll check with you later. We have a photographer coming from *The American Lawyer.* I'll have him take your picture."

"Over my dead body. And yours. This is an associate thing. *If* I wear this all day, I'm dead anyway, but no pictures. Got it?"

"Okay. But, Kathleen, you *are* doing the right thing."

Midmorning, Kathleen stopped by the library, which throbbed as the nerve center of the movement. Howard sat at a table in the center with a stack of files and a long white stand-up card that said "*Pro Bono* Assignments." "How's it going?" she said to Howard. She hoped he would comment on her courage in wearing the armband.

"I think Rachelle counted 62 percent participation."

"Right on!"

Howard barely looked up. Kathleen returned to her office, closed her door and ordered lunch in, a prerogative of partners she seldom exercised.

Jimmy called her about 2:00 and she went down to his office. He was wearing an orange and brown dashiki shirt, and the arm band was tied around his forehead. As she walked in, he got up and twirled around for her.

"Fuck 'em, Kitty. Fuck 'em," Jimmy whooped the way he did sometimes when he was feeling particularly delighted in his opponent's bad fortune and was well into that second celebratory martini. Ernie Gordon, the old man of the Management Committee, the one from Iowa who had asked Kathleen to sign the partnership agreement way back when, strolled into Jimmy's office, apparently returning from the men's room. He and Jimmy had lunched together. They were an odd match—Ernie the former farm boy and Jimmy, the first token African-American partner—although they both had ended up someplace neither of them could've expected.

"You're the one who should have ribbons in your hair," Ernie said, standing with his arm propped up against Jimmy's doorway as if it were a milk barn. Ernie had a twinkle in his eye. He'd learned to drink the day he slaughtered his first chicken. He'd been in fourth grade.

"She's one of us!" Jimmy whooped.

"Maybe time for some coffee, Kathleen," Ernie said and winked. He stepped through the door, and Kathleen realized he was asking her to get it. She pulled off her arm band and tied a quick bow around her hair, the loops sitting on top of her head like a cartoon character.

"Cream and sugar? One lump or two?" she asked in a high, subservient voice.

"Black, strong and quick." Ernie sat down on Jimmy's couch. Kathleen couldn't find a secretary, so she brought two coffees. She tucked a can of Coca-Cola under her armpit for herself. It was strike day and she was serving coffee. The irony was not lost on her. But for all of Jimmy's faults, he was her colleague, her partner, and she got to work on Anthony's matters because of him. He needed coffee, and she was, she told herself, senior enough and secure enough not to have to stand on ceremony.

Ernie took a loud slurp of his coffee, and she put Jimmy's in the center of his desk. She knew better than to expect him to drink it, and wondered if Ernie really thought he could stop Jimmy's loose train with a single cup of steaming coffee.

"Anthony's got a new joint venture," Ernie began. Jimmy stood like a statue facing out his window, quietly ignoring them both. "We're going to meet him Sunday in New Orleans. We're on the 7:30 flight."

"New Orleans," she muttered.

"Great town!" Ernie said. "We'll have a good time."

Kathleen grimaced in Jimmy's direction.

"He'll be fine."

"Easy for you to say."

"I'll watch him. We won't get in any trouble, will we, Jimmy?"

Jimmy didn't answer and Kathleen saw an opportunity. If she was wearing a rose arm band to stick up for someone she didn't even like, then she had better stick up for herself. "Ernie, if you want me to be there, you must keep his hands off of me."

Ernie's blue eyes lost their twinkle. "He's getting worse," she whispered. She didn't say at what, and she assumed she didn't have to say. Ernie and Jimmy had had enough restaurant meals together for him to have witnessed Jimmy's behavior.

"I said I'd take care of it," Ernie said seriously.

Kathleen took the armband off of her head and retied it as best she could around her arm. It occurred to her that she was entitled not only to wear it, but to flaunt it. If the partnership wanted the truth, she could goose them with a truth that would make their skins crawl. She could tell them about Jimmy.

She went back to her office, answered a couple of calls from clients, and, since she would be on a plane to New Orleans, canceled her Sunday racquet ball date with Jill. She wrote two pages about freedom of expression and at 4:30, her arm band securely back on her left arm, she walked the three flights to 48G for Judge McMillen's speech. Maybe half the partners were there, and a sprinkling of male associates in their three-piece suits. The women associates had either participated in the strike or were "out of the office on business." She saw three young woman partners huddled together, and knew that partnership was new enough to each of them that solidarity with the strike had not crossed their minds. She waved to Sally, who for so long had stood alone and who finally was feeling part of her partnership, but she purposefully did not make an effort to sit with her. She did not want to appear soft. Jimmy stood by a seat in the first row and waved his arms wildly when she came in. She pretended not to see him. She didn't want to take sides with so visible an outcast. She took a seat in the second to last row, on the left, near the end but not the very end, so as not to draw attention to her own solidarity.

Through no particular fault of the Judge's, the speech, which by its very nature had to be platitudinal and melodramatic in its tales of the accomplishments of *pro bono* lawyers for their clients, was enough to put Jimmy to sleep in the first row. She heard two gentle pulls before a loud snort punctuated the climax of one of the Judge's stories. Although she hoped for his sake it wasn't, she knew it was Jimmy because she saw the orange flurry of his dashiki as Ernie's swift elbow straightened him in his chair.

Polite applause welcomed the end of Judge McMillen's remarks. Finally, the bar was open. Kathleen slipped her arm band off, wadded it into her shirt pocket, and ordered a glass of red wine. Out of the corner of her eye, she saw Ernie guide Jimmy towards the elevators, away from the bar. It wasn't a very good cocktail party, anyway, more of a quick fix, one-for-the-train sort of affair. The bartenders, in white shirts and black bow-ties, worked feverishly for half an hour and then it was over.

She stopped by her office to pick up her jacket, purse and briefcase, and found a note from Rachelle. The associates were celebrating at a Rush Street bar, further from Albright & Gill than their usual after work get-togethers. She appreciated the invitation, but it didn't give her a sense of belonging. At the end of strike day, Kathleen Hannigan went home to drink alone.

NINE

Q: *You were Chair of the Committee?*

Ernie took care of Jimmy in New Orleans, and the three of them blended uneventfully into Anthony's entourage. They ate well, drank moderately, slept a little, and managed to put a joint venture and two big pay-per-view concerts together, at least on paper. Anthony had a tendency to treat his contracts as statements of his good intentions. His view, like Blake's, was that if something was good for him, it was good for everyone. If an event failed, he didn't care what was on the piece of paper entitled "Agreement." He would forge a new agreement by the sheer dint of his will—he simply told the participants and the investors the amount of their new share, reduced from expectations. "We're in this together, my friend," he would say, and those who wanted to stay friends would say "okay" when he told them that they should take the long view. After all, he said, the losses were as illusory as their wild hopes for profits had been inflated. This was the entertainment business.

Thursday, Kathleen returned to an Albright & Gill that had forgotten the strike the way poor golfers forget two muffed strokes— they just don't show up on the scorecard. Ann Rose was in New York again on business, but her supporters hardly noticed. She'd become a principle, not a personality. Hers was not a charismatic or cult following, and the rebellion among the associates was quieted by the weight of billable work thrust upon them. There'd been some disillusionment when Ann Rose was rumored to have said the cause was in fact personal, not political.

Within a month of leading the only rebellion Albright & Gill had ever endured, Rachelle Fineberg took personal action and left the Firm. She found a job as the assistant director of a legal services clinic on the near west side of Chicago which paid maybe a third of her starting salary at A&G but promised her people-oriented legal problems. She did not encourage her fellow associates to follow her.

"Some have to stay and work within the system," she told Kathleen. "I don't have the patience. I also don't have the need— either financially or professionally. I can see how if I stayed, I'd get stuck, like you."

Kathleen was flattered, again, that Rachelle had come to her office to say good-bye. She liked the woman's straightforward manner, but the word "stuck" was like a stab in the chest. She reached in her desk drawer for a Rolaid. There'd been a time in her life, too, when she'd enjoyed all the freedom that is the privilege of the well educated, well-to-do and unattached. Some of that freedom had dissipated, but she couldn't pinpoint exactly when it had slipped away. Some of it, no doubt, she'd ceded to the Firm, to its criteria for partnership, for power, and for remuneration. Was she stuck? She was, she assumed, employable elsewhere, albeit most likely at a lower salary. She could live on less, certainly, but she was acutely aware that she was her only source of income, and she rather liked the comfort—even wealth—that A&G afforded her. Besides, could other places be that different? At least here, at A&G, they knew her, and seemed to respect her, and she, for her part, thought she knew what they wanted from her. It would be a lot of work to start over, and somewhat risky. You could call that stuck.

"Well, I'm happy you found such an ideal position, Rachelle," Kathleen said, perhaps with too much cheer.

The following spring, Kathleen was named Chair of the Evaluation Committee. Since chairs of this Committee normally were highly respected, she was inclined to see it as a reward for her handling of the rebellion, but it could just as easily have been interpreted as punishment. According to the outgoing chair, Marshall Long, heading the Committee took several hundred hours a year, but these were over and above a lawyer's normal workload. He said he was pleased to be done with it and shipped six heavy cardboard file boxes to her office.

At her first meeting, the Committee clicked through its work, class by class, the youngest, easiest, first; the balance on a beautiful April Saturday when every member of the Committee had someplace they would rather be. On Saturday, only Marshall wore a jacket and tie, the rest came in jeans or khakis. If it weren't for his seeming formality, she noticed again that Marshall was the type of man she still hoped to meet someday.

The Committee behaved itself beautifully, avoiding long quarrels over "A" associates from corporate and "B" associates from tax. If they finished early, perhaps they could each salvage something of the afternoon. The Committee—all men except for her—was also watching its words. Associates whose hours were low because of maternity leave were "normalized" to see the pace at which they were billing. No one said "maternity," they referred, haltingly at first, to "personal leave." As the afternoon wore on, "personal leave" sounded more natural. Kathleen thought Rachelle would approve of their process and of their rhetoric.

The oldest class, of course, got the most attention, because no one knew for sure how much his or her evaluation would matter when it came to partnership. Dozens of evaluations for senior associates read, "Make him a partner," or "ready for partnership now," or "functions at the level of a partner," or simply "superb lawyer." Unlike the files of the junior associates, the files of senior associates were filled with written evaluations, as if every partner wanted to have his or her say, cast his or her vote, as if they were in fact voting for new partners. The actual partnership ballots were perfunctory. The Management Committee would put a slate to the partners and give them 48 hours to cast their affirmative votes in a box held in the mail room. No one who made the ballot ever failed to make partner, so the partners took this last go-round of associate evaluations as their last chance to be heard.

"Ann Rose," Kathleen announced. Hers was the third-to-last file for the day, and it was only 3:00 p.m.

Marshall summarized Ann's evaluations in a calm, even tone. They were uniformly superior. Two partners had commented in writing that they thought "certain personal issues" had been "adequately addressed."

The Committee sat silently, as if to wash its hands of the whole business.

"Is there a motion?" Kathleen asked.

"Based on the file, it's an 'A'," Marshall said.

Kathleen thanked him with a smile. All were in favor. Two abstained. They dispensed with the final two associates, both clear "As" and were done by 3:30.

F our times a day, every day, the mail room staff delivered mail, both intra-office and external, to the lawyers of Albright & Gill. Gerard was the Head Floor Clerk on Kathleen's floor, and usually he just said hello, put her mail in her always-full in-box, and hurried out. Today, he stood waiting for her to read the white "To All Personnel" memo on top. She hadn't picked it up. She knew what it said.

Gerard said, "Ann Rose's name's not there. Will you be having another strike? With arm bands and all?"

"Who knows, Gerard," she said gently. "It's not my decision. Neither who makes partner nor whether there's a strike. It's too bad, but I'm sure there are reasons we're not aware of."

"Yes, ma'am. I guess it's more important to be a nice person, huh? Miss Rose, she never smiles, not like you." Gerard obviously believed guys who weren't nice deserved to finish last. He smiled a smile that was naturally crooked, and a bit of a shiver crawled up her spine. She couldn't help the fact that she was nice—her mother had drilled "niceness" into her. How could Ann Rose be *that* nasty? How could she have survived this long, how could she have established at least some client relationships, if she were so *un-nice*? Kathleen was sick of being nice. She answered Gerard.

"Well, Gerard, I guess we have to believe that all things work out somehow for the best, don't we?"

"Yes, ma'am," he said, looking very pleased with himself.

Kathleen closed the door after him. Through the rumor mill, she had known for a week that Ann had been told, this time by Jules Steinberg himself, that the Firm was trying to place her in an appropriate spot with a client. The Firm apparently hoped that her considerable skills would put her in line for a general counsel position, which, he didn't say, might not require general congeniality.

Kathleen swallowed hard, her throat dry. All that she wanted to say, no, to scream, weighed like cement in her stomach. She stared out the window thoughtlessly. Ten minutes passed.

"Oh, God," her own words woke her, a plaintive cry from a different realm. When did this happen? How did this happen?

"I'll be gone for the day," she told Carol, who looked surprised but for once didn't pester her for the details of her afternoon whereabouts. It was mid-May, but the Lake's bite was on the brisk wind. Why couldn't Chicago have spring like everybody else? Why couldn't Chicago in May be nice? Kathleen walked into the wind, towards the Lake, and then turned north, over the Michigan Avenue bridge, in the direction of home. She missed her street and kept walking. When she got to the top of Michigan Avenue, to the Drake, she stopped, and then decided to go in. The doors to Harry's favorite bar were to her right, their stained glass giving them a religious cast.

She sat at one end of the bar, against the wall. Two men in business suits occupied the other end of the bar, talking in low voices, and two white-haired ladies sat behind them at a dark square table, sipping red wine. The bartender brought her a Chivas on the rocks and a water chaser. She took a big sip and held it in her mouth, letting the burning liquid trickle down her throat until she couldn't hold her breath any longer and then let it rush down. Her stomach was empty, and she thought she could hear it splash. She finished the scotch and silently got the bartender's attention. An hour passed and a gray-haired gentleman with thick glasses came into the bar and sat next to her, although there were plenty of empty stools where he could have had his space. He wanted company and tried to start up a conversation.

"I'm sorry. I don't feel like talking right now," she said, and he moved down the bar to the two men in business suits, who readily included him.

On her fourth scotch, a couple of hours later, she realized that the palliative effect of the first two had worn off and she was no longer mellow, just depressed. She started to order another, but the bartender looked at her funny, and she ordered a seltzer water instead. The bar doors opened as he put a large glass in front of her.

She recognized the duet of laughs before she saw their faces—one "ha ha ha" half-swallowed in an elite sort of way, above the joke; the other flowing as if it never stopped. Harry and Ned. Why were either of them in town? Why hadn't one of them called her? She turned away, staring into the mirror behind the bar bottles. Harry and Ned settled on stools in the middle of the bar, Ned closest to her, two stools away. In the mirror, she saw him subtly turn his head her way, confidently checking her out. He had done this before. She saw him turn away and nudge Harry.

"Kitty! You old whore, what the hell are you doing here?" Harry got up and strolled over.

Kathleen shook her head. What made him think she would welcome such a greeting? "Having a drink, you old fart. You come to town and don't call?"

Smiling broadly at Harry, the bartender washed two glasses a second time and winked.

"Have I taught you nothing? When you drink alone, you drink in the middle of the bar, like you mean it. Why are you hiding, my lovely?" Harry put his arm around her and sat, uninvited, on the stool next to her.

"Chivas for the lady," he said. "Doubles."

Ned moved down a stool, and for an awkward moment Kathleen didn't know how to explain her presence. In the middle of an afternoon on which she should've been at work, she was instead alone in a bar playing eye games with a bartender who obviously would not have served her again but for the presence of these two relatively sober gentlemen. She felt compelled to explain herself, but she could not. She could recite the facts pertinent to Ann Rose, but Harry would say it was hogwash and no one in his right mind would want to be a partner at a place like this, that sucks the very blood out of one's viscera and he himself wouldn't give them another breath of his life if he were good for anything else. Ned, on the other hand, didn't know Ann, and had never shared Kathleen's political or philosophical take on things. To Ned things just were what they were.

Didn't Ned and Harry have just as much explaining to do? It was too early in the evening to expect that Ned would volunteer. His easy going nature doubled when necessary to mask a deep denial of even the most major of life's crises, and he usually had to work up to disclosing the big stuff, even to his closest friends. The only reason she suspected that anything was out of the ordinary was that he hadn't phoned to say that he would be in town. Harry, of course, wouldn't have called, and wouldn't now offer an explanation, so they sat, three old friends, drinking expensive booze in a fancy bar and not talking.

"Okay. So. Kitty. Down in the dumps?" Ned sounded reluctant, as if the answer might ruin his whole evening.

"Long story. They passed over a woman—who deserves to make partner—because of her personality. They're right, of course, she's a pain in the ass, and everyone knows it. But still, I'm chair of the Evaluation Committee, and this happens under my watch, as it were. It just gets me going on my own life, and what the hell I'm doing with it."

"The sensible thing, my dear," Harry put his glass down and signaled to the bartender. "You're drinking fine scotch in the fine company of like-minded fellows."

"I don't want to be a fellow, Harry." A boozy tear slipped out of her right eye, and then one escaped the left. She touched them both away.

Ned ignored Harry and leaned on his left elbow to see past him to Kathleen. "I know what you mean, Kitty. Amy and I split up a couple of months ago, and—that's okay—but here I am alone again, and *I* don't know what *I'm* doing. And, I'm doing it in Champaign! I only went there for her and the kids, and they don't want to see me, and I sure as hell don't want to see Amy, and right now I'm thinking I never should have left A&G, for godsakes, if it was going to come to this."

"Then you should have kept it tucked in," Harry winked at Ned, "and you could still be coming home to apple pie on the sill."

"Symptom, not a cause," Ned dismissed Harry. "You, my friend, were born old, so middle age is not the shock to you that it is to Kitty and me."

Kathleen hurried to piece together Ned's apparent marital infidelity, his getting kicked out of his marriage, and how on God's earth Harry's idiosyncrasies were tolerated by a Firm that couldn't tolerate Ann Rose. "I beg your pardon. I can't be middle-aged. I'm not married. All the personals I write say 'sweet young thing.'"

"I think you'd have better luck with 'old whore,'" Harry gave her hand a squeeze. She squeezed it back and held it tight.

"Lookit, you can't fix the Firm overnight, and you really shouldn't let them get to you. It's a job, not a crusade. Every family has a black sheep. Ann Rose will end up as General Counsel of some bank and take all its business away from A&G and laugh while she pulls out their fingernails, one by one. Hang in there, and you'll get to watch. Your alternative is to find yourself some rich widower and fuck him to an early, but for you, lucrative, death."

"A rich widow, for me," Ned said with false hope, "but my luck, *she'd* be the death of *me*."

The three had another round, their issues dissolving into Chivas on the rocks and a swirl of stories from the old days when they were young and believed that it all mattered. And then they went their separate ways, the men off to steaks and perhaps more talk, Kathleen home, alone, resenting every nuance of the word "nice."

TEN

Q: *You are familiar with how it works?*

A nn Rose must have believed that something about Albright & Gill mattered. She resigned and hired the most aggressive, best regarded sex discrimination lawyer in the entire Midwest.

On behalf of Ann Rose, Helen Bornstein filed a complaint in the United States District Court for the Northern District of Illinois, alleging that Albright & Gill had discriminated against her on the basis of sex in violation of Title VII of the Civil Rights Act of 1964, 42 U.S.C. §2000e *et seq.* Helen Bornstein's theory was that the evaluations of Ann Rose had been based on sexual stereotyping. What she intended to prove was one of several things: that the Firm had intentionally discriminated on the basis of gender, or that it had consciously maintained a system which gave weight to biased criticism and did not discourage sexism, or that it should have investigated whether the evaluations of Ms. Rose were in fact influenced by sexual stereotypes, or....

First a wrong, and then a right. The constitution was inching along towards guaranteed happiness for all. Kathleen herself had trouble focusing solely on the *pursuit* of happiness as the constitutionally guaranteed right. She had a late twentieth century tendency to work from the outcome backwards—if the end didn't turn out as she thought it was supposed to, there must've been a failure, or a wrong committed somewhere. The smart thing Helen did was to frame her complaint with an "or" that actually accused the process rather than the outcome. That would make it that much more difficult for even a socially conservative judge to rule against Ann Rose.

The Firm's Insurance Committee announced the lawsuit in a sealed memorandum to All Partners, urging them not to discuss the matter with any members of the press, particularly *The American Lawyer.* The Firm denied all charges and had every expectation, it said, that the matter could be resolved "appropriately." The Memorandum repeated the Firm's long standing commitment to equal opportunity in hiring and promoting associates. A small but prominent employment law firm, Darby & Blythe, had been retained to represent the Firm's interests, and the progress of the litigation would be monitored by Marshall Long.

Each and every partner of the partnership was individually named in the Complaint, with the exception of the new class of partners. If Ann Rose won her lawsuit, the women partners of the Firm might rejoice as women for the principle, but they would pay, like their male counterparts, as punishment. On the other hand, if the partnership won the lawsuit, then perhaps something would be lost for women, at least for women who were perceived to be acting too much like men. In addition to the particular wrongs suffered by Ann Rose as an individual, her lawsuit also alleged a pattern and practice of discrimination by Albright & Gill in its dealings with women generally. Thus, her case, although framed as an individual matter, also had political implications beyond the Firm.

Kathleen was stuck in the thick of it. Having been a member of the Evaluation Committee, and thus privy to the discussions of Ms. Rose's professional performance, the Firm would no doubt call upon Kathleen, as it had called upon her when Randy died and when the rebellion loomed, to testify on its behalf. The Firm would expect Kathleen to say that the process of evaluation was free from sexual bias. Wasn't the Evaluation Committee itself chaired by a woman?

Kathleen thought that part was true, that her Committee had done its best. How then to explain that the Committee gave Ann Rose an "A" as an associate? Shouldn't "A" associates expect to become partners? Hadn't all the male "A" associates become partners? Kathleen suspected that Helen Bornstein would demand to know, in depositions and perhaps at trial, what *sub rosa* comments the Committee had passed on—verbally, if not in writing—to the Management Committee about the real issue in this case—the personality of Ms. Ann Rose. As Kathleen studied the announcement of Ann's lawsuit, she realized that beyond the financial implications of the case to the Firm, and beyond the political principle at stake for women, there was something at stake of more immediate importance to her—her own promotion to Management Committee.

"Damn," she said out loud. She dialed Jill's number.

"I'm so glad you're home. Ann Rose filed suit."

"I'm not surprised. What did she have to lose?" Jill said, without sympathy for Ann, but also missing the implications for Kathleen.

"Well, she probably just cost me my career."

"That would be hard to believe. What do you mean?" Jill didn't get it.

"I mean, she'll want me to testify that some of the members of the Evaluation Committee thought she was too macho—and, by the way, I'm not talking to you about this—and the Firm will want me to say that we're just one big, happy, sex- and color-blind family, and that she was treated absolutely equally."

"Well, she was, wasn't she?"

"Jill, to tell you the truth—and I'll deny I ever said this—how the hell do I know? I'm not on the Management Committee, and at this rate, I never will be."

Jill was late for an appointment with her OB/GYN and had to go. Although she'd been gone from the Firm for two years, Jill still wasn't pregnant. Kathleen assumed she was pursuing fertility treatments, but Jill hadn't yet admitted it. She crossed her fingers for her friend. Jill said she was sure the Firm would settle up and Kathleen wouldn't have to worry.

Kathleen was, however, worried. She dropped by Brian's office. While he wasn't necessarily in the loop of Firm life, he nonetheless seemed to understand the Firm better than she. Brian was agitated about the announcement.

"I don't like her, although I thought she was a pretty good lawyer." That was about as high a compliment as Brian allowed anyone who in any way threatened him. "But we don't need her, do we? I think we still have a shot at getting Gloria Ellens, don't you? They love me."

"It's *me* they love, Brian. *You*, they tolerate. Besides, Ann doesn't really have much to do with them. It was just that one deal. Do you think we'll win?" she said.

"Who, the Firm?" Brian shrugged. "We don't have to make every smart lawyer a partner. It's our prerogative to choose. That doesn't make us sexist. There are quite a few of you now, aren't there? But I think in the long run most women don't want to work this hard. You know, they want to have families."

"You realize, don't you, that you can't say any of that to anyone except me? Tell me you understand that it is sexist to say what you just said."

"It's not sexist, Kitty. It's how I see it."

She let the Kitty go. "I hope you're never called as a witness."

Brian started to laugh and stopped. "Do you think you'll be called? Yes, I guess you would be. Well, that will certainly put you in the limelight!"

"Geez, Brian, what do you think I should wear?" She left his office, furious that Brian didn't see her dilemma. Of course he wouldn't. He didn't consider her a candidate for Management Committee under any circumstances.

Ann Rose's case did not settle quickly, and Helen moved the case to the top of her agenda. Within months of filing the complaint, Helen scheduled the deposition of Kathleen Hannigan. To prepare her, Darby spent an afternoon with Kathleen the week prior, but because she was an attorney, and because he knew she didn't like Ann Rose, he'd not drilled her the way he could've been expected to drill a lay witness.

Kathleen had attended a few depositions—not many, since she was not a litigator—and had been elated or horrified, depending on which side she was on, to watch the witness shine or wither under the barrage of questions asked, answered and asked again, and again. Slowly, every word of any answer would be analyzed by the lawyer in charge of the deposition, whipping a subject dry.

"Let me get this straight."

"Let's make sure I understand."

"Didn't you just say...."

"What do you mean by that?"

"Is that what you thought at the time?"

"Why?"

In between, the witness, frustrated, would try—if she were a good witness, from the point of view of the party who didn't want the witness to say too much—to listen to the question, understand the question, and say as little as possible in response. The lawyer would ask the question again, a slightly different way. The lawyer for the witness would object every so often, but objections didn't matter. They were procedural ploys and the witness would be instructed to answer anyway. Darby told Kathleen that he would use objections to alert her to tricky questions, or just to disrupt Bornstein's tempo. Like the Bar Exam instructor so many years ago, Darby had only one cardinal rule, *"Do not volunteer."*

On the appointed morning, Kathleen showered twice. She got out of bed at 5:00, uncharacteristically early for her, and drank three cups of very strong coffee. She paced her apartment for 10 minutes, shaking out her dangling arms like a swimmer before a race. At 5:45, she couldn't stand her own nervous energy any more and took the elevator to her building's exercise room, where she cranked the treadmill up to five miles per hour and watched a morning news show for 28 minutes. She went back upstairs, showered again, and clipped her toe nails. Just after 7:00, she hailed a cab for the office. She was supposed to meet Philip Darby at 8:00 at A&G. Helen and the court reporter would be there at 9:00.

Darby brought with him his young, African-American—stroke of trial genius!—associate, Michelle Richardson. He immediately removed his jacket and slung it over a chair to the right of what would be Kathleen's seat at the end of the long, grey, marble table. They were expecting seven people altogether, but the conference room table was designed for 16 and gave them plenty of room to spread out. Darby took two of the Firm's trademark cinnamon buns and began to pace.

"You know the rules, right?" he asked Kathleen. "I mean, you know the drill on depositions, right? Don't volunteer, and all that?"

Kathleen said she understood.

"Don't argue with her, okay? She can be tough and annoying, but don't argue. I'll be here to protect you," Darby said, and Kathleen smiled. Darby was no taller than five-six, balding and borderline roly-poly. He would be dwarfed by the statuesque Helen Bornstein. "I'll object if you need time to consider your answer. You can always ask her to repeat the question or clarify. But don't argue. Don't spar. Okay?"

She nodded, amused.

"Lawyers tend to argue," he said. He cleared his throat. He walked over to the platter of breakfast pastries and studied them as if he'd forgotten he'd already had two. "If she asks how 'charming' you've been to clients or partners," he said, too off-handedly to be anything but calculated, "can I presume the answer is negative?"

It took Kathleen a full, awkward five seconds to understand his meaning. "Right," she said, finally. "I'm not a virgin, Philip, but I'm not a whore, either."

"No hanky-panky with the partners or the clients?" he turned to face her.

"I said, 'no,'" she said firmly, but she wondered how she could feel safe under the protection of someone who used the words "hanky-panky."

Marshall Long rushed into the conference room at a quarter to nine, apologizing for being late.

"Didn't they give us any cinnamon buns?" he asked.

Kathleen nodded discreetly towards Darby.

"Maybe they'll bring us some more," Marshall said, and dialed the Firm's catering department. She listened while he sweet-talked the catering manager. As the Firm's liaison to Darby & Blythe, Marshall was the embodiment of the institutional client, relaying trial counsel's advice to the Firm and carrying back the Firm's approval of strategies and tactics. In effect, Darby would tell Marshall who would tell Blake who would tell Marshall who would tell Darby. Neatly, no single individual had to take much responsibility.

Helen Bornstein arrived precisely at 9:00, accompanied by her associate and the court reporter, and, although Kathleen had hoped against it, Ann Rose. Kathleen could feel both Marshall's and Darby's eyes searching her for a reaction. She nodded to Ann, but did not smile. Darby immediately grabbed Kathleen's arm and steered her into the hall.

"They are just trying to rattle you. Don't let it bother you. Don't volunteer. Don't argue. Don't even look at Ann Rose. Got it?"

They went back to the conference room table, and Kathleen took her seat without looking again at Ann. She took a deep, meditative breath to relax. Darby had said the first hour would be all background, all warm-up, routine sort of stuff. She was ready for that.

Darby was wrong. Helen Bornstein did not start Kathleen's deposition with the routine. She started near the heart of her case.

"I have read your personal evaluation of Ms. Rose," Helen Bornstein began. Kathleen stared deliberately away from Ann. Helen was wearing wire framed reading glasses. She was an attractive woman, at least 10 years Kathleen's senior, but of indeterminate age. Her blond hair was obviously dyed, but the right professional shade of golden white. "You are not a commercial lawyer, are you?"

Kathleen decided not to spar with Ms. Bornstein, even though that required that she volunteer, just a little, "I'm an intellectual property lawyer."

"So you don't have contact with clients of the commercial lending group?"

"Not usually."

"And how often do you work with commercial lawyers?"

"Sometimes."

"Ten percent of your time?"

"Maybe."

"That's what, a couple hundred hours a year?"

"I guess."

Helen Bornstein wanted Kathleen to admit that she didn't know the expectations of commercial lending clients. Wanted her to admit that she didn't know the meaning of "team," when it came to banking and other big, corporate clients. Kathleen's little advertising and entertainment clients were a "looser" crowd, weren't they? Kathleen dutifully kept her answers short. There didn't seem to be much harm in admitting her clients were sociable.

"You used the word 'charming,' Ms. Hannigan. Can you define that for me?" Helen looked at Ann Rose and smiled.

"The dictionary could define it for you." That was, she thought, a spar, but Darby didn't look upset.

"What I want to know is what *you* mean by 'charming,'" Helen Bornstein pronounced the word slowly, letting it slither out in twice its normal length, like a long black dress with a deep, deep cut down the front, showing a little breast.

"Charming," she said again.

"I guess I mean it like everyone means it. Kind of pleasing, or attractive. Sociable." Kathleen kept her gaze soft and focussed on Helen. She had no desire to confront Ann Rose.

"What you wrote was, 'i.e., engage the client in conversation, social or otherwise.'" She paused. Kathleen looked past her, waiting, like a good witness should, to hear a question mark.

"Am I to understand that Ms. Rose did not speak one word to her clients on the night in question?"

"She spoke at least one word."

"How many words did she speak?"

"I wasn't counting."

"So you don't really know, do you, now much she spoke to them?"

"I was there. I know there were awkward silences. I know I felt I had to engage the clients in conversation."

"Or what? They'd take away their business?" Bornstein raised her hands in an exaggerated gesture of alarm.

Kathleen, staring at Bornstein's squared off, French manicure, thought her question was rhetorical. The night in question was way off the main point. She didn't answer.

Helen looked at Ann Rose, as if to coax a smile. Kathleen didn't need to look at Ann Rose to guess she did not oblige.

"Please instruct the witness to answer," Bornstein said, crossing her arms and leaning across the table. Kathleen caught her own reflection in Bornstein's reading glasses, and it gave her courage.

"We wanted them to think of us as facilitators—people they would want to work with on other deals. We were putting two companies together. It was supposed to be a friendly, happy atmosphere."

"And it was your job to make it 'happy'?" Bornstein pitched her voice to imitate a happy high school girl's. "Happy, happy, happy?" she goaded.

"This is boring, boring, boring, Ms. Bornstein," Kathleen said in imitation. Out of the corner of her eye, she caught a congratulatory smile on Marshall's face. It reminded her of how much she had at stake, personally, in how this deposition was perceived. Whatever interest Bornstein had in the truth was not, in Kathleen's mind, as important as her own performance, her own ability to withstand, and perhaps outwit, Ann Rose's renowned lawyer. She could stand up for the Firm, and for her own credibility as a partner in Albright & Gill. Marshall could report to Blake that Ms. Kathleen Hannigan was indeed Management Committee material.

Bornstein pounced. "An example of 'charming,' Ms. Hannigan?"

Without taking her eyes off of Bornstein, she said, "Philip, I don't want to get into a pissing match." He had, to her mind, been less than protective during these exchanges. "I have clients who would like me to get to their matters sometime this...*month.*"

"Then let me direct your attention to your evaluation interview with my client," Bornstein went on. "Did you tell Ms. Rose she had been described as bitchy?"

"I don't recall." This was the rehearsed answer. Darby had said that if she didn't remember the exact words she used in the evaluation interview, that she should not recall. How could she be expected to remember every word said to one of 15 associates that many months ago?

"You don't? Did you tell her she was too aggressive?"

"I don't remember."

"That she was too harsh?"

"I don't specifically recall." She glared at Darby, who sat passively at the conference room table, his hands folded on his empty legal pad.

"Too mannish?"

"I don't recall." Geez, Kathleen thought, this is why she didn't do litigation.

"To act more femininely?"

"I don't recall."

"Perhaps, Ms. Hannigan, I can refresh your recollection." Bornstein's associate reached into his briefcase and brought out a small black Dictaphone, perhaps twice the size of a credit card. He pushed a button. Kathleen Hannigan's voice began to speak.

"My fear, Ann, is that they will tell you to practice elsewhere when it comes time to make partner. The Evaluation Committee doesn't decide those things, but your file is filled with people's perceptions that you are too aggressive, too bitchy, too harsh. One guy even went so far as to say you ought to wear make-up and act more femininely, that you were too mannish. You know as well as I do that this place runs on perceptions, true and false, and that there's a certain culture here. You either fit into the partnership or you don't. Why shoot yourself in the foot? You're such an excellent lawyer, but it might not matter. The only thing holding you back is your attitude— the perception of your attitude. Why not be a little softer, if that's what it takes? There aren't that many women partners here. We need you to join our ranks, but sometimes I think you're deliberately making it harder for us, like they'll think we all are as...as hard as you."

Bornstein's associate turned off the machine. Kathleen's mouth was dry. Despite Darby's instructions, she dug her eyes into Ann Rose, who refused to look at her. Kathleen pressed her lips together and stared past Bornstein into the glare of the picture windows. A small plane ducked behind a building, approaching Meigs Field. Marshall cleared his throat. Darby and Richardson straightened themselves in their chairs. Kathleen could tell that they were all trying not to look at her. She tried to look bored.

Darby jumped to his feet. "What in hell is that? Let the record show Ms. Bornstein played an unidentified tape of an unidentified voice. I object!"

Bornstein feigned amusement. "Perhaps I should ask Ms. Hannigan if she recognizes the tape."

Kathleen looked at Darby. It was, unquestionably, her voice. Those were her words, she knew, but they were out of context. She had been provoked by Ann, but she had, in fact, expressed her concern—she recalled expressing her concern for Ann's happiness. Bornstein, if she had a complete tape, had excised that part of her conversation with Ann.

Darby objected, and instructed Kathleen to answer.

"It sounds like my voice," she said evenly.

"Do you *now* recall your conversation with Ann Rose?" Bornstein demanded.

"I always recalled *speaking* with Ann Rose. You asked me if I recalled using specific words." She wondered again why Darby wasn't defending her more.

"Does your voice on this tape use the word 'mannish'?"

"We haven't established that it is in fact my voice, Ms. Bornstein, only that it sounds like my voice." Where the hell was Darby? He told her not to spar, but someone should. The woman was so smug! Darby didn't seem to be paying much attention. He was standing behind his chair. He leaned down to Michelle Richardson and she nodded and left the room.

"Ms. Rose will testify that her voice-activated Dictaphone recorded your entire conversation," Bornstein said.

"We'll object to the unauthorized taping of a private conversation," Darby said, although Kathleen suspected that he had just sent Michelle off to see if that was, in fact, the law.

"Of course you will," Bornstein said. "But, you should look at *People v. Beardsley*, first." His reluctance showing, Darby scribbled a note.

"You didn't play the entire conversation," Kathleen said. "You took a portion out of context."

"Let's go back over that context again, Ms. Hannigan," Bornstein said in a tone that reminded Kathleen of a hungry cat.

They adjourned at 5:00 only because the court reporter couldn't stay over-time, and Bornstein said they had at least another day's worth of questions.

"We'll deal with it," Darby said. Then, again, in utter disbelief, he added, "She never told you she had a tape?"

"She wasn't exactly confiding in me, Philip." The defense team had retired to the bar in the Downtown Club.

"Yeah. Listen, you did fine today. It's not that damaging. She only used it today to force us to settlement."

At Philip's mention of the word settlement, Marshall sat up straight and leaned the full length of his torso across the little table. "You know we won't settle. Ever. On any terms. Tape or not," he said, and Kathleen knew, as she had not known for certain before, that he was absolutely right.

"I'm going to look ridiculous if they play that at trial," she moaned. She wished Marshall was wrong.

"Not necessarily, Kathleen," Marshall smiled with the good-natured malevolence of a big brother. "But the Firm would sooner brand you with a red 'A' and send you to the stocks than settle." She wasn't sure if the image betrayed a literary or an historical bent, but in either case she was impressed. It reminded her a little bit of Harry. She was searching for an erudite and witty comeback when Darby broke them up.

"The real damage is in the written evaluations," he said. Marshall grimaced, annoyed. Darby hurried to add, "Damaging but not fatal. The whole defense is that her personality was judged by the same criteria applied to men. The partnership is free to choose its partners." He sipped his martini, straight-up. At that moment, after a day of Helen Bornstein's depositions, he did not sound convinced that the partnership indeed had that right.

It must have been the tape that jarred him, the language. The objectionable, uncivil words, the vernacular "bitchy" and "mannish" had come from his own client's mouth. As a messenger, any one of them would probably have done the same. Did Darby think she should've known about the recorder?

She should've stayed out of it, Kathleen thought. She could've given Ann her well-deserved "A+" and not said anything about the upcoming decision on partnership. Was it her own ambitious ego, the overly protective mother taking credit for her daughter's success, that had said too much? The partners would no doubt have rejected Ann Rose anyway, and she still might have sued, but at least Kathleen herself would not have felt so much in the vise of it.

After the deposition, after the drinks, Kathleen wanted to be alone, but not as alone as she was. She went home and poured a scotch, ran a bath. She sat in the sudsy water and cried. Staring at the grout between the tiles, she was lost in the kind of thought that has no specific content. Every so often, she would get a slight chill, take a sip of her scotch, add a bit more hot water and try to articulate for herself just why she, the stoic, was crying. She hadn't cried when Jill was passed over or when she'd left the Firm. She'd sobbed when Randy had died, but that was different. She had no personal interest in Ann Rose or her career, so why was she crying? She shivered, toweled off and crawled into bed. It was only 9:30.

The phone rang.

"Come get me." Kathleen recognized Jill's voice at once. She felt a drumbeat in her stomach and Jill struggled on. "I'm at Prentiss."

Jill didn't say what was wrong. She didn't have to. Kathleen asked if she could bring anything.

"No. Just come."

Kathleen pulled some jeans from her laundry basket and threw on a sweater. She didn't stop to put in her contacts, and the doorman of her building looked surprised when he flipped on the cab light.

"Are you okay, Ms. Hannigan?"

"Fine, Ali, thank you," she said, conflicted again that he insisted on calling her Ms. Hannigan but, being single, not wanting any more familiarity than that. At the same time she was keenly aware that he was one of the few people who knew her well enough, if only through her comings and goings, to pay attention to the fact that she was leaving her apartment on a weekday night at 10:00, and that he noticed, and probably speculated, on such things.

When she told the cabbie to take her to the Prentiss emergency room, he looked at her with genuine concern and peeled away from the curb.

"It's okay," she said. "It's not me." He apparently didn't hear her, and they arrived at the hospital in less than five minutes. She gave him $5 and he peeled away from the curb again, all things being of equal urgency.

It was relatively quiet in the E.R., and the nurses were sympathetic when she asked for Jill. Jill was lying on a bed between two curtains.

Jill had been crying and her face looked swollen. She held out her hand and Kathleen took it.

"I lost it," she whispered, her chin trembling.

"I'm so sorry," Kathleen said. Never herself having been pregnant, and never having wanted to be, she could only observe the depth of her friend's hurt. In her dispassion, she saw both the pregnancy and its loss as the same biological accident, to be survived. It was not, to Kathleen, as if Jill had lost someone she knew and loved. It was not like losing Steve, or a parent, or a friend, like Randy. It was a loss she couldn't fully comprehend. She wished Steve were not in London on business. As the father, it was his loss, too, one he was better equipped than Kathleen to understand.

Helplessly, she stroked Jill's hand, relieved that her friend was okay. Even though they were best friends, Jill had been very private about her efforts to conceive. Jill hadn't even told Kathleen she was pregnant until a few weeks ago, and at that time she hadn't yet told Steve, because she said she wanted to be "sure." Kathleen had thought that Jill was not as giddy with her news as she could have been expected to be, and Jill had admitted, but not for repetition, that she was indeed a little scared. She said to Kathleen that she might be too old; that 18 years until the kid went away to college seemed like a really long time; that she sometimes missed the urgency of a full time legal practice; that sophisticated maternity clothes were hard to find. Did she know how to be a mother? They giggled a little between themselves, appreciating the irony of their professional competence being reduced to performance anxiety over pink, blue and yellow bunnies and "How To" books on the most basic of all instincts.

Kathleen asked Jill if she needed anything.

"I just want to go home," Jill said. "Can you ask the nurse?"

Kathleen helped Jill into the cab and into her dark apartment. It was after midnight, and Kathleen thought to make some tea. She felt warmed by the notion of tea, sweetened by milk and sugar, but Jill declined. "You won't believe this, but do you think I could have a glass of red wine?"

Feeling like a bad influence, Kathleen fetched two glasses and a bottle and stretched out next to Jill on her bed, taking Steve's place.

"Can we call Steve? Is it too late? I mean, too early?"

"It's like six there?" Kathleen said, holding the phone.

"I probably shouldn't wake him. I just want to hear his voice. I'm not going to tell him."

Kathleen sat up. "You didn't tell him yet you were pregnant?"

"In case something happened," Jill started to cry. "Now if I tell him," she struggled for the right words, "that I, I had a miscarriage, he'll not want us to try again." Kathleen took her friend's free hand. She marveled that Jill could want something so badly that when it happened she'd been too afraid of losing it to tell the one person who would've wanted most to know. Within a few minutes, Jill was asleep, and Kathleen crept over to the light on her side of the bed, turned it off, and sat in Steve's La-Z-Boy.

She wondered if this was what it felt like to keep a death watch. The room was dark, but not pitch black. The bathroom light was on, and the door cracked just a bit to serve as a night light. Venetian blinds let in the filtered light of the street 20 stories below, and the old stone façade of Jill's building muffled the drone of the steady midnight traffic on Lake Shore Drive. Kathleen heard the alarm of an ambulance in the distance. The external noises seeped through, but inside this old building, there were no human noises: no opening of doors or flushing of toilets or whirrings of dishwashers. Twenty-five floors and 50 apartments' worth of people slept or watched TV or nursed an infant, without a sound.

Jill lay motionless, and Kathleen panicked. Had they given Jill drugs at the hospital? Should she have mixed them with alcohol?

An odd thing, she thought, not to know, as an observer, the difference between sleep and death. Would the sleeper know? If Kathleen weren't there, how long would it take someone to notice if Jill did not wake up? Even as witness, Kathleen wouldn't be able to say when sleep became *dead* asleep. How would she know when she'd lost her friend? If *she* couldn't, what about the rest of them? Would they know, at the moment of their waking, that the world had changed slightly since they laid down? It was a very slight change, wasn't it? Too slight to be noticed, although she supposed that there would be an obituary and perhaps a picture, and it would say "law professor" and "former partner in the prestigious law firm of Albright & Gill," and that Jill was survived by Steve. Kathleen remembered that the newspaper hadn't used her name in the story about her baby brother's death. By someone's mistake, she'd not been included in the list of survivors.

It had been only the shortest of announcements, as if the infant's death were something to be ashamed of. Sometimes still, when Kathleen was told very bad news, she would hear her mother's wail the morning that baby Michael did not wake up. The paramedics had shaken their heads; he'd been dead a few hours. At the door, clutching her yellow plush bunny, Kathleen watched her mother bury her face in her father's shoulder, her body limp. Her father struggled to lay her mother gently on the floor and the paramedics knelt down and put a plastic mask over her mouth. It'd been very quiet, and Kathleen had been too frightened to make a sound. Her mother twitched, came to and turned on her side, her knees to her chest, crying. Finally, one of the paramedics, a tall young man with brown curly hair, saw Kathleen at the door. He picked her up in his arms, took her to her room, and told her everything was going to be okay.

Kathleen poured herself another glass of red wine and noticed that her hands were cold. *Everything had not been okay after that day.* Kathleen, the precious, unnamed survivor, had become everything to her parents—both daughter and lost son—and very little of herself. What of *her* had survived?

Baby Michael had lived but a single year. He hadn't been given time to play out his parents' dreams—no time to please or to disappoint or to make a difference in the world—just a bundle of potential, a potential left to her. Only now did it occur to her that she would never be able to make up to her mother or to her father for that loss. She wondered how much of her own potential she'd already lost in the trying.

She had the urge to shake Jill, to wake her up, to confirm that it did make a difference, to her, anyway, whether Jill slept or stopped breathing. Was there something else Jill wanted in her obit? Something else that mattered to her? Jill turned over. Kathleen, relieved at this confirmation of life, put her fist in her mouth to stifle her confused tears. She was pissed at Ann Rose for interfering with her five-year plan towards Management Committee, towards the time when she could possibly make a difference. Albright & Gill avoided controversy like cats avoid water, and now she would forever be tainted by her association with the Rose controversy. Unlike Jill, she didn't have a Steve. She didn't have Jill's easy solution to the problem of meaning and making a difference. When it came right down to it, she wasn't sure when she'd made the decision to let A&G define her, to put so much of her sense of self in the hands of an institution that, like her parents, wanted her to be something or someone she was not. But she knew of very little else that mattered to her.

When Kathleen opened her eyes it was almost 7:00. She tiptoed to Jill's kitchen and found a can of premium Colombian coffee in the refrigerator. She added two extra scoops for the pot and watched it drip. She used the guest bathroom in the hall to splash cold water on her face, which, she thought, didn't look *terrible*, considering. Pouring two cups of coffee, she took them to Jill's room.

"Good morning," she whispered, but Jill did not stir. She tried again, a little louder, trying to hit a chord between cheery and routine. "Your morning coffee, ma'am." Jill opened her eyes, and rolled over to Steve, and only seemed to remember Kathleen when he wasn't there.

"How do you feel?" Kathleen asked.

"Okay. Tired."

"You can go back to sleep. I only woke you up in case you wanted to call Steve. It's 2:00 there." Kathleen rushed through her apologies. She had to go home, dress and be at the deposition table at 9:00.

"I know, I know. I'm sorry you had to come last night."

"No, no. I wanted to be here for you. I would've been furious if you hadn't called me. I wish I didn't have to go. Will you be okay?"

"If your coffee doesn't kill me," Jill said. "Geez, that's strong."

"Like you." Kathleen gave her a kiss on the cheek. "I'll call you as soon as Helen's done with me. If I survive!"

Helen finished Kathleen's deposition in a few hours, mostly repeating the testimony of the day before. There'd been no real reason, Kathleen thought, for the continuation to the second day, except to harass her. Ann Rose didn't even bother to be present. Darby could have protected her, could've said that the important Intellectual Property partner of the prestigious Albright & Gill law firm could not be expected to be unavailable to her clients two days in a row (to say nothing of being unbillable for two days in a single week). Darby could've said that Ms. Hannigan would be willing to return the next month, should that prove necessary. Darby was bending over backwards to give the appearance of playing fair, and he produced Kathleen for the second day without objection. Bornstein, Kathleen knew, was using the subject matter of the lawsuit to her advantage.

When it was over, Kathleen stopped to see Brian, whom she found standing over Holly's desk. Brian was in an unusually good mood. He told her that Gloria Ellens Golf had called him earlier in the afternoon because they were naming a new line of clubs and needed some trademark advice, just like Brian had hoped. She was too tired to even think about asking him to share the billing responsibility with her. She would have to fight that battle another day. At the moment, all she really wanted to do was be with Jill.

She went back to her office and called her. "Shall I bring pizza or Mexican or both?"

"Both," Jill said, "and chocolate chocolate chip ice cream."

Kathleen changed into one of Jill's oversized tee shirts and sat up in bed next to her. Jill flipped the channels on the TV. A woman lawyer was having a baby. Click. A woman doctor was delivering a baby. Click. A woman interior designer was suffering the world's worst blind date. Click. ESPN was reviewing the Great Moments of the NBA.

"If they could see us now," Jill laughed.

"They'd have to raise our billing rates!" Kathleen said. Then she remembered that Jill was out of law firm politics. "You're so lucky. I never expected to be caught in this game. You know, I thought you studied hard, got an A, collected your medals and that was it. All this other stuff—jockeying for position, worrying about billings, being judged by appearances—it's the worst part of high school!"

"Get out," Jill said.

"I can't."

"I did."

"But you had other reasons. If you hadn't wanted to have a...," Kathleen realized too late what she was saying, so she blundered ahead, "a baby, would you have left?"

Jill didn't answer. She squeezed Kathleen's hand.

"I'm sorry. I guess I don't have a good reason to leave. I don't know what else I'd do. Besides, if I left the Firm, it would just feed the fires. Women with children don't want the Firm. The Firm doesn't want the Ann Roses of the world. I see myself as kind of the middle ground."

"Well, of course you are. But if *you* don't want the Firm—*on their terms, mind you*—then why keep beating your head against a wall? There are other things. You could go in-house someplace, be general counsel."

"I'm not sure I could, really. I don't have enough corporate and securities experience, and besides, now they've made me mad. I'm not a quitter."

Jill started to cry. "Do you think I'm a quitter?" she said.

"No! No! You had your reasons, your dreams. You made choices."
Jill switched the channel back to the woman in labor.

Feeling very, very sorry for herself, Kathleen touched away her tears.

ELEVEN

Q: [*He*] *is a highly respected lawyer*
at your firm, is he not?

A year after Kathleen's deposition, the Ann Rose suit was still
pending in the courts, but Kathleen's professional life had
returned to normal. One fall evening, she was alone in her
apartment, reading the newspaper, the television providing
background noise. Young men with long ponytails or with no hair at
all—the two extremes of rock style—were standing in front of a
microphone saying "check, check, check," and then giggling
inexplicably. A stark stadium stage was awash in spotlights, catching
in silhouette a tall figure with his arms raised. A man's voice filled
the night, "Ladies and Gentlemen, I give unto you...." The voice
from the TV sounded familiar. She looked up and groaned. "Give
unto you,"—vaguely sacrilegious—was Anthony's pet phrase.
Whatever they were selling, she could hear Anthony's indignation
that they were using an imitation of him to sell it. The phone rang,
and she missed the name of the advertiser. "Geez, I'm sorry. Wrong
number," a man's voice said. Kathleen returned to her paper. She
hoped the commercial was something local or just a favor Anthony
had done for someone and not told her about.

Two days later, Anthony called. Jimmy was on vacation, and he
was trying to track him down—this is why he shouldn't go on those
damn cruises—but Anthony wanted something done, and done now,
about the nerve of Sconsin Beer to imitate his voice, to make people
think he was in their commercial, and not to pay him. Kathleen said
she would send a demand to the president of Sconsin Beer that they
immediately cease and desist from running the commercial, and she
would file a complaint with the television networks, who could be
expected to stop running the commercial. Anthony said that wasn't
good enough. He wanted a lawsuit filed immediately. Kathleen said
he might want to think twice before suing an important potential
sponsor like Sconsin Beer. Anthony said he wouldn't take their

scumbag money if it was the last on earth. Kathleen said they'd draft some papers and then he could decide. If they did the initial work, they'd have a better idea of his chances of winning the suit. Anthony said he'd *better* win, and she better file it, and meanwhile he was going to find Jimmy, wherever the hell he was. Kathleen told Anthony not to bother Jimmy, that she and Marshall could do what needed to be done, that Jimmy needed his vacation.

"Only if you can win without him," Anthony said.

"We can win without him," she said. In her view, winning had nothing to do with Jimmy and everything to do with luck. Some judges would be more sympathetic than others. Whether Anthony won would be only half-dependent on how well she argued the case. The other half was the out that experienced trial lawyers left themselves for the sake of saving face.

"Jimmy promises me."

"I promise you," she said, although she thought it was a risky promise.

She drafted a cease and desist letter in her most formal legalese. It was a professional courtesy a court would expect her to extend to the potential defendant, even if she was completely certain that it would be ignored. Then she met Marshall in his office to divide up the tasks necessary to draft a complaint and a motion for a temporary restraining order which would stop the broadcast of the offending commercial. Marshall was hesitant about the TRO—he thought that whatever damage Anthony was suffering was not, as the law required, "irreparable"—it could be resolved by the payment of money to Anthony. Kathleen argued that no, it couldn't. Anthony had a right not to be exploited at all, if he didn't want to be. He had the further right not to be associated with a "controversial" subject like beer. Marshall scoffed out loud at the notion that beer was controversial, or that Anthony would be harmed by his association with it, but he nodded his approval of her arguments.

"You're good, Hannigan," he smiled. "But we still have the slight problem that the commercial does not use his name and does not use his face. I'm not sure voice is enough."

"It'll be new law in Illinois, that's for sure. Although there is a California case that gave Bette Midler a ton of money for a vocal imitation," Kathleen said. "Of course, Bette makes her living singing and recording, and California is a pro-entertainer state. It's going to be a little harder to make the case for Anthony, since his voice is not his livelihood."

"Then we can't bring it. It's not worth the risk. Anthony can't bear the embarrassment of a loss." Marshall looked disappointed. "We ought to put together our best shot and then talk him out of it when he cools down."

"You mean A&G's crack litigation team is afraid of a loss?" She liked that she could speak honestly to Marshall and that he could laugh at his own defensiveness.

"I mean Anthony might need Sconsin's money some day, and he shouldn't sue them over hurt feelings, especially if it's at all iffy whether they've done anything wrong."

"That's the beauty of it! It's just sexy enough and unimportant enough that both sides will get some good-natured press, and Anthony loves press. They are a beer company, so chances are, we'll win. Then we'll settle prior to appeal, and Anthony can give them something like a concert, and everybody will get rich, including us. I've told Anthony we'd expect a two-fifty bonus if we win and five hundred if we settle with a sponsorship deal from Sconsin."

"No!"

"Yes!"

"Takes balls, Hannigan. Puts the pressure on me. Did you clear this deal with Blake?"

"No need to. I just thought it would make it interesting for you, and be good for my billing book."

"How are you getting the billing from Jimmy?"

"We have our ways," she said. She hadn't quite figured that part out yet, but she would, if it all worked out the way she hoped it would.

For the next 24 hours, Kathleen claimed a table in the library, which didn't have the privacy of a carrel but allowed her to spread out piles of cases and books fetched for her by a young associate. She had decided to write the first draft of the brief herself. If they brought this case, it would be what was called a "case of first impression" in Illinois. If they won, it would be big news, at least in certain, small legal circles, and she, Kathleen Hannigan, would "own" a little piece of publicity law. In addition to the possibility of her own fame, the issue of voice intrigued her. It was after midnight when she began to write:

> "A person can be instantly recognized by his voice. It is the instrument we use to express our innermost thoughts and desires, loves and fears. We use our voices in the most sacred of human endeavors, to express that self which, without a voice, would remain secret and unknown, inaccessible to our fellow human beings. We use our voices to admire a new baby, to vow fidelity, to warn of danger, to tell a story, to create a human record. We use it to entertain and to worship. And indeed, we can use our voices for baser purposes as well: to manipulate, to lie, and in this case, to sell. For Sconsin Beer to steal Anthony's voice is to steal from him the right to choose that to which he will give his voice. So closely is voice associated with an individual that this Court must conclude that Sconsin Beer stole Anthony's very identity, in violation both of his right to privacy and of his right to control the commercial exploitation of his identity."

She didn't have a lot of law to go on but she liked the inflamed tone of her rhetoric. It sounded lofty and noble. She hoped it would obscure the fact that Anthony would, in his own crass way, be more than willing to sell his voice, his face and his very identity to the highest bidder.

Marshall took a look at her draft the next afternoon. They had, over the years, developed a fairly efficient working relationship, free of the rancor of the penis case. He skimmed areas of the law that were "hers," and she skimmed areas uniquely "his." They each used a pencil to make corrections and suggestions, but as the litigator, Marshall had the final, final say.

"Geez, Kit," he said, "makes me want to weep. 'The most sacred of human endeavors.' Where do you get this stuff?" Sometime over the past few years, without permission from her, Marshall had adopted "Kit" as his special name for her. She rather liked it.

"Just an idealist at heart, Marsh. Is it too much? The truth is, I do think voice is one of our most recognizable features, though not as honest as the eyes. Ever call a girl just to see if she was home and then throw your voice when she answered?"

Marshall raised his eyebrows.

"It never works," she said. She stopped short at the sound of her own words. Marshall abruptly turned his attention back to the brief. She looked at him quizzically. He cleared his throat and looked up.

"Well, if a voice is so damn recognizable, and so uniquely individual, then we've shot our own argument in the foot, haven't we? This voice isn't Anthony's. Anybody would know it was an imitation. If it is an imitation, it's not him, and so, where's the harm?"

"Harm is" she used a voice of proclamation, "of all the voices in all the world…"

"…they chose *his* for the sole and specific purpose of alluding to his personality and good will. I get it." Marshall said. "We can file yet this afternoon. Get Anthony into town, if you can."

Anthony was in the air somewhere, and hadn't returned Kathleen's call by the time she went home that night, at 8:00. They'd gotten "lucky," Marshall said. Judge Lawton had agreed to hear their arguments at 3:30 the next day. Marshall told her again to get Anthony in town ASAP. Kathleen didn't like Marshall's change of tone: he was assuming the command, giving her an order. Although she never would've forgiven Brian for such a lapse, she understood Marshall's anxiety—Anthony had made her promise, and she herself had raised the Firm's financial stakes.

She had a bigger problem, though, than finding Anthony. She felt she really ought to speak with Jimmy—as between herself and Jimmy, Anthony was unmistakably Jimmy's client. He would take it as a territorial threat if they filed suit on behalf of his largest and best-known client without his personal *imprimatur*. He would be irreparably insulted. In addition, she'd made an unusual financial arrangement with Anthony, and it would be good if Jimmy blessed it. She knew Jimmy well enough to know that his own unavailability would be quickly forgotten, if, God forbid, Marshall and she didn't win this one. Jimmy would defend his turf by blasting them. She left another message for Jimmy on his ship.

It had been a long day after her all-nighter, and as soon as she got home, Kathleen kicked off her heels and sprawled on her bed, fully clothed, just to collect her energy for a shower. She thought she might reread the brief before going to sleep. It was a solid—no, brilliant—piece of work on extremely short notice, and she'd nailed it. When the phone rang at midnight, Kathleen was jarred awake, shocked out of a deep sleep, and when she finally recognized the sound, she was immediately relieved that it wasn't the morning alarm.

"Kitty, baby," the voice boomed. "Shouldn't you be at the office, drilling the troops? This is hand-to-hand combat, baby!"

"The troops need sleep, Anthony, so they'll be fresh and strong," she said. Anthony had just landed at LAX from New York. He'd gotten her message and would be on the red-eye to Chicago.

"Have the bloodies ready, baby," he said. "Nighty-night." Anthony already sounded as if he were on a first-class transcontinental roll, and, after a two-hour layover and another half-continent, the last thing he would need was a Bloody Mary. She hadn't had a scotch herself in two nights now. She turned off the lights.

She awoke at 6:30, both exhausted and edgy. She made coffee and opened the refrigerator, thinking she should have a bit of breakfast. With any luck, there would be some milk and she could have cereal. Instead, there was a half-bottle of Bloody Mary mix where the milk could—should—have been. She'd never had a drink this early before—wasn't that a sign of being an alcoholic?—but having worked all night two nights before, she figured time was a matter of perception. It might as well be happy hour. Gingerly, she poured an ounce of vodka into a tall glass of the mix and retrieved the paper from the hall. The top headline on page three blared,

"ANTHONY GIVES NIX UNTO SCONSIN COMMERCIAL." She read quickly:

"Legendary concert promoter Anthony filed a federal lawsuit yesterday to stop Sconsin Beer from using an imitation of his voice to pitch its beer in a commercial that began airing nationally last week. The 30-second commercial, created by Chicago advertising agency BDB, opens on a silhouette of a stage announcer in a stadium who says, 'I give unto you.' The phrase is familiar to concert-goers as Anthony's usual opening line. Federal judge William Lawton will hear arguments in the case this afternoon, according to Chicago lawyer Marshall Long of the prestigious law firm of Albright & Gill, which filed the suit on behalf of Anthony. Although celebrities in California have successfully sued for similar imitations of their voices, Long says this is the first time an Illinois court has been asked to rule squarely on the issue. In his brief, Long called Anthony's voice 'sacred' and accused Sconsin of stealing it from him."

The article was two columns wide, six inches long. It didn't mention her name, although it was on the brief, right under Marshall's. Kathleen got up and added another shot of vodka to her half-full glass. Marshall hadn't told her the press had called. Yet he'd been quoted, "They are stealing his right to choose that to which he will give his voice, his prestige, his very identity." It took her about 20 minutes to finish the Bloody Mary, staring blankly out the window of her apartment. She got in the shower and let it pound her face.

She was in her office at 9:00 when Anthony called from O'Hare. Had he been a normal client, she would've insisted he come down to the office immediately, so that they could prepare him for the court hearing. They would want him to read the briefs, understand the strategy, and help them think through the possible weaknesses in their case. For instance, had Anthony ever endorsed a beer? Certainly he'd promoted festivals and concerts sponsored by beer companies; they'd backed off the moral issue in the brief, and had simply emphasized that he had the economic right to choose which companies—beer or not—with which he would associate.

"Honey, I'll come down for lunch. While I'm here, there's one or two folks I need to speak to. That steak place I like. Gene's? Yeah, let's do that. I'll swing by. Where is he anyway?"

Kathleen said she hoped to hear from him before noon. She asked Anthony to try to make it to her office before lunch.

Anthony sighed and said okay, but she knew that she wouldn't see him until noon. Several young associates and Marshall were camped in a large conference room at the Firm, when Kathleen walked in. She reported her conversation with Anthony and Marshall jumped to his feet. His voice was a pitch higher, almost breathless.

"Get him here, now!" he said to her in a near-shout. Marshall stood at the end of the long mahogany table, his suit jacket sprawled over the back of the chair. He'd rolled up his shirt sleeves.

"He'll be here, Marshall," she said in her lowest, calmest voice. She was afraid he would lose it when she told him the rest. "He wants to have lunch at Gene's."

"No way. Order lunch here!" He crossed his arms. "I want to go over his testimony in case we have to put him on the stand."

"You're getting crumpled. Do you have another shirt?" Marshall sat for the first time, and straightened his shirt, rolling down the sleeves. Kathleen called Carol and asked her to order lunch. She read over the affidavits the associates had prepared, statements they'd gathered from friends attesting to their thinking that Anthony was involved in the commercial. They had evidence from a survey begun two days before that the phrase, "I give unto you…" meant, to a certain age group, Anthony, with the same frequency that another age group recognized "Here's Johnny," as the once famous talk host, Johnny Carson, or "Only in America," as the boxing promoter Don King, or "Here's looking at you, kid," as Humphrey Bogart.

"Good stuff," Kathleen said as she read.

"Could be a little better," Marshall said. "Are those percentages enough? Anybody got a case on percentages?" The associates culled through their photocopies.

She told Marshall he had a good case, and offered to hear a practice argument. He leaned back in his chair.

"Kids," he said. "That's it for now. Let's meet back here at 11:30." When they left, he said to her, "Alone, at last." She laughed. "It wouldn't be so bad if our clients weren't so nuts."

"All clients are nuts," she said.

"I'm including our partner as a client, and he has no idea what's going on."

"And that's different how?" she joked. "Enough avoidance, Marshall. It's going to be okay. Remember, I promised! If it's not, you've only cost us $250,000. Now, begin."

The associates were staring at the pile of deli sandwiches which had been brought in when Anthony called the conference room at noon. He was waiting downstairs in his limo.

"No, Anthony, let's do that for dinner. No. Maybe you won't, but you need to be prepared. I don't think we have time. My best professional advice, Anthony..." Kathleen smiled as she watched Marshall squirm.

"Nuts," he said, grabbing his jacket and a copy of the court papers.

"Good try. Who's buying?" She rolled her eyes.

Anthony had arranged—how and when was a mystery of the rich and famous—a private dining room at Gene's. He sat at their table, serious for the first time. He ordered three Bloody Marys without asking them, and addressed Marshall.

"Okay, boy, you've got my attention."

Marshall outlined the case, with heavy emphasis on the possibility that the court would not enter the requested cease-and-desist order on an emergency basis, in which case there might be another hearing in a week or so. Kathleen had heard Marshall refer to this as "hanging crepe," meaning he always prepared his clients for the worst of outcomes. Since the worst of worsts rarely happened, the use of this tactic conveniently left Marshall in a position to salvage some claim to at least partial victory at the end of the proceeding. It also tested his client's stomach for the gore of legal combat. Anthony listened to Marshall and ordered another drink.

"Anthony, I might have to call you as a witness," Marshall said. He himself had not touched his cocktail.

"I understand," Anthony said, refusing to follow Marshall's logic. "Drink up. You're the one with the case of nerves."

"I don't drink before court appearances, Anthony."

Kathleen had finished half of hers. One drink a couple of hours before they went to court couldn't matter. Marshall scowled at her as if to say that she should know better.

True to his word, Anthony ushered them out of the restaurant and they were back in their conference room at 2:10. The team left for court at 3:00. Although court was only two blocks away, Anthony insisted on taking his limo, but he refused Marshall's offer to arrange to use the building's secret, high-security entrance. The paralegal carried a large trial case of documents, including photocopies of cases, a videotape of past concerts promoted by Anthony, a copy of the survey and a summary of results, and a trademark search on "I Give Unto You...."

When they arrived at the court building, Anthony was rushed by two local television teams and a number of radio and press reporters. Kathleen deliberately hid behind Marshall. Not being a litigator, she didn't know exactly what she was allowed to say or not say about the case. Recently, saying stuff out loud had caused more than a few problems for her, and while she'd been somewhat aggravated that morning to see that Marshall had been the one cited by the *Tribune*, she had to admit that she was relieved not to be in the spotlight on this one. Anthony walked straight up to the closest camera and, with a mischievous twinkle in his eye, told it, "I give unto you a solemn order: Do not buy Sconsin Beer." The reporter, who hadn't even had a chance to ask a question, laughed and thanked him.

Marshall and Kathleen stood together at the podium when their case was called, Marshall directly behind it, Kathleen flanking him to his right.

They showed the judge the commercial.

"How can they do that?" Judge Lawton asked.

"They can't, Your Honor. Courts around this country...." Marshall began.

"I'm not asking you, Mr. Long. Mr. Weaver, what's your defense?"

"Your Honor, this commercial depicts a generic type." At the counsel's table with the young lawyers, Anthony chuckled loudly. The judge shot him a skeptical look.

"If you rule in Anthony's favor, you would tie the hands of every major advertiser in this country. They would be open to suit by every Tom, Dick and Harry who thinks a voice sounds vaguely like him." Kathleen leaned around Marshall to look, pointedly, at Mr. Weaver.

"Or her," Mr. Weaver corrected himself.

"But every Tom, Dick and Harry doesn't promote rock concerts, and every Tom, Dick and Harry doesn't say 'give unto you,'" the judge said, and Marshall and Kathleen nodded in unison.

"Your Honor, this commercial cost five-hundred-thousand dollars to produce. It would work a disproportionate hardship on Sconsin Beer if they couldn't run it. They've already committed three million dollars in media time over the next month."

"They don't have other commercials?" the judge asked.

Mr. Weaver hesitated. "It's a matter of free speech, Your Honor. Stopping this commercial would be a prior restraint, which is clearly prohibited by the First Amendment."

"The First Amendment doesn't have the same appeal to me, Mr. Weaver, when you're talking about purely commercial, instead of political, speech. Mr. Long, I'll enter the temporary order. You can come back in 10 days for your preliminary."

Marshall thanked the court and conferred with the clerk and Mr. Weaver on a time for the preliminary injunction hearing. Mr. Weaver told Marshall he would call him. He said perhaps they could work this out.

Outside the courtroom, Anthony smiled broadly for the television cameras, plugged his plans for another mega-concert at Soldier Field, and called to the executive vice-president of Sconsin Beer, who had sat silently throughout the entire court proceeding. "We need to sit down, Butch, talk about some big ideas coming your way."

Butch smiled a smile that reminded Kathleen of the good old boys and the Gloria Ellens golf deal. "Do you ever stop?"

"That's what makes me indispensable to you, my friend. How many times do you think your commercial was run on the news? How much press did you get? Can't buy this kind of exposure, Butch. We'll be in touch." Anthony patted him on the back, off-camera, and waved to the small crowd that had gathered to see why there were television cameras in the courthouse.

"Gene's" he told his limo driver. "We're all going to Gene's."

The young associates, of course, were thrilled to be in Anthony's presence. This was their reward for three 18-hour days—a big name to drop at singles bars in answer to the question, "What do you do?"

Anthony ordered crab legs for the table in the private dining room he apparently had claimed as his for the day, and dry martinis all around. It was just after 5:00. Marshall took off his jacket, rolled up his sleeves.

"Crumpled?" he said to Kathleen.

"Well done," she said, and lifted her glass.

Anthony reveled in the success of the afternoon. Not that he complimented Marshall or Kathleen or otherwise suggested that he understood that the case could just as easily have been dismissed. Instead he told them about his childhood, in Detroit, in the ghetto, and the gift that had been given unto him, which apparently was the gift to talk anybody into anything. Kathleen slipped away for a few minutes, called Jimmy's ship and left a victory message. At 6:30, after he'd ordered three rounds of martinis, he handed his platinum credit card to the waiter and told him to keep the tab open for the young folk—dinner and all.

"Send the bill for that big number," he said to Kathleen. "For superb services rendered. The best is yet to be." Then he was gone. He had a plane to catch, back to L.A.

"I guess we've got a settlement," she said to Marshall. He nodded, although she could tell he was still figuring out how she knew that.

The associates drifted away in the next 15 minutes, too tired to be tempted by the restaurant's famous steaks, and left the last round of martinis largely untouched. Marshall and Kathleen were alone. Kathleen reached for one of the martinis.

"Congratulations, Marshall," she said. She felt a genuine respect for his organization of the case, his restraint in the courtroom, his willingness to let the other side hang itself rather than force himself to be a star.

Marshall nodded. "But you're the one who's called it thus far. Sconsin sounded ready to settle, and Anthony's sending you a bonus. You're so good, Kathleen. I can't imagine what you would be like if you got that monkey off your back."

Kathleen looked at him, not sure she'd heard him right.

"What do you mean?" she said.

Marshall pointed at the martini in her hand.

She was genuinely surprised. "Problem? This is the solution!" she laughed. Harry's drinking was problem drinking, not hers. "It's not a problem, Marshall. I mean, I do like to drink but its…um…not a problem."

"You drank at lunch." His tone was factual, with just enough of a question in it so as not to sound to her like an accusation. Still, there was an edge to her voice when she answered him.

"To keep Anthony company, for godsakes."

"It's none of my business, Kathleen. I apologize."

She nodded. They'd been having a great day together, professionally and, she'd thought, personally. She didn't want it ruined by something that was none of his business.

"Shall we go, then?" she said, pushing the martini away.

"Let's finish these," Marshall said. "I'm already crumpled."

The next evening, Kathleen was mildly annoyed as she waited for the doorman to Jill's building to announce her presence. He'd started to say they weren't home, and she'd started to say she was expected, when someone finally answered the phone and the doorman sent her up. Jill had gone into labor the same day that Anthony had called Kathleen about his lawsuit, and all Kathleen knew—from an exchange of voicemails, was that Jill had been in labor for 16 hours, and had named her baby Caitlin, which, the voice message gushed, was for Kathleen. Kathleen had bought a little sterling silver brush and comb set and had it monogrammed in swirling letters. She took a deep breath before lifting the brass knocker on Jill and Steve's apartment door. She would've expected them to be standing in their entry way, waiting for her. Instead, it took Steve a full minute and a half to come to the door. He was friendly, but distracted. He led her into the living room, where Jill, nursing baby Caitlin, looked up and put a finger to her lips. Steve gestured to Kathleen to sit down on the couch, and she put her gift on the end table. No one said a word. Finally, Steve said, "She's our miracle baby." Kathleen remembered the agony of Jill's miscarriage a year before, and agreed.

After five minutes of looking and looking away, Kathleen got up quietly and said, "I'll help myself." Luckily, she found a half bottle of white wine in the refrigerator, and returned to the sofa. Jill looked surprised to see her.

"Pretty amazing, isn't she?" Jill giggled.

"Amazing," Kathleen heard herself say. For the first time since Steve had come into Jill's life, Kathleen was feeling like an intruder. Jill noticed the present on the table and opened it with her right hand while Caitlin suckled. When Jill thanked her and said, "Oh, how cute!" Kathleen felt not only the insignificance of her present, but of all she wanted to tell her friend about Anthony and the bonus and her case of first impression in Illinois. Jill listened to her news, and tried to show interest, but Kathleen could tell she didn't care. Despite the late hour, when she got home Kathleen called her mom, who answered in a sleepy voice. Immediately, her mother brightened in genuine excitement.

"I'm so proud of you," she said.

"Thanks," Kathleen said. It was some satisfaction, anyway. At least her parents were proud of her; she hadn't let them down.

In the next few weeks, Marshall and Kathleen settled Anthony's case, exactly the way Kathleen had said they should. Both sides agreed that they'd gotten a pretty good public relations bang for their legal buck. She sent a bill for the bigger number and sent a carbon copy to Jimmy.

Jimmy didn't say much about the trial or the copy of the bill. As soon as he got back to Chicago, he joined Anthony on the road. Officially, the court papers dismissed the suit in consideration of Sconsin not admitting any kind of liability, but agreeing to donate $25,000 to Anthony's designated charity, the Boys and Girls Club of America, because he believed in the youth of America and wanted to set for them a good example of "Anybody Can," which he was thinking of adopting as a new trademark, given the immense popularity of Nike's "Just Do It." The press reported the gift and the settlement as gossip rather than news.

At the same time, Butch, the executive vice-president of marketing for Sconsin beer, decided it was also a pretty good deal for them to kick in seven million dollars to become the presenting sponsor of Anthony's MegaMillennium Tour, which was still a ways off, but the effect would be to cut other beer sponsors out of Anthony's events until the Millennium. Anthony had also decided that imitation was the sincerest form of flattery. Kathleen decided that as a lawyer she made a pretty good businessperson.

The day after the settlement, she got a call from Marshall, asking if she'd seen the morning *Trib*. She had.

"I feel badly that they didn't mention your name," Marshall said. "You know, Kit, I told them, honest, that it was really your case."

Kathleen was surprised that Marshall had called, and even more so that he was apologizing for something beyond his control. While her folks would have gotten a kick out of seeing her name in the *Tribune*, she figured she would be able to make the necessary professional hay out of the case as a speaker at law seminars and such, and two colleagues from other firms had called her to congratulate her. Perhaps because of them, this time she'd not been so troubled by the newspaper's giving the credit to Marshall.

"That was nice of you, Marshall. I appreciate that. But you *are* the litigator. It makes some sense. Had we lost..."

"I still would have told them it was your case!" he laughed. "Listen, how about we celebrate, you and I? Saturday night? Le Titi?"

She hesitated.

"Oh, maybe you don't know. I was divorced about two years ago now."

"I'm sorry to hear that, Marshall. I really didn't know."

"I just asked you for dinner. You're not supposed to be sorry!" Marshall laughed in self-mockery. "She left me. Well, maybe that's a warning. Hell, Kit, it's just dinner with a partner."

Kathleen had had dinner with a fellow lawyer before. "Okay. Let's just do it," she said. "Or should I say, 'Anybody Can'?"

S aturday night, Marshall came to Kathleen's apartment to pick her up, even though he wasn't driving. She'd said she would meet him at Le Titi, but he'd said no, he'd rather pick her up. He let the doorman hail them a cab. "I had to let my driver go," he apologized. She didn't mean to look shocked, but she must have, because he winked. He gave the taxi driver the address. "Did you really think..."

"You never know!" she said gaily. "Sometimes I think everybody in the whole world has grown up, except me." She laughed a hearty but wistful laugh.

"If having a driver is the measure of maturity, there's no hope for me! Now, my ex-wife, she wanted all the trappings—country club and live-in maid, stuff like that. She was looking at a house in Lake Forest—with a pool! That's when we broke up. I was working to keep her in Nieman Marcus, and she was spending afternoons at the Ritz with her boyfriend."

"Ouch!"

"She's got a Harvard law degree, unused. She can work. Thank God the judge saw it that way, too."

"You were lucky."

"I don't mean to sound so bitter. I'm not, really. But I will say that I am amazed at what financial success is doing to our colleagues."

"Me, too!" Kathleen was animated. "You know, I don't have kids, and I don't have extravagant tastes. There's only so much money a person can really use. I don't know what to do with half of it except to give it away."

"I'd trade half my income today for a 40 hour work week," Marshall said. They'd arrived at Le Titi. Kathleen tried to notice what kind of tip Marshall gave the driver; she hoped it was a decent one.

"Shall we share a bottle of wine?" Marshall preempted Kathleen's taste for a scotch.

"Sure," she said, feeling a little curious about Marshall and why he'd asked her to this dinner. She wasn't sure it was a date, although he had picked her up and had paid for the cab. If it were a date, wasn't he being a bit directive, about the wine? Maybe he had business he wanted to discuss?

"How about a four day week for half the income?" she said.

Marshall took a sip of wine and nodded. "What would you do with a free day?" he asked.

Kathleen rattled off every hobby she'd put on hold. "I'd play golf and tennis and sail and write a novel and volunteer at a homeless shelter and bake Viennese sachertortes." Something about this conversation with Marshall was different, certainly different from her outings—rare now—with Harry and Ned, and different, too, from the strategy sessions she'd had from time to time with Marshall over Anthony's business issues. She felt relaxed and expansive, and it wasn't the wine.

They talked like old friends who hadn't seen each other in years. Marshall played lead guitar with a rock and roll band that practiced twice a year. He'd play more if he had a four day week, and he wanted to learn the banjo.

They weren't rushed. They talked so much the bottle of wine lasted through the entire dinner. After a triple chocolate dessert— profiteroles with chocolate mousse filling and bittersweet chocolate sauce—Marshall ordered cognacs for them both.

"I thought you thought I shouldn't drink hard liquor," she said, remembering his comments the day of Anthony's hearing.

"Special occasion," he said, and held his snifter in toast.

She raised her glass, thinking that it was indeed some kind of special occasion, although she couldn't quite put her finger on it. For the first time that night, it seemed, she had a thought she didn't share out loud.

The taxi had to pass Marshall's apartment to get to hers, but Marshall insisted that he would see her home. He'd somehow paid at Le Titi without a check being presented at the table, and he asked the driver to wait while he walked Kathleen into the lobby and gave her a friendly peck on the cheek.

"See you Monday!" He waved again as he pushed through the revolving door. It was 11:30. She washed her face and changed into a long silky peach nightgown her mother had given her one Christmas. It had a lace bodice and she rarely wore it. However, tonight—a night she didn't fully understand—it felt rather right.

TWELVE

All rise.

Sixteen months after Ann Rose had left the Firm, and several weeks after Marshall and Kathleen's celebratory dinner, they sat together again at the defendant's table, watching the court watchers as they waited for Ann Rose's case to be called. Marshall had told Kathleen about the court watchers. They were the dozen or so old men and women who spent their retirements watching trials the way others watch daytime TV, surfing from courtroom to courtroom, gossiping about the lawyers and judges, and laying small wagers on verdicts and judgments.

While technically each partner of Albright & Gill was a defendant, the Firm had decided that it was not necessary for each to attend the trial. In a confidential memo to each partner, the Firm said it would be adequately represented by counsel and designated members of the Management Committee. Kathleen read the memo as Blake's attempt to distance himself from his own decisions as Managing Partner of the Firm, to recast the lawsuit as a problem created by the Evaluation Committee. Blake expected Marshall and Kathleen to attend, as former and current chairs of the Evaluation Committee, which, Kathleen wanted to scream, was not, in fact, in charge of partnership decisions. Silver-haired Jules Steinberg, the former head of Ann's department, and litigator Leonard Stonehill had both eased up on their practices in recent years and were to be Blake's eyes and ears.

Despite the veiled warnings to stay away, most of the Management Committee and most of the Evaluation Committee found a reason to be in the federal courthouse—by happenstance, they said to one another—just about the time the opening arguments were set to begin. They appeared minutes before Judge Jasper's gavel and feigned mild surprise, like at a family reunion, that so many of their partners were there as well. Four of Albright & Gill's female partners—specifically requested by Blake to attend—sat in the first row of spectator seats, just behind the defendant's table.

At the table opposite them, Helen Bornstein wore a gray silk shirtwaist dress, buttoned at the neck. From under her collar, a modest strand of pearls hung just to the top of her bosom. Ann Rose was wearing a black wool suit—a skirt and jacket—with a starched white blouse, uncharacteristically unbuttoned at the neck. It must have been Helen's coaching, Kathleen thought. Ann always wore pants.

The judge entered the courtroom. All rose, all sat. The judge made some opening remarks to the jury and called on Helen Bornstein. Taking a legal pad with her, she stood at the podium in front of the jury and began. She told them the law, which was, strictly speaking, the court's job. She said that Title VII, the Civil Rights Act of 1964, 42 U.S.C. §2000e *et seq.*, a statute they had no doubt heard bandied about their own offices, forbids an employer "to discriminate with respect to his compensation, terms, conditions or privileges of employment" or "to limit, segregate or classify his employees or applicants for employment in any way which would deprive or tend to deprive any individual of employment opportunities or otherwise adversely affect his status as an employee, because of such individual's...sex." With what Kathleen presumed was restraint, Helen didn't comment on the sexist language of the statute itself. Then she told them precisely what facts to listen for in the testimony she was going to present, and exactly what she was going to prove. She was pleasant, even friendly. Her style was simple and straightforward. Nothing about her threatened to draw attention to herself or to distract the jury away from the simple facts of her client's case.

"Ladies and Gentlemen of the jury, what this statute means is that gender must be irrelevant to employment decisions. During the course of this trial, we will prove that Ann Rose's gender—the female gender—was highly relevant to Albright & Gill's decision not to advance her to partnership. *Because of her sex.*" Bornstein paused, letting those words become a refrain. "Albright & Gill discriminated against her. They did not offer her the ultimate privilege of employment—partnership—despite the fact that for nearly eight years, she was recognized as a star associate. Her hours were the highest of any associate. She brought in more business, and had primary responsibility for some of Albright & Gill's most important work for their most important clients. Because she was a woman, *because of her sex*, she was denied those privileges of employment.

"I want you, ladies and gentlemen, to pay special attention to what Ms. Kathleen Hannigan has to say. She is the chair of Albright & Gill's Evaluation Committee. She will testify, as she did in depositions, that not only is Ms. Rose a superb lawyer—no one in her class, no man in her class, received better evaluations—but *she* is the one who told Ms. Rose that Albright & Gill wanted Ms. Rose to act more femininely and to wear jew-el-ry and make-up and frilly clothes!"

The court watchers perked up, twittering softly among themselves. Bornstein's inflection of "jew-el-ry" was the kind of theatrics they liked. Kathleen stared passively at the jury, hoping that her expression didn't look mean or worried or dark, the way it could sometimes when she was lost in thought and the corners of her mouth dragged down. She parted her lips slightly, innocent and open, not defensive. She held her breath for as long as she could and then tried to sneak a bit of air through her mouth, her shoulders steady. She didn't want to look like she was breathing hard or that she was at all anxious. Her show was as much for her partners and herself as it was for the jury.

Helen Bornstein continued. "To judge Ann Rose by standards of some outdated notion of femininity—her jew-el-ry and her clothes— was to deprive her of an opportunity to become a partner in Albright & Gill because she was female, and, because she didn't fit their nineteenth-century notion of what it means to be a woman."

Kathleen heard the back pews shuffle as the court watchers strained to get a sideways glimpse of Ann Rose. The plaintiff herself sat motionless, a leather portfolio open before her at the counsel's table. The yellow legal pad inside seemed to have one five-letter word on the first line. Twenty feet away, it would have taken telescopic vision to read it, but Kathleen wondered if it said, "smile."

Helen Bornstein didn't smile, but she didn't bark either. She looked each juror in the eye, neither favoring the seven women nor scolding the five men, and then she sat down.

Immediately, Philip Darby rose to address the jury, buttoning his jacket as he got up. He folded his hands together, prayer style, chest level. He started at the beginning, which may have been a desperate move.

"In 1877," he said, and Kathleen thought she heard the court watchers yawn, "two childhood friends, farmboys from Springfield, had a dream, a dream that they could follow in the footsteps of a lawyer named Abraham Lincoln. They read the law, just like good old Abe, and were admitted to the bar of the State of Illinois."

Kathleen looked at the jury, which looked impressed, even though nearly every firm in town tried to trace its roots, one way or another, to the overused Abe.

"They brought that dream to Chicago, where they shared a 10 by 10 office over here on LaSalle Street. They worked hard, skipped meals, and eked out a living, until one of them, Winston Albright, met the daughter of a railroad tycoon, and Albright and his buddy, Jeremiah Gill, became two of the busiest lawyers in town. They had so much business they took on a young lawyer who worked for 15 years for Winston and Jeremiah, and, when the young man was 40, they finally made him a partner. So they had three partners, and hired two other younger lawyers, who got into a brawl in a saloon over a point of law, and Albright sent them both off on their own. Albright then hired three other young men, and one of them was a regular Clarence Darrow in the courtroom. He had so much business of his own, he didn't have time for Albright's business, but he was the brother of Gill's younger sister's husband, so they made him a partner, and you see, ladies and gentlemen, that's how partnerships grow."

Kathleen took a deep breath. It was a long way to go to get to some kind of point.

"Lawyers come together to practice for a variety of reasons, from economic to social to downright nepotism. When they do, they trust their professional reputations to each other. Albright & Gill, the firm founded by those two farmboys, today has 315 partners, in five cities, and more than 500 bright, young associate lawyers. The successor of that first railroad client is still its client, and its biggest clients are household names you trust, the best companies in America. This case is about how Albright & Gill decides who to trust with a name that has meant excellence since 1877."

It wasn't the most gripping of beginnings. Kathleen had not been consulted by Darby & Blythe on this part of the Firm's defense strategy. Had they asked her, she would have said history was the poorest of defenses when it came to discrimination. She wondered if the African-Americans, the Asian-Americans, the Jews, the gays or even the women on the jury could take any solace from history. Apparently Darby was trying to establish that a variety of factors—some fair, some not—go into partnership decisions, but his statement so far left open the possibility that sex was one of those factors.

"We're going to show you the incredible lengths that Albright & Gill goes to in order to ensure that it selects only the best people— and here I emphasize people, not the best lawyers—as its partners. Twice a year, the young lawyers are evaluated. These evaluations are performed by all of the lawyers that each associate works with. They fill out a four-page form and grade each associate on legal research, writing and oral presentations; on attitude, interactions with clients, staff and other lawyers, and on public service." Kathleen tried not to smile. "Public service" was not, in her experience, one of the Firm's decisive criteria—either for success as an associate or for partnership.

"These evaluations are reviewed by the Evaluation Committee which Ms. Bornstein mentioned. There are 15 lawyers on that Committee and they spend several days, twice a year, including weekends, making sure the evaluations are fair. Each associate is interviewed before the Committee meets, and again afterwards. The associates are told what people think of them, and how they can improve their performance. Those for whom the demands of Albright & Gill are too great are helped to find employment elsewhere. The Firm spends hundreds of valuable billable hours to make sure that each associate gets the best chance to reach his or her potential, and a fair chance to become a partner. At the same time, the Firm makes sure that it doesn't get fooled by an associate who bills thousands of hours but doesn't have the interpersonal skills, the special qualities, of an Albright & Gill partner. Since 1877, hundreds of lawyers, including dozens of women and other minorities, have exhibited those skills, and have become partners of the Firm."

"In the case of Ms. Rose, what came to the attention of the Evaluation Committee, as well as others at the Firm, was that Ms. Rose swore in front of clients, yelled at staff, and was generally thought to be irritating and annoying. We'll hear from Ms. Hannigan, who interviewed Ms. Rose, exactly what she said to her— how the Firm wanted Ms. Rose to improve her interpersonal skills so that she *would* become a partner, not that she was supposed to wear jew-el-ry." The court watchers shuffled.

"Ms. Hannigan conveyed to Ms. Rose that she was *perceived* as being overly aggressive, even hostile, to clients, to staff and to other lawyers in the Firm. This was two years before Ms. Rose was considered for partner, and Ms. Rose refused to change her behavior. Now, ladies and gentlemen, how would you feel if you were forced to marry someone you thought was hostile?"

Finally, Kathleen thought, an argument with some emotional punch. But Darby still hadn't unclasped his hands.

"The newspapers are full of stories about how frustrated judges are with lawyers and how uncivil they've become. Albright & Gill holds itself to the highest standards of professionalism, including professional demeanor. If a lawyer doesn't meet those standards, he or she is not invited to partnership. It's that simple.

"Ms. Rose is, by all accounts, a fine lawyer, and that is not the issue here. Albright & Gill did not choose to make her a partner— the positives on her lawyer side, which Ms. Bornstein will tell you about again and again in the coming week, simply did not compensate for the negatives on her personality side. If Ann Rose were a man, she would not have been invited to partnership. Albright & Gill's decision has nothing to do with sex, ladies and gentlemen. If anything, it has to do with civility."

With a slight bow, Darby nodded to the jury and returned to the defense table with his hands stiffly at his sides. There, he quickly folded his hands, and looked straight ahead at the judge. It occurred to Kathleen that he was hiding a slight trembling, the kind actors get before they take the stage. His voice had been steady, and he had looked at the jury, although he may have looked at the men more than the women. Having seen Darby when he was relaxed, it was clear to Kathleen, although the jury might not have noticed, that Darby was nervous. Nervous! Here he was, supposedly the very best of the very best, and he was plain old nervous. Of course, there would be some tension. A substantial audience of the most prestigious lawyers in town were staring at his backside while he argued that they had a right to pick and choose their partners. Any member of the jury who'd ever been excluded from a fraternity, a sorority, or a childhood treehouse, would naturally lean towards the excluded plaintiff, Ann Rose. The press, the champion of underdogs, would be more favorably disposed towards Helen Bornstein's client than Darby's. Kathleen thought he might have done better to admit to all those difficulties and to his own nervousness—to have made himself into an underdog representing the Goliath that everyone loved to hate. But that was not the chosen tactic. It was apparent Albright & Gill was going to defend this one based on its sacred right to choose: Gender never crossed their lofty minds.

It was almost noon, and the judged declared a recess. Helen Bornstein could call her first witness after lunch.

The Albright & Gill partners shuffled out, some back to the office, some to lunch. Darby went off with his associates to discuss things between themselves. Marshall and Kathleen looked at each other.

Marshall looked to the empty jury box and said in a low voice, "Unless you're running back to the office to do public service, I'll buy you lunch." Then he leaned over and whispered in her ear, "You sexy thing."

Kathleen's laugh bounced off the courtroom's walls. One of the court watchers at the back turned and tossed her a toothy grin. The clerk, straightening our her papers, looked up and smiled.

"It's that laugh," Marshall said.

Kathleen realized that, like Darby, every muscle in her body had been clenched, all morning, braced against an expected blow.

It felt good to breathe, and little tears licked her eyes. She felt like a *papier maché* mannequin of herself, a hodgepodge of conflicting emotions and loyalties, slapped together to look like a person she wasn't. The trial had begun, and she couldn't yet articulate what it was she wanted to say to Helen, to Ann and to her partners. She smiled, a little more sure of herself when she was smiling. She knew that under the bright light of the witness stand the layers would, in time, shrink and begin to peel away, revealing the wire-mesh skeleton of truth.

"Tuna salad?" she said as Marshall opened the courtroom door.

"Not now," he said to a reporter.

They went to lunch at a deli around the corner from the courthouse, but they didn't talk much. There wasn't time. First, they stood in line for 10 minutes, studying the menu posted above the counter. Actually, they both knew what they wanted, but it gave them a polite excuse not to talk. Talk would only have been disheartening, as "could have" and "should have" usually are.

"Do they put pickle in their tuna?" she asked Marshall. She detested anything other than celery and onions in her tuna salad, and while she might tolerate chopped eggs, pickles soured her on the whole notion of lunch.

"As I recall," Marshall said, "in 1877, when Uncle Mort's great, great uncle on his mother's side founded an ale-house—although some say it later was a whore house—on this very spot, tuna salad was only the dream of a humble innkeeper..."

"Shush!" she said, chuckling at Marshall's credible impersonation of Darby's opening statement. "I didn't know you were an actor!"

"We all have our secrets," he said. Recklessly, she ordered the tuna.

After lunch, Helen Bornstein called her first witness.

"I do," Ann Rose said as she sat down in the witness box. The after-lunch crowd was thinner—most of the Albright & Gill contingent had seen in Darby's morning performance what they wanted to see. Kathleen realized with a jolt that it probably had never occurred to them to stay to hear Ann Rose herself. Either

her personal story didn't matter to them or they already had their own opinions of the truth. However, the court watchers were curious, and filled in the benches toward the front of the gallery.

In the hall, after lunch, Kathleen had heard an old woman, her wool coat buttoned around her, say, "She looks a little severe to me." Her companion, a distinguished looking gentleman in a suit and tie, leaned down to her and whispered, "We used to have a name for them." Kathleen stopped and looked at them, considering whether she'd heard them correctly. They had assumed, based on nothing more than appearance, and before a word of truth was spoken from the stand, that Ann was a lesbian. Kathleen didn't know for sure Ann Rose's sexual orientation, and, in fact, thought they were wrong, but she'd heard, as clearly as she'd ever heard, classification of a person because of that person's failure to satisfy a sexual stereotype.

Ann's testimony was simple and without rancor. Bornstein ran through Ann's educational background, asking her to explain each honor listed, including her double major in math and economics at Indiana University, where, she recalled, only 15 were elected to Phi Beta Kappa in their junior year.

"You were elected as a junior?"

"Yes, ma'am." Kathleen had never heard Ann use the word sir, let alone "ma'am." To her, it sounded fake, a bad line from a bad play, performed badly. The jury nodded its approval—how could they tell the real Ann Rose from the coached one?

Bornstein got Ann to say that Albright & Gill had recruited her while she was still in law school, as if that somehow set her apart from other law students. She asked her, without a question in her voice, if she'd been editor of the law review, and Ann said smoothly, "Yes, I was an editor of the law review." Kathleen silently shook her head. Bornstein cleverly let the jury think that Ann was *the* editor, the top dog, when in fact she was only *an* editor, one of six beneath the editor-in-chief. It was a distinction, Kathleen realized, which would be lost on a jury which probably had never seen a law review and would not, in any event, appreciate the fine tunings of its rankings.

Bornstein and her client presented a tight duet of Ann's progress at the Firm. After two hours, they were as far as the pitch to First Credit and the Gloria Ellens matter.

"Mr. Steinberg told me that they were looking for counsel on this deal, due to a conflict at their other firm. Another lawyer and I made an appointment to talk to the officer in charge of the deal at the bank. At the very last minute, he had to cancel, and so I went alone and presented our credentials. They called me the next day and hired me."

"So the Firm trusted you to represent it and its professional reputation to this major, potential client?"

"Yes, ma'am." It had been Kathleen's impression that from time to time First Credit called upon A&G when its usual firm had a conflict, and that different partners, often Steinberg himself, headed up those deals. Steinberg had been the billing partner for First Credit in the past, and was, still, the billing partner.

Helen looked at her watch. She told the judge that she expected Ann's next testimony, on the events immediately surrounding her last two evaluations and the partnership decision, to take two hours. The judge said the jury had heard enough for one day and sent them home.

D arby turned to Marshall and Kathleen. "We need to review the cross." He started to suggest that they go back to his office, but Marshall cut him off.

"Home is where the heart is," he said lightly. Back at A&G, Darby took off his tie and put it in his jacket pocket, and then took off his jacket. Marshall peeled off his suit coat, but not his tie. Taking a seat at the conference room table, Kathleen slipped out of her shoes. Darby asked if they could get some Cokes or coffee.

"Which?" Marshall said, and Kathleen was relieved that he hadn't turned to her to play "hostess."

"Both," Darby laughed. "The worst thing about being on trial is the water."

"A caffeine addict?" Kathleen asked.

"Big time," Darby said, and folded his hands against his chest. Marshall called the floor's after-hours secretary and ordered coffee and Cokes—no diet—and said they'd call later about dinner.

"They'll finish up tomorrow with Ann Rose, I hope. Then maybe they'll get to her character witnesses for another day, and then this kooky psychologist they've got who's going to say some gibberish about subconscious stereotyping. The way I see it, we cross Ann pretty hard, get a little of her edge out in front of the jury to counteract this ma'am crap, and let the character witnesses say whatever they want. Then we'll get to the psychologist and go after her. Right now, I think the jury likes Ann Rose well enough. Helen did a good job on the lesbian question. She got Ann to say she dates men but hasn't had time in her busy schedule to marry. Poor thing! By the time Helen has presented the character witnesses, Ann'll be up for sainthood!"

They drank an entire pot of coffee and Darby had three Cokes besides, one before the coffee, one with the large everything pizza they ordered at 7:30 and one after. Kathleen picked mushrooms off while Darby picked away at Ann's testimony. They just needed to cast a little doubt, he said, to let the jury see how she slanted things. The partner who'd canceled the First Credit meeting at the "last minute"—the day before—actually had asked her to reschedule. Why hadn't she done so? *An* editor, Ms. Rose? One of six? By the way, ma'am, have you ever sworn in front of a client?

At 9:30, they went home. Marshall and Kathleen shared a cab.

In the cab, he said, "We'll make a litigator out of you yet, Kit."

She faked a gag. "It's pretty tedious, Marshall. Makes me wonder about the system. It's such theater. So rehearsed. How's the jury supposed to know the woman is a…?" She caught herself before she spit out, "bitch."

"You'll tell them," Marshall said.

"It's not that clear," she said.

"It will be," he said, with the confidence of a coach who does not acknowledge defeat.

"But it isn't, don't you see?" She clutched his arm without thinking. "I call her a bitch because I don't like her. I don't like her style. But hell, Brian's the best client-getter we've got, and I don't like *his* style either. I think maybe she *does* have a case."

"We are allowed to discriminate based on style," Marshall said quietly. "That is the crux of our defense." He put his hand on top of hers. "I know you're in a bind. You're a woman. You're a partner. And this is your Firm. They want all their women attorneys to be like you."

She flipped his hand away to cross her arms. "Because I'm such a weenie, that I let Brian get away with crap that Ann would cut his balls off for." She was shocked at her own language. She was, indeed, angry with herself for not being more like Ann Rose. "They want all their women partners to be grateful they even get to play."

The cabbie pulled up in front of Kathleen's apartment and Marshall gave him five dollars. The meter said four. Without asking, he got out of the cab with her and said good evening to the doorman, who held the door open but showed no surprise that he would be going up with Ms. Hannigan.

To her own surprise, Marshall silently got in the elevator and punched the thirty-ninth floor. She fumbled for her keys. Inside, she headed for the kitchen, took out two glasses, poured two scotches to the brim. She left her shoes by the sink, handed him a glass, and walked into her living room, where she dumped her coat on a chair and sprawled on her couch. She took a long, sullen sip of her drink.

Marshall sat in the low-slung leather swivel chair opposite her head. He put the glass to his lips briefly and then took a cork coaster from the little basket on her coffee table and set it down. Kathleen was staring at the ceiling. Marshall's watch beeped the hour.

Tentatively, he said, "This isn't really about Ann, is it?"

She didn't know what he meant.

"It's about your personal future at the Firm, isn't it?"

"They can't kick me out—not after all this—if that's what you mean. *That* would be *per se...*"

"No," he cut her off. "I think you have other ambitions. Like Management Committee?"

"What makes you say that?" she said, sitting up.

"You work hard. You seem to care a lot about the Firm, do a lot of recruiting and all. Your name is in the newsletter a lot." Marshall's tone was matter-of-fact.

"Of course I've thought about it, but that's impossible now, " she said in what she hoped was a neutral tone.

"But *why* would you want to do Management Committee? You'd have to hang around with the very guys you complain about all the time." Marshall's voice hit a whiny note of frustration.

"Because then I could make a difference. I could change the place." Marshall didn't react. "For the women at the Firm."

"Like what?" Marshall demanded. "I'm not being hostile," he said.

"Could have fooled me," she snapped back.

"I wonder what, for instance, you *would* change, setting aside for the moment the question of what you *might be able* to change. Like what, the maternity policy?"

"Well, maybe," she said. Marshall's silence forced her on. "It needs to be looked at. And daycare, maybe, for the staff, which is primarily women."

"Those issues don't affect you, personally. What else? How have you been held back by the fact that there have not been women on the Management Committee?"

"How could I know the answer to that one?" She hated his cross-examination, and was aggravated not to have a concrete example to shove in his face. A law school professor had drilled it into her as a first-year student: *Concepts without facts are bullshit. Facts without concepts are trivia.* She immediately moved to depersonalize the discussion.

"How can I know what might have been, in the absence of bias? How do we know what great discoveries we've missed in this country because women, blacks, native Americans, whoever, have not been given opportunities?"

"I'm not so sure this is about any feminist agenda, Kitty," Marshall said in a noticeably impersonal way. "It could just as easily be about feminist ego, and that's the same trap the good ole boys got themselves into in the first place."

"Ego?" she shouted. "You think this is just about my *ego?*"

Marshall cleared his throat. "Most of the issues the Management Committee deals with are gender-neutral, like billings and collections, not grand policy-based issues," he said flatly.

"They are not gender-neutral as long as they are decisions being made solely by one sex. I don't know, for instance, how those decisions would be decided differently if the Committee were balanced. My guess is that today women lag behind their male partners in points and compensation. I would bet that when someone dies, women don't get their hand-me-down institutional billings—the boys look around for one of their buddies who's a little behind and give them to him."

He leaned forward in this chair and held her gaze. She stared back, holding her breath. "You want to be on the Management Committee so you can say you were the first woman to make it, but it's not like anything is going to change around here except that you are going to get a lot of national press as the woman who shattered the glass ceiling in the legal profession." She felt the blood drain from her skin. She had, in fact, fantasized about the cover story *The American Lawyer* would surely run.

"Hey," Marshall continued when she was silent. "I'm enough of a feminist to think that if you and Sally and whoever—if the entire Management Committee were women, you'd reach the same decisions, because you have to: economics are economics."

"You really don't understand, do you? The economics might be the same, but the values underlying distribution would be more cooperative, less greedy. We might fund on-site day-care or paid sabbaticals or 12 frigging months of maternity leave."

"Bull. You threaten to take one dollar away from Blake and he splits the Firm in two, like a pair of matching towels—'his' and 'hers.' Now, what would the feminist regime do, preside over the dissolution of the Firm? It's not about your agenda, Kitty. It's about your *ego*. At least be honest about that much."

"What if it *is* about ego? Am I not entitled to the same e-go as men?" She exaggerated "e-go" the way Bornstein had exaggerated "jew-el-ry."

"Sure!" Marshall said, laughing victoriously. "Then there's no dilemma! You *must* support Ann Rose. You want the freedom for women to be just like the people you want to replace. Ann Rose, being most like them, is most likely to succeed at their game. You *must* support her. For feminist reasons, of course. But I think you want her to succeed only if she does it your way, fits *your* stereotype of what a woman lawyer should be like."

Kathleen wasn't sure if Marshall was toying with her for argumentative sport, or if he was being brutally honest. She didn't know anyone—not Jill, not Harry, not Ned, not even her own father—who would hold up such a harsh mirror. What *did* she care, anyway, about most of the issues—maternity leave, day-care, part-time—that women groused about? She didn't have children. Hell, she didn't even have a husband. She'd watched Jill meet Steve, lose ambition, conceive, lose, conceive again, and she'd felt lonely, but she'd not been tempted. What her personal life might be lacking she could make up for in professional success. That part, she had to admit, was selfish. Marshall could be right. It might not make a difference if one woman made the Management Committee.

"We've got to start somewhere, Marshall. You can't change a culture overnight. One generation of women lawyers, or even two or three. It could take ages. But, not to make a start...." Her mouth was dry. She wanted to cry, but no tears came—it was deeper than that. She leaned back on her couch, swung her feet up, avoided looking at him. "When men don't make the Management Committee or president of the company or whatever," she said slowly, "it's mid-life crisis time. They realize their own limitations. I feel like this is more serious. The professional woman's depression is not merely personal, but political as well. We feel like it's not just that our individual egos are bruised, but somehow, that the whole movement failed. All the sacrifices and indignities that women had to face to even knock on the door of the Management Committees of this world, what were they for, if...if we're not going to make it?"

Marshall's voice was soft. "Maybe it's just about the effort, the process. You, as one person, don't need to take the whole thing on. If you don't want it for its own sake, or for the ego of it, then move on! Do something else. If it's for the grand cause, the big difference, the change-the-world revolution—well, then, you *are* going to feel frustrated and angry and depressed. I've got news for you. It's not worth it."

Marshall's watch beeped again. Fifteen minutes had passed. Kathleen's scotch was gone, his barely touched. Tears formed and she struggled not to wipe her eyes for fear of drawing attention to them. She closed her eyes.

S he smelled coffee and she heard a shower running. She squinted and saw that it was light. She tried to remember why she'd fallen asleep on her living room couch. Marshall, and one scotch—just one—and then she'd been so tired, and it'd been so peacefully quiet.

Marshall shook her gently. She must've drifted back to sleep. The coffee smell was closer. Marshall's dark hair was wet and beginning to curl. He was fully dressed, completely pressed.

"How do you do that?" she said.

"The coffee goes in the filter in the top, and the water...."

"No, that's a clean shirt."

"I'm a trial lawyer, Kit. Have shirt," he reached in his pocket and took out a disposable razor, "will travel."

"I'm not a morning person," she moaned, sitting up and reaching for the coffee.

"Toast or cereal?" Marshall said. He apparently had learned his way around her apartment, and knew what little there was to eat. "heel of rye or heel of wheat?"

"Coffee, shower, cab," she said, getting up. Marshall had retrieved the paper from outside her door and was reading in the same chair he'd occupied last night. She didn't remember asking him up. Why on earth had he stayed? Why was he acting like this was normal?

"Lawyers watching the case of Ann Rose versus the prestigious law firm of Albright & Gill were fascinated yesterday by the stark contrast between the mannish and some say boorish Rose and the firm's expected star witness, senior woman partner, the beautiful and charming Kit Hannigan."

"You are so full of shit," she said. "Or, as Ann would say, you are so full of shit, sir."

As soon as they got in the cab, Marshall said, "Okay, so, today, we sit, we listen, we see if Darby has any wits about him at all, and tonight, I treat for dinner and we discuss your feminist dilemma."

"It's morning," she moaned. "I can't argue with you." About two blocks from the office she started to tell the cabbie to pull over, she wanted to get out.

She didn't have to explain to him that she wanted to avoid starting any rumors. "Nonsense. No one's following us, if that's what you mean. We had an early morning meeting, if 'no one' asks. Besides, a feminist can do as he or she pleases."

She scowled.

"A feminist can be a he," he smiled.

THIRTEEN

Ms. Hannigan, I have one last question.

At the beginning of the second morning of trial, Helen Bornstein played for the jury the tape of Kathleen's interview with Ann Rose. First she played it all the way through, starting with Kathleen's fear that Ann would not make partner. Sitting at the defense table, Kathleen lifted her chin slightly, and, as she'd been coached, thought pleasant, unrelated thoughts while looking in the direction of the jury. Then Bornstein played the tape, over Darby's objections, line by line, asking Ann to comment on each of Kathleen's words, explaining what she'd understood by Kathleen's use of "feminine," "bitchy," "harsh," "softer," "mannish," "shooting herself in the foot," and "perception of attitude." Kathleen directed her attention to Ann Rose, who avoided Kathleen's gaze and fixed her eyes instead on Bornstein.

"I understood Kathleen Hannigan to be telling me that I needed to do whatever was necessary so that the partners would perceive me as feminine, like wear jewelry and make-up and such."

"What did you mean, 'I'll take my chances'?" Bornstein asked.

"Objection!" Darby said, mostly to aggravate Ann Rose.

"Yes, but I'll allow it," the judge said.

Ann Rose turned to the jury. Her voice was even, and she sounded to Kathleen rehearsed. "I meant that I am who I am. I am a highly skilled and competent lawyer. It so happens that I am a woman. I am not particularly out-going. I didn't think my sex mattered to partnership decisions. The partnership is organized for the purpose of making money. I saw the qualifications of the men who made partner in each of the past five years. I met or exceeded each of them on every financial criterion. Billings. Hours. Collections. I had a strong relationship with a substantial commercial client. I didn't need to wear jewelry or win any Miss Congeniality contests to meet the Firm's traditional standards for partnership."

D arby began his cross examination of Ann Rose with a deliberately cordial air.

"Ms. Rose, I am impressed, as surely the jury must be, with your superb credentials. You have my sincere congratulations on a fine career, one which I am certain will continue to prosper. I apologize that we need to go over your testimony again. I know you understand that I am not questioning your legal ability." He cleared his throat. His hands were folded on the podium, on top of the legal pad of questions he'd written the night before.

"Did Ms. Bornstein play the entire tape of your conversation with Ms. Hannigan?"

"She played the relevant part."

"There's more, isn't there?"

"There's some of Ms. Hannigan's chit-chat at the beginning."

"I think the jury should hear that part," Darby said, and introduced the part of the tape that Bornstein had not played, the part where Kathleen had asked Ann if she were happy, and had told her the Committee had concerns about her interpersonal skills.

"...*tell them, in whatever interpersonal way you find appropriate, to fuck themselves.*"

The jury didn't gasp, but one or two of the women looked down, and two middle-aged men smiled broadly. There was a gentle rustle among the court-watchers.

"I apologize to the jury," Darby said. "We don't mean to offend."

Kathleen half-expected Bornstein to object to Darby's characterization of the tape as offensive, but she sat passively, apparently not wishing to draw attention to what Darby was trying to play as a bombshell. Ann Rose, too, was still. Darby'd been wrong to hope that she would lose her temper, that she would perhaps slip and swear in front of everyone.

Darby let the silence in the courtroom rise, while he consulted his notes.

"I take it, Ms. Rose, you don't care to apologize now."

"Objection! He's badgering the witness." Bornstein was on her feet, pretending Ms. Rose could be badgered.

"I'll withdraw it." Darby said, and tilted his head to the jury, as if to say, "see, that's how it is." He took the entire afternoon for his cross, and when he was through apologized again to Ann that it had gone so slowly. Ann didn't respond, but smiled demurely at the jury and nodded quickly to the judge as she left the witness stand.

With only character witnesses scheduled for the next day, neither Marshall nor Kathleen felt the need to go back to Darby's office to help him prepare. Marshall had said he'd treat, and she said she needed comfort food. They'd agreed that the landmark Italian restaurant around the corner from the federal court house, a favorite of the city's litigators, had the best lasagna in the city. It was just about 5:00, a little early for dinner, but the bar was full, and Marshall stopped to greet a small group of older men while she followed the maitre d' to the last table, in the darkest corner, against the wall. With a flourish, he opened her napkin and placed it on her lap for her. She smiled weakly and waited for Marshall.

When he sat down, the waiter brought a bottle of good Chianti, a gift, apparently, from one of the bar crowd.

"So, were you really Prom Queen?" he said.

"Heavens, no! I wasn't even asked to the prom!" She shivered in an exaggerated attempt to shake the memory, but for a moment she was a high school girl again, and miserable. Glasses. Braces. Unmanageably curly, uncool hair that her mother wouldn't let her straighten. "I didn't even have a damn date," she confessed for some reason that was not immediately apparent to her.

"Valedictorian, no doubt."

"There were six of us with straight "As." None of us had dates. You'd think at least we could have dated each other, but the boys were worse than the girls. It's that age when you can only have one: looks or athletics or personality or brains. In that order of preference!"

"Just wanted to make sure you were normal!"

"All my life I've wanted to be normal. Not to have to carry this Ivy League baggage around. I feel like I've never been normal."

"But you have been. Normal for us, that is. These guys probably didn't even have one of your four in high school! Late bloomers, all. Heavens, they were absolutely nobody until they made law review somewhere. Then that became their life. They learned only the minimal social skills necessary to maybe get some girl to marry them for their income potential and to talk a little shop and some football with contemporaries of the same ilk. Totally dysfunctional. No, not dysfunctional, a-functional! All of us. Branded in high school. Only the exceptional few got out."

She raised her glass and he clinked it with his. She was laughing so hard little tears were filling her eyes with sympathy for herself and for him. "How did you get out?"

"I had an older sister. I eavesdropped when she and her girlfriends talked about boys. The big difference between the boys they liked and the ones they didn't, it turned out, was that they liked the ones who talked." Marshall said that his father had made him join the debate team because he needed something to put on his college applications. The debate team had taught him to talk, no matter what. "Mostly, though, with girls—and I'd say with most people—all you really need to do to be a great talker is to listen. But you know that."

"I do?" She was fishing, she knew for a compliment—she wanted Marshall to say that she was an empathetic listener, and that's why people liked her. That there was an upside to "Prom Queen."

Instead he said, "Listening to others is how you avoid letting people get to really know you."

In the light of the table's votive candle, she studied the color of her wine, less purple than the hearty burgundies she favored.

"Oh?" she said sarcastically. "Exactly how long did you go to marriage counseling, anyway?"

"See? Flicked away like a gnat," he said, pushing his index finger against his thumb. "Back in my court, so to speak, and you avoid saying anything personal in response."

"Not exactly true, Mr. Litigator. I just told you about high school."

She turned her attention to the salad. As a person, she liked Marshall well enough, but she wasn't sure she wanted one of her partners to know all that much about her. As a topic of conversation, high school was safely in the past.

If her partners knew her, they might suspect that she didn't like them that much, or remind her she didn't care about the game except to prove it could be played as well by a woman as by a man. The game itself—representing the rich, protecting their money, making her own money in disproportion to her contribution—that game didn't matter to her. In that sense, she wasn't a normal partner. Somewhere along the line, her vision of justice, the reason she'd gone to law school in the first place, had become myopic. She'd been so caught up in the fairness of the Firm's internal playing field that she'd forgotten her own antipathy for the game itself.

"I...I think Ann Rose is right," she said, nodding gravely. Her eyebrows arched in an uncontrollable reflex. What would Marshall think of that?

"Of course you do!" he said.

"What's that supposed to mean?" she said in disgust.

"Just that I don't like her either, and a lot of people don't. How am I supposed to know if I would like her better if she were a man, or if I don't like her because she doesn't fit my stereotype? That's what the psychologist is going to say...that we subconsciously let our gender stereotypes get in the way. It's hard enough to prove outright criminal insanity, let alone subconscious motivation. Ann can make a credible argument—and a jury could reasonably believe—that sex was a factor."

"Yes, they could reasonably believe...."

"In your heart of hearts, Kathleen Hannigan, you aren't one of these Firm-type guys. You've tried your damnedest, and you've succeeded beyond their expectations, but you aren't, and never will be, one of them."

She wasn't sure if he'd read her mind, or was imposing a stereotype on her. "And you, are you one of them?"

"No, but I don't have as much to prove as you do. I'm *presumed* to be one of them because I'm a guy. I can come in and try my cases and kind of leave the politics aside. My gender is the norm. Yours, you see, is not. I can see how you want to change things, so that you or women after you will have the freedom to take it or leave it. But, quite frankly, it's going to take longer than 15 or 20 years, and, if you ask me, it's costing you too much of yourself." He looked at her wine glass, which was empty.

"Waiter?" she signaled. The young man asked Marshall if he wanted another bottle, but before he could respond, she said, "No, just another glass for me," and her smile faded as she turned back to Marshall. He was looking at her with a sadness she resented.

"I know I need to stop," she sighed. Her voice broke up in little chunks. "I need to stop...drinking...working so hard...living alone...worrying. I need to stop everything! Stop! All the pressure, all the time. It's like a tightrope and I'm hanging on by my toes." She scrunched her eyebrows, not sure tightrope walkers hung by their toes, but she blustered on. "I think I'm saving myself from being one of them, and I don't see how every day I lose a little more of myself to them—conform a little more, measure myself and value myself more and more by their yardstick and their criteria. And now, now what they want me to do," her voice was urgent, "is to say that Ann Rose was measured by the same yardstick and it was totally fair. You know what I think? There is no yardstick!"

The waiter put a new glass of wine in front of her, and she was, again, angry at Marshall. "What were your billings the year you made partner? Zero? Damn close, probably! If it's not the money, what else do they really care about? Ann Rose has the billings, and now they find some other pretext..."

"Then stop. If you really are serious about stopping. I know someone who helps people get a handle on things. It's not easy, but..."

"In my spare time," she said. She wondered if they were talking about the same thing.

"Tomorrow?"

She looked at him. His eyes were translucent, brown, soft. She searched them for a flicker of judgment or condemnation. There was none.

"Maybe." She forced herself to make the new glass of wine last all the way through the rest of dinner. The truth was, she liked to drink, liked how it made her feel relaxed, how it removed her from the frenetic pace of her thoughts and feelings.

They talked about other people's vacation plans, and sports, and Marshall's home town of Bloomsburg, Pennsylvania, which was just like it sounded, but they could not avoid talk of Ann Rose. As they were waiting for coffee, Marshall slid his hand across the table and covered hers. "This isn't all on you, you know," he said. "What you think happened doesn't matter, really. What matters is the facts. If you can just state the facts, without characterizing them, then the worst that happens is the jury, maybe, thinks you're waffling. They already know you're in the middle. If you say one thing, then you're a raving feminist, and if you deny any stereotyping, you're just another partner on the defensive. If you ask me—and I know you haven't, and even Darby hasn't yet, either—it's a trial on the numbers and the documents—the written evaluations. You, my dear, are not that important."

"I know, I know. I hate being in the middle."

"You know what Yogi Berra says" He didn't wait for a reply. "When you come to a fork in the road, take it."

She was still laughing to herself when Marshall dropped her at her apartment.

For the next two days, Helen Bornstein moved swiftly through her character witnesses on behalf of Ann Rose. One man had gone to law school with Ann and said she was the smartest person he knew. Another, a mid-level manager formerly at First Credit had worked with her and found her work exceptional. (He'd also asked her out, but she'd declined.) Another woman client, with long blond hair and an engaging smile, said that Ms. Rose was one of the most effective lawyers she'd worked with in her 10 years in investment banking. Another said Ann volunteered one night a month at a homeless shelter on the northwest side. Darby didn't object to much of what they said, nor did he cross them vigorously, although he did get each of them to admit that they'd heard Ms. Rose swear.

One of the good old boys from Gloria Ellens, which technically was a client of the Firm, stumbled through his testimony, remarkably uncomfortable even though he had agreed to speak on Ann's behalf. He was the one who'd asked Kathleen for a nightcap, and he said he liked Ann's tough style, and that although she technically had been on the other side of his deal, he found her very fair. Bornstein got him to say that he didn't remember her swearing. In fact, he said, he didn't remember her talking very much at all. So as not to add credibility to his testimony, Darby told Marshall and Kathleen that he wasn't going to cross examine him. He didn't, and the startled good ole boy left the stand, which brought to an abrupt close the first day of testimony to Ann's good character.

Kathleen declined Marshall's invitation to dinner. She'd resolved, although she'd not told him, that she wouldn't drink until the weekend, and she thought that would be easier if she weren't in a restaurant. She told Marshall she was tired and was just going to go home and watch television, but when she got there, anxiety literally threw her to her knees, from which position she scrubbed the kitchen floor and nearly knocked herself out with the fumes from the ammonia. She only took two breaks, both short. When the phone rang, she hoped it was Jill—they hadn't talked since the trial began—but Sally's voice surprised her. Sounding both motherly and conspiratorial, she asked how things were going, and whether Kathleen felt ready to testify.

"I will be," she said cavalierly, but then, because she had a notion she needed to test out on someone, she ventured, "but you know, if they ask me point blank whether Ann should have made partner, I think I have to say yes."

"Oh...my...." Sally started. It occurred to Kathleen that Sally's understanding of the trial was the one nurtured by Blake's propaganda. It was the Evaluation Committee's problem, and Sally's question about whether Kathleen was ready was really a question of whether she was rehearsed. Sally apparently thought Kathleen's testimony didn't pose a dilemma so much as an opportunity for her to save the Firm from the embarrassment of Ann Rose and to earn her place on the Management Committee. As far as Kathleen was concerned, however, any chance of that had been destroyed the day the papers were filed.

"Well, if there is anything I can do to help," Sally said brightly, and Kathleen said thank you with the gratitude of a new widow. The person she really wanted to talk to was Jill.

Steve answered the phone. He hesitated, and said, without apology, that Jill might be too busy to come to the phone. He went to check. After a minute, Jill picked up, sounding terribly rushed. Kathleen offered to call the next day, and, to her surprise, Jill said that would be better. She hoped, however, that the trial was going okay. Kathleen hung up and dug into a scuff mark with a vengeance. Together, they'd been through the bar exam and dating, the corporate group and changing groups, Randy's death, leaving the Firm, having a miscarriage. Now, Kathleen's career was on the line, but Jill's baby needed her more. Kathleen fanned away the damn ammonia fumes. They were making her teary.

A fter the end of the second day of character witnesses, Darby, Marshall and Kathleen went to Albright & Gill's offices to review Kathleen's testimony. Bornstein had—as a courtesy—told Darby that she planned to call Kathleen before the psychologist. That meant that Kathleen would have to decide how to testify a day or two earlier than she anticipated. As Darby began his review of Bornstein's likely questions, Kathleen cut him off.

"The bottom line is, Philip, that if she asks me point blank whether Ann Rose should have been made partner, I'm going to have to say yes."

"You're a partner!" he cried. "How can you say that?"

Before she could answer Darby's challenge, Marshall broke in. "How can she not?"

Darby shook his head. He stared at the corner of the conference room, where the ceiling joined the panel of windows and the white textured wall. He looked back at Kathleen, without hostility, but with a trial lawyer's acceptance of bad facts—something to be explained to the jury if it came out at trial.

"If that is your opinion, Kathleen, it is irrelevant. I will object. You're not on the Management Committee. It wasn't your decision to make, and you aren't competent to make it." He leaned across the table, holding her gaze, and Kathleen punctuated his thoughts with her own silent recognition that she would, indeed, *never* sit on that Committee.

"No offense, Kathleen. I can argue that what any given partner thinks is irrelevant. We're not saying that partnership decisions have to be unanimous, or even right. Reasonable people can differ. All we have to show is that it was not a sexually stereotyped decision, and, as to that, you are not a psychologist, and you can't testify to stereotyping." Darby learned back in his chair, pleased with himself.

Marshall looked at Kathleen and raised his eyebrows, his head bobbing from side to side as if he were weighing the strength of the argument and found it adequate. For once in her life, having her opinion called irrelevant seemed to her like a good thing.

On Friday, Bornstein called Kathleen, and asked the court's permission to treat her as hostile, which was only a technicality that allowed her to ask leading questions, as if Kathleen were being cross-examined.

"I do," Kathleen said, and gave a calm and pleasant nod to the jury. She waited for the first question, and Bornstein waited an extra couple of seconds before she asked it. Kathleen knew that Bornstein was deliberately using that silence to let the jury form an impression of Kathleen, and Kathleen was determined, as she'd been all week at the defense table, not to convey the slightest tick of nerves or defensiveness. She folded her hands in her lap, palms up, meditation style. She'd chosen the right suit, and had deliberately sat on her jacket so that it wouldn't bunch up or look disheveled—a trick she'd read that news anchors used. She crossed her legs, uncomfortably but elegantly, at the ankles. It was too bad, she thought, that the jury couldn't still see her leopard shoes. She thought they'd gotten some attention when she walked past the jury box to the stand. She tilted her chin lightly up and towards the 12, and she remembered her mother's words, "You will rise to the occasion. You always do."

"Ms. Hannigan, will you state your name for the record, please." Not a very interesting first question, she thought. Hardly worth the silence.

"Kitty Hannigan," she said reflexively, and was surprised to hear herself so informal in such a formal setting. For years, she'd practiced being Kathleen, the name she attached to her professional persona.

"Is that your given name, Ms. Hannigan?" When she didn't answer right away, Bornstein raised her voice slightly.

"Let me repeat, Ms. Hannigan," Bornstein said, as if the question were difficult or the answer somehow incriminating. "Is Kitty your given name?"

"Kathleen Ann," she said, and she thought she caught the beginning of an ironic smile on Marshall's face.

"Ms. Hannigan, do you know the plaintiff in this case, Ann Rose?"

"I do."

"And how do you know her?"

"I am a partner at Albright & Gill, where Ann Rose was an associate."

"Were you a friend of hers when she was employed by Albright & Gill?"

"I would say we were friendly in the sense that we worked on some matters together, and after that, I took an interest in her career." Darby had wanted Kathleen to position herself as a mentor who'd told Ann Rose the things she had as a friend and not in her capacity as a member of the Evaluation Committee.

"Were you what one might call a role model for Ms. Rose?"

"You would have to ask her who her role models were."

"You were on the Firm's Evaluation Committee in 1988 and chair of that Committee in 1989?"

"Yes."

"So you are familiar with how it works." Bornstein put on her reading glasses and had Kathleen describe, in excruciating detail, the Evaluation Committee's process, and had Kathleen read the evaluations of Peter Banks, who had given Ann "As" but had commented on her profanity; of Gregory Bleecher, who'd said Ann needed charm school, and her own, where she had said that Ann would be more successful if she developed her social skills to match her legal ones. Bornstein had a particular interest in the evaluation of Stanley Whitestone, the old geezer who'd given Ann "As" and had said, without apology, "Someone ought to tell this young lady to act and talk more femininely."

"Mr. Whitestone is a highly respected lawyer at your firm, is he not?"

Double bind, Kathleen thought. How could she say that one of the senior members of the Firm, who'd been part of the management that had overseen its spectacular growth, was not "well-respected?"

"Yes, he has an outstanding reputation as a lawyer."

"How did the Committee treat this Evaluation from one of the outstanding members of the bar?"

"Honestly? We laughed. We knew his comment was inappropriate, and that his attitude was generational—that it didn't represent the attitude of the Evaluation Committee or the management of the Firm." She could've added that "femininely" wasn't even a word, but she didn't.

"Did anyone from the Evaluation Committee talk to him about this evaluation?"

"Not that I'm aware of."

"Did the Evaluation Committee take any steps whatsoever to screen out sexist evaluations?"

"Objection!" Darby shouted. "Ms. Bornstein is characterizing the evidence as sexist, which at best is a legal conclusion…"

"I'll rephrase," Bornstein said without waiting for the judge to rule.

Bornstein played the tape and they went over the make-up and mannishness, and Kathleen defended herself as being only a reporter. They examined Ann Rose's attitude, and Kathleen corrected Bornstein to "perception of attitude." Kathleen gave a little speech about how large firms run on perceptions and first impressions, for both men and women. Sloppy offices, being overweight, dressing poorly, leaving at 5:30 and not being there on Saturdays and Sundays. It all went into the mix, she said.

Helen Bornstein sighed wearily. "Ms. Hannigan, I have one last question. From your years on the Evaluation Committee, do you believe Ms. Rose should've been named a partner?"

For a long moment, all of the rustling noise of life—breathing, coughing, shuffling, yawning, scratching—stopped. Darby and Marshall and Kathleen had all hoped that Bornstein would not ask that question. She should've expected Kathleen to say no, that Ann Rose shouldn't have been named a partner, and, coming from a woman, that would've carried some weight with the jury. Kathleen, however, was prepared. She'd told Darby and Marshall that Helen Bornstein was so aggressive, she would ask the question and then explain away Kathleen's answer as evidence of how pervasive the stereotyping was—even the women bought into it.

"I don't run the Firm, Ms. Bornstein. I don't make partnership decisions." The courtroom unfroze, resuming its normal activity.

"But if you did, based on your knowledge of how all the associates in the Firm are evaluated…?" Bornstein persisted, but the dramatic import of the moment had been lost.

"Objection!" Darby tried again. "Ms. Hannigan's opinion is irrelevant! She is not qualified as an expert of any sort!"

"Overruled." The judge looked curious, and turned his attention to Kathleen.

"I personally would not choose her as my partner, but that's true of many of my partners," her voice cracked slightly. She paused, took a deep breath, and made a decision, for herself as well as Ann Rose. "But I believe that Ms. Rose met the general criteria for partnership at Albright & Gill."

Helen Bornstein looked up from her notes and took off her reading glasses. She held Kathleen's gaze until the judge interrupted, asking her if that was all. She fairly whispered yes, and sat down, almost as if she felt defeated by the enemy's surrender.

Darby gathered a big black binder and walked to the podium to begin his cross-examination. Much to his credit, he didn't look at all flustered. She'd warned him. He couldn't claim to be surprised.

"Let's make sure we've got this straight," he began. "The Evaluation Committee evaluates young associates and the Management Committee chooses its partners."

"Yes."

"The Management Committee does or does not look at the Evaluation Committee's files?"

"I don't know."

"You don't know what the Management Committee does?"

It was brilliantly redundant and perhaps rehabilitative. "I don't know what the Management Committee does," she parroted.

"What percentage of your current partners would you have chosen as your partners, to use your words?"

It seemed to her an odd question for him to ask, especially since he'd objected to her opinion as being irrelevant, and he hadn't prepped her. She waited for Bornstein to object. Bornstein didn't move. At the counsel's table, Marshall pointed his right thumb up in his folded hands. Subtle, Kathleen thought.

"Seventy," she said. Where she came from, 70 percent was a failing grade. Marshall quietly clapped his two thumbs together in what could have been misinterpreted as a nervous gesture.

Darby continued, eliciting examples of Ann's swearing and her unwillingness to begin conversations at dinner with the Gloria Ellens people, and her gruffness with staff. Kathleen looked straight at Darby as she answered each question. To herself, she sounded petty, and she didn't want to appear to be baiting Ann Rose. Darby finished with a bravado Kathleen thought was false. Helen Bornstein got to her feet with feigned weariness.

"Just a few questions on redirect, Your Honor," she said. "Ms. Hannigan, can you explain to me how Ann's interpersonal skills would be strengthened if she wore jewelry?"

Kathleen laughed, hoping Darby would jump in. When he didn't, she answered, "They wouldn't be, necessarily." In her mind, it was just one of many factors.

"But you told Ms. Rose to wear jewelry," Bornstein pretended not to understand.

"No. I told her *one* of the evaluators had suggested she appear more feminine. The point was that perceptions...."

Bornstein didn't let her finish her thought, to say that sometimes people's perceptions can be wrong, that if they only get part of a story, they'll get an impression which is inaccurate. Bornstein didn't let her say that perceptions make a difference, that if someone thinks you look harsh, and then they overhear you saying something harsh, they will conclude that you *are* harsh.

"Perceptions based on her failure to wear lipstick, or frilly dresses or jewelry. Isn't that what you would call sexual stereotyping?"

"Objection!" Darby was on his feet, pretending to be angry.

"Withdrawn," she said. "No more questions for this witness."

"Thank you," Kathleen said. She made it a point to look calmly at each and every juror as she walked back to the counsel's table, and she saw one man in the back row wink at her when he noticed her leopard shoes.

The judge dismissed them for the day, and the courtroom quickly emptied. Ann vanished, the way Blake vanished, and Bornstein and her two associates were picking up her files.

"I like your shoes," Helen Bornstein smiled to Kathleen. "Nieman's?"

"Heavens, no! El cheapo! That place on Randolph. Thirty bucks. The other pair are zebra-striped."

"Good job," Marshall said to Kathleen when they were out of earshot and had said goodbye to Darby. "I thought it was very effective testimony, and whether you like it or not, I think you probably helped the Firm. Seventy percent!" He chuckled.

Outside, he hailed a cab. "Get in," he ordered. "I'm in charge of your post-trial recuperation." He gave the cabbie a Lakeview address, and they stopped in front of one of the vintage buildings overlooking Lincoln Park. Kathleen was mentally spent from her day on the witness stand, and the crash from her adrenaline high was turning her arms and legs to dead weight. Marshall opened the door to his apartment, and was immediately greeted by a young man who took their coats.

Marshall quickly introduced her to George, an assistant to someone named Ron, who supposedly was in the kitchen preparing dinner for two. She hung an arm off of Marshall's shoulder, saying, "You, my friend, are too much."

"I am," he said. "Come see what I saved from the divorce." He gave her a tour of a huge, old-style apartment. The gallery entry hall was larger in square feet than some studios she'd looked at her first year. To the right, it led to the formal dining room, kitchen and three bedrooms—not including a tiny maid's quarters off the kitchen—and to the left, the living room and adjoining library, both overlooking the park and the lake. The floors were oak, newly stripped and polished, covered only in part by Oriental style rugs of various, custom made shapes. A cream colored leather sectional couch curved around the living room, facing the view, and in the corner a Zen water garden gurgled in broad layers of slate.

"This is beautiful," she said. "So grown-up! I'm still living early student, compared to this."

A silver wine bucket sat on the glass and chrome coffee table in the center of the room, chilling a bottle of something. As if on cue, George appeared, a white towel draped over his starched white shirt. Kathleen heard the pop, and he poured two flute glasses of champagne, which he left on a silver tray on the table, and withdrew.

Marshall handed her a glass. "To a beautiful partner, a beautiful person, and a hell of a witness. Strike that. A heck of a witness!"

How could she have had a friend as dear as Marshall and not fully realize it? When exactly had they become so close, close enough that he would cater a dinner in his apartment just for her? "Thank you, Marshall, for everything!" she said, a crack in her voice.

He took her champagne from her, put it down on the silver platter, and took her in his arms in a hug that became a kiss as naturally as if they'd always been the most romantic of couples.

"I'm going to marry you, Kit Hannigan," he said, his voice softer than she'd ever heard it.

She thought he was embarrassed. They were, after all, partners, and they'd become friends. The kiss was, she assumed, part of some fantasy that had nothing to do, really, with her.

"That won't be necessary, Marshall. It was just a kiss."

She started to reach for her glass and he took her wrist. His eyes filled. "I mean it. I'm crazy about you."

"You can't be serious! We haven't even, you know…"

"We can change that."

"Why, all of a sudden?"

"Not all of a sudden, although I know it seems that way. I've felt this way for a really long time, Kit, and maybe it's not the right time to tell you, with the trial and all, but we both know, and now you know for sure, there are things more important than that trial."

He kissed her again.

They were on the couch, kissing, touching, laughing. They hadn't said a word in 10 minutes when they heard a set of chimes, like in a Zen temple, coming from the kitchen.

"Dinner," Marshall said, and they walked hand in hand down the long gallery to the other side of the apartment, where the dining room was dimly lit by six candles in glass holders and the lobster bisque was steaming.

FOURTEEN

A: *I don't run the firm, Ms. Bornstein.*
I don't make partnership decisions.

"Darby at eight! Don't be late!"

"Ugh!" she groaned involuntarily, and Marshall grabbed the sheet and pulled it down. He was, of course, already dressed. She smiled as best she could, given that she was not, she repeated for his benefit, a morning person. She pulled the sheet back up over her head. "There's coffee," he reminded her, and she reached out to her nightstand. After a fantasy weekend, they were back at her apartment, and only a few hours away from the testimony of a social psychologist and then the Firm's own witnesses.

Saturday morning, Marshall had let her sleep until 9:30, and swore that he wouldn't have awakened her even then except for the fact that he'd arranged for a masseuse who was coming at 10:00.

"How did you know I'd be here?" she said in mock horror that he would have presumed such an immodesty.

"I told you, I'm a good talker," he said, and threw her a white terry robe. "It only looks stolen from the Ritz," he said. "At least, *I* didn't steal it. The 'ex' did."

She'd never had a massage. She hadn't even known that a masseuse would make house calls, or that they worked in teams. A man and a woman had arrived at Marshall's at exactly 10:00, each with their portable tables and fluffy towels. They set up their gear in his living room and Marshall and Kathleen groaned at each other for an hour. Marshall told her to shower while he took care of the pair, and just as she had her hair lathered up and her eyes shut tight against the suds, he joined her. They went back to bed and back to the shower, and around 2:00 he said they should walk to her apartment. He had tickets for an early play off-off Loop, so they could grab a bite first.

Sunday, a rainy, stay-at-home day, they spent the morning in bed with the *New York Times* and croissants and walked around the aquarium in the afternoon. Marshall hadn't repeated his offer of marriage, but he'd presumed to pick up his things at his apartment and accompany her back to hers Sunday night. She hadn't told him not to, but she hadn't accepted his proposal, either. In fact, she was harboring a nagging fear that she was only saying yes because of the trial and her dashed hopes for Management Committee. Whatever resolution she came to about her future at the Firm and the rest of her professional life, she wanted it to be independent of having a man to marry her. If she did leave the Firm—as she might have to—she didn't want people to say it was because she'd found a husband. If she left, it would have to be because in the past week she had admitted to herself, to Marshall, and to a courtroom of people she didn't know, that she didn't respect three out of 10 of her partners, didn't care that much about their game, and probably never would have tried to play but for the fact that for so long women were not even invited to play.

A t 10:00, the social psychologist began her testimony. She had adequate academic credentials, having published one study in an extremely prestigious journal and several others in well known but less snooty ones, and she was writing a book called "Ms. Typed," that she said would expose the sexual stereotyping of a nation. Since the woman had no hands on experience in real businesses with actual financial bottom lines, she clearly was banking on paperback success for her own retirement. She seemed to Kathleen anxious to please Helen Bornstein. Under Bornstein's skillful direction, the woman expressed her expert opinion that some partner comments about Ann were influenced by sex stereotypes and concluded that stereotyping played a major determining role in the Firm's decision.

Darby had promised Marshall that he would put on his boxing gloves and go a few solid rounds with the psychologist, but when he got up to hammer her testimony, he was his usual deferential, mild mannered self. With his hands folded on his legal pad, he did get her to admit that she couldn't determine the precise effect of whatever stereotyping may have gone on. She told the court that in traditionally male dominated organizations, sexual stereotyping can lead to a negative judgment of women. What was confusing to Kathleen, and perhaps to the jury, was that most of the expert's studies were done with women who were in fact blond and stereotypically ultra-feminine, which had, according to the published papers, gotten in the way of their being considered for promotions. Here, it was Ann's *failure* to come at all close to the feminine stereotype—if Darby were to admit that such a stereotype in fact existed—which tripped her up. Stereotyping can be conscious or unconscious, the psychologist said, and a negative fact could be expressed in words that imply stereotyping—words like "bitchy"— and yet be wholly non-discriminatory. Kathleen saw several jury members rub their eyes, and she knew that the concept was confusing them.

Darby did his best to further obfuscate the issue, feigning his own non-understanding and repeatedly asking for judgments on various words: macho, aggressive, charming. The famous social psychologist was unwilling to say that any given written comment was in fact based on a sexual stereotype, because she hadn't interviewed the evaluator. She wasn't being asked, she said, to judge the sexual-political correctness of each partner in the Firm, simply to judge that sex had played a factor. Yes, she said, how could an evaluation like Mr. Whitestone's be characterized as anything other than sexist? His entire generation, as she would prove in her book, was sexist.

On her next round of questioning, Bornstein asked the psychologist what a firm could do, under the circumstances, to rule out any possibility of sexual stereotyping. Here, the psychologist began to talk to the jury, which had that "yeah, so what were they supposed to do?" look about them. She said that Albright & Gill should've seen that Mr. Whitestone's comments were sex-based, and easily could've issued guidelines to help their partners identify sexual stereotyping. They could've investigated. They could've called Mr. Whitestone in—presumably for a stern talking to—to talk him out of his old-fashioned ideas. They could've made an attempt to separate out those evaluations tainted with sexual stereotyping from those which weren't. It would've been so simple for them, she said, to root out stereotyping.

Bornstein finished and Darby got up for one more question.

"Can you say, based on your review of these evaluations, that Ms. Rose would have been made a partner but for what you have identified as stereotyping?"

The question was a good one. Darby didn't question stereotyping. He simply said that even if the Firm stereotyped, if it would've made the same decision without any such stereotyping or discrimination whatsoever, the Firm wins the case. Darby asked the question because he knew the social psychologist could not answer it with certainty. No one could.

The next day, Darby began to call the defense witnesses. The courtwatchers packed the room. Darby first called the partners who had evaluated Ann Rose, starting with Stanley Whitestone because he had said she should "act and talk more femininely" and his comments would be the hardest to defend. Then, Darby called the others, some of whom had given her rave reviews, and some of whom had not. He dispensed with each quickly, letting them give again their conclusions about Ann's performance, this time in less inflammatory words. When Helen Bornstein crossed them, each stonewalled, apologizing, if necessary, for their imprecision in language, but repeating that they'd filled out so many evaluations, they often used a shorthand. Each—except Whitestone—denied that sex influenced their thoughts on Ann at all, and Whitestone was so disarmingly honest about his views on "lady lawyers" that even Bornstein didn't go after him.

Darby disappointed Bornstein by not giving her an expert to either interpret the lawyer's evaluations or dispute the social psychologist's opinion. Blake had judged it unnecessary.

Darby also would've liked to have called each member of the Management Committee and asked him to explain his vote, but Blake had said that he would speak for the Committee. He said he didn't want the Firm's petty disagreements to be so exposed. Helen Bornstein had ultimately agreed. At first she'd threatened to call each one, just to raise the Firm's stakes by the added expense, inconvenience and possible embarrassment, but when the Firm steadfastly refused to even discuss settlement, she'd agreed that the jury might resent the waste of their time in hearing 22 identical stories, and had told Darby she would take on Blake.

So after the evaluators, Darby immediately called two secretaries who had done stints for Ann in her last two years at the Firm. He'd taken a fair amount of time to prepare each of them. He didn't want them to sound like they had any particular ax to grind. Angeline, an African-American woman in her late twenties, wore a raw silk navy dress and jacket with pearls, an outfit almost identical to Helen Bornstein's that day. She spoke softly and elegantly, and told Mr. Darby how Ms. Rose repeatedly made her miss her train home to her three children because of an "emergency," even though there was always a night-time secretary available who could have completed her work.

"She made it seem like it was my fault that the work wasn't done, when sometimes I wouldn't even get the project until 4:30. She would stand in the hall and shout that she was going to ask the supervisor for a competent secretary, that a sixth-grader would do better work. Mr. Darby, I have two years of business college and 10 years of experience. I type 90 words a minute, and she's the first attorney I ever worked for who criticized me like that. One time she was so angry, for some reason that had nothing to do with me, she slammed a big huge document down on my workspace so hard that a picture of my little boy came crashing down, and the glass in the frame shattered into a million pieces. She made me finish her document before I cleaned it up, and she never even offered to pay for the frame!" Kathleen thought she heard a tsk! tsk! from the back of the courtroom.

The jury could relate to Angeline, although the specifics of her testimony, separated from the emotional heat and urgency of the moment, were the kind of subtle insults that on their face don't seem quite as bad in the retelling as they do in the experiencing. Clearly Ann was a demanding boss. But she didn't make Angeline get coffee or buy presents for "the wife" or call home with white lies about working late. This boss didn't ogle her breasts or her legs or drink too much at lunch or otherwise fit the stereotyped nightmare of a boss. This boss demanded that a memo to the file be retyped if so much as the date were a pica off center, hurled insults just short of racist at the secretary and her skills, and never remembered her with more than a card at Christmas. Becky, the other secretary, who had served Ann for about eight months, testified to a similar experience.

Blake slipped into court the third day of A&G's defense, just before he was called. He wore a dark suit and a navy tie salted with little red university crests. Against his healthily tanned face—a cover for physical lethargy—his starched shirt blazed stark white. Blake looked expensive, powerful, and dignified. He also managed to convey, at least to those who knew him, a slight irritation that his busy time was being taken up by this nonsense. He took the oath, sat down, and raised his monogrammed shirt cuff to take a meaningful look at his watch. He gave no indication he even knew which one Ann Rose was.

Blake had a reputation, which he did nothing to correct, of being a man of few words. Darby said he would be a difficult guy for the jury to get a feel for—Kathleen thought he meant "a good feeling *about*"—but that Blake would have to try. It might have been weariness, but the night before, while Darby was trying to prep him, he had just blurted it out—Blake should try to be personable and to relate to the jury. Blake had nodded, but his already thin lips disappeared.

Blake sat in the witness stand with the command of a king on his throne, his self-possession completely overshadowing the judge in his robes above him. He spoke in barely audible platitudes which to Kathleen sounded thin, but to the uninitiated, majestic.

"I serve my partners as their Managing Partner, but," and here he tried a bit of uncharacteristic humor, "I can assure you that 315 of the finest lawyers in America do not wish to be 'managed.' I am only a conduit for their collective will."

Kathleen looked down. Blake hadn't spoken to her or to Marshall since the trial began. He must've been aware of her testimony, but had dealt with it, as she should've known he would, by ignoring it, and her. Kathleen knew he meant for her to suffer the brilliance of that ultimate insult—she and her testimony were irrelevant.

"We are a law firm which for more than 100 years has served the law," Blake intoned. "I can assure you that it is not enough at Albright & Gill to be a brilliant lawyer—that is our minimum requirement for partnership. It is another, higher quality that we look for, and we are blind to whether that quality is packaged in white skin or black skin or female garb or male. I think you will find, Mr. Darby, that statistically, we are one of the three most diverse firms in the city."

By his direction to Darby, Blake's testimony was short. When he was finished, Helen Bornstein stood, matching his dignity with her own. Kathleen nearly beamed with pride—she found herself rooting for Helen.

"Mr. Mills, when you joined Albright & Gill, how many women lawyers were there?"

"None, Ms. Bornstein. It was 1956."

"Who were the senior lawyers at the Firm, the ones you admired?"

Blake mentioned two or three men, one of whom was still alive and in a retirement home in Palm Beach.

"Could you point me to two or three Albright & Gill lawyers who today exemplify this, this 'higher quality' you spoke of?"

"I would hesitate to single out any one of my partners," Blake said before Darby could object.

"Well then, how about naming *any* lawyers at *any firm* whom you admire?"

"Objection!" Darby drew himself up to his full, but insubstantial, height. "Where is counsel going with this? Who any given lawyer admires is totally irrelevant to the Management Committee's right to make a decision about who will become a partner."

"I agree," said the judge, who happened to belong to the same country club in Lake Forest as Blake. It was not an important ruling, just professional courtesy. So far, Kathleen ruled the Mills-Bornstein exchange a draw. She clenched her folded hands, waiting for first blood.

"Mr. Mills, can you help the jury understand what you mean by 'higher quality'? So far, I think we've shown that whatever it is, it's a quality most typically found in men." There was a twitter that sounded like applause among the courtwatchers.

"I can tell you what it is not, Ms. Bornstein. It is not offensive in speech or manner. It is never uncivil to undeserving staff."

"Do any of your male partners, to your knowledge, swear, Mr. Mills?"

"Only in the most provocative of situations, and normally out of earshot of those who might be offended." As much as she didn't want to, Kathleen had to admit that Blake was very, very smart.

"The good ole boys," Bornstein mused. Blake looked at his watch.

"Objection!" Darby cried, but Bornstein ignored him as she would a gnat and asked her next question at the same time as the judge said, "Sustained, the jury will disregard Ms. Bornstein's comment."

"Can you tell me what steps the Firm took to protect Ms. Rose and others against sexual stereotyping?"

"Let me make this perfectly clear, Ms. Bornstein. We were not aware of, nor were we influenced in any way, by sexual stereotyping." Kathleen remembered a time in her life when "perfectly clear" was a political punchline, but Blake made it sound like a solemn oath.

They were at a stand-off. Bornstein understood that in some ways Blake's testimony was irrelevant, just as Kathleen's opinion was irrelevant. Blake was merely the head of a committee whose collective mindset *was* relevant, but which could only be known by what little had been written down by others, mostly by people who were not on the Committee at all. She wanted the jury to see the man, to judge him arrogant and unfeeling and ruthless—the kind of man who exemplified an entire club of men who, like a fraternity, chose only their own clones and punished difference with exclusion. Helen Bornstein wanted to keep Blake Mills on the stand long enough for the jury to feel his disdain for them. In the jury room, she wanted them to remember Blake's arrogant chill and know what prejudice Ann Rose faced. If Bornstein were lucky, she could badger him into saying something like "for godsakes, woman!" but that would be too much to hope for.

"How many women partners at the Firm today, Mr. Mills?"

"I believe there are 15, including one or two who are part-time partners." Blake had considered the part-time partnership a remarkable innovation, although he had hardly been the one to invent it, and it rarely was in fact part-time.

"How many are on your Management Committee? The Management Committee is 22, right?"

"The Management Committee is 22, but no woman is yet senior enough to qualify for that Committee."

Bornstein pounced. "Did Sally Streeter withdraw from the partnership?"

"No."

"Sally is the same law school class as Jay Greene, Jack Limer and Tod Turley, isn't she?"

"I don't recall each partner's law school class, Ms. Bornstein," Blake said, obviously annoyed.

"But you said, without hesitation, that no woman was senior enough."

"If your information is correct, Ms. Bornstein, I stand corrected." Slimy bastard, Kathleen thought.

"Your Management Committee selects its own members, doesn't it, Mr. Mills? So, why isn't Sally Streeter on the Management Committee?"

"Objection! Irrelevant!" Darby tried.

"Overruled."

"Ms. Streeter has not yet demonstrated the requisite leadership abilities."

"Are there any women in the partnership today who, in your personal judgment, Mr. Mills, are at least beginning to demonstrate that leadership ability?" Without consciously meaning to, Kathleen sat up a little straighter, expectant.

"I am not personally familiar with each woman partner and whether or not she would exhibit such qualities." Kathleen leaned back.

"But you have chaired the Committee long enough now that each and every one of those women, with the exception of Ms. Streeter, was elected partner under your leadership!"

Blake looked mildly surprised. "I suppose that is correct. As I said, I am a servant of the Committee. I have every confidence that in due course, one of our woman partners will be asked by my partners to join the Management Committee." Blake's partners would never ask any such thing, Kathleen knew, unless Blake told them to. She was furious that Blake could sound so convincingly self-effacing, and worried that the jury would believe him. She put her hand over her mouth. She definitely was pulling for Helen.

"And which stereotype will apply to them? I'm sure Ms. Hannigan, for instance, would like to know." At the sound of her name, she uncovered her mouth and looked up. She was oddly flattered that Helen Bornstein had corrected Blake, had mentioned her by name. She figured Blake would evade the answer, which was too bad because she would've liked to hear from him what indeed it would take for a woman (which, in her mind, had meant her, prior to this whole mess) to be anointed.

"We value loyalty, Ms. Bornstein," Blake smirked. Making a show of weariness from the routine of objecting to her questions, Darby had gotten to his feet too late to prevent Blake's answer.

"Sustained," the judge said and asked Bornstein if she had any further questions. Helen shot Blake a look of disgust and shook her head. "More questions than Mr. Mills has answers, I'm afraid. That will be all for now."

Blake nodded to the judge and bowed his head as he walked past the jury. He left the courtroom. Darby said he had no more witnesses, and the judge said counsel could present closing arguments in the morning.

Darby, Marshall and Kathleen trudged back to Conference Room A, where they were going to work on Darby's closing. They were still discussing whether to order pizza or Chinese or deli sandwiches when Blake, Leonard Stonehill and Jules Steinberg strolled in. Blake sat silently at the head of the long conference room table and nodded to Darby, "whenever you're ready." Darby's ears reddened. He'd told Marshall and Kathleen that he usually talked through the closing first, made notes as he went and then did a final prep, the way some people wrote out a rough draft and then a final. He'd not expected to do his talking draft in front of the triumvirate. He stumbled badly, and beads of moisture formed on his forehead. Kathleen casually left the room and returned two minutes later, a Coca-Cola in hand. She popped the top and slipped it in front of him on the table. He took a long swig. It revived him.

"Blake, we're still working this through. Perhaps you and the rest would like to have dinner and come back in an hour or so."

Blake looked at his watch. "No dinner. I'm on the 7:02."

"Then I hope you understand this is a work in progress."

"I understand, and I assume that you will make such progress." He didn't need to add that what he'd heard so far wasn't the superior work Albright & Gill demanded.

Darby continued, tossing ideas at Marshall, who sat halfway down the conference room table. "I should say something like.... Remind me to hit the point about...." It was cruel of Blake not to leave. He waited until 6:46 and then rose.

"Remind them, Philip, that we, as a partnership, are each responsible for the actions and judgments of our partners. Accordingly, we have a right to choose for whom we will be liable and accountable. If a person's interpersonal skills are so questionable that we believe that in the long run there is a potential for liability or embarrassment, we are free to reject their candidacy. It is that simple. We have admitted women to the partnership in the past, admitted women this year, and will continue to do so as they meet our standards."

Jules, who'd not said a word since joining them in the conference room, held the door open for Blake and followed him out. Leonard, the legendary litigator on the verge of retirement, asked if he could stay.

"Gets the old juices flowing, you know," he said to Darby.

"That was terrible," Darby said, sinking into a chair.

"Stunk to high heaven," Leonard said. "That's how I know you're for real. If it hadn't, I'd have no hope for you."

Darby put his feet up on the table and loosened his tie. He beamed, and Kathleen understood that he felt admitted to the legendary trial lawyer's private club. Anyone could litigate, shuffling papers back and forth. Only the cream of the crop could stand up to the rigors of trial. She didn't know if Leonard was being genuine or gracious, but in either event, she admired his class.

"The good news here," Leonard said to Darby, "is that you got your client's input. Do it his way, and you can't be second-guessed tomorrow. You heard him. 'Ladies and gentlemen of the jury, we screw whoever we want whenever we want.'" Kathleen smiled. Leonard continued, "The partners understand that. Hell, maybe the jury does, too. There are no CEOs on this jury. They're all just regular folks who've had an unfair boss or two along the way. They either want revenge or they've accepted their lot in life. It's not really about the law, is it?"

Darby heaved a sigh. "Blake doesn't get it, does he? He thinks this is a nuisance suit, a no-brainer. I think, Leonard, that he's missing the subtlety of it."

Marshall jumped in. "You'll find, Phil, that Blake doesn't miss the subtlety of things. He may, however, choose to ignore it."

"I think it's called 'denial,'" Kathleen said, but Marshall ignored her. He continued, "It's not that Blake is convinced that sex was not a factor and that we're 100 percent innocent. He just thinks that even if we're wrong, we have a right to be. Not that Albright & Gill is often wrong, mind you. People pay us for our judgment—it's our only real asset. For Blake, I'm sure this is as much about our judgment—of people, of cases, of judges and who's likely to do what to whom—as it is about sex discrimination."

"In other words, Phil," again Kathleen summed up their discussion, "Blake is not outraged because he strongly believes his own bullshit."

"I wish we'd brought in an expert," Darby moaned. He was on his feet, beginning to pace. "Or that I could point to non-tainted evaluations and say, here's why she didn't make it. But all the ones that commented on interpersonal skills may or may not be tainted with the language their expert called stereotypical. What do I have left?" Darby was now personalizing the case, as if he had been persecuted not only by Helen Bornstein, but by his own client as well.

"The jury," Leonard said, with a note of majesty.

"Jury's on the fence, Leonard," Marshall said. "I agree we have to play it Blake's way, but what the jury will relate to is the swearing, the mean-to-staff stuff."

"I think they're leaning towards Ann," Kathleen said. Darby grimaced. Leonard pointed at her and then the door. She knew he liked her, so she explained.

"I talked to some of the courtwatchers in the hall. They hated Blake and Ann. They liked me and they liked Helen. Didn't understand a word of the psychobabble. Comes down to this: Ann is so much like Blake, she deserves to be his partner! Oh, they think she ought to wear jewelry, too, and one lady told me she thought Ann ought to color her hair, but they wouldn't hold all that against her. They thought she was smart and dignified, just like Blake, and they want her to be a partner. But me! They think I'm too nice to be a partner! And they love my shoes!"

Leonard nodded his understanding. "So we need to distinguish Ann from Blake. Blake might be arrogant, but he's not intentionally disrespectful of others."

There was a silence which suggested only the most uncomfortable acquiescence with Leonard's assessment of Blake's character.

"So, back to Blake's basic rule," Marshall said, which rescued them from their impasse. "Keep it simple."

A night secretary brought in sandwiches. "The Last Supper," Leonard intoned, and patted Darby on the back. They ate in relative silence, watching Darby scribbling an outline, and then listened to his final draft, which Leonard generously interrupted at least six times with rowdy cheers.

Friday morning, Darby kept it simple, and so did Helen Bornstein. Bornstein used the phrase, "Because of her sex," 12 times in 28 minutes. Darby said, "it's just that simple" seven in 31.

FIFTEEN

Objection!

F riday afternoon, after the closings, a number of A&G lawyers stopped by her office. It amused her because she'd said—in open court and under oath—that she didn't want to be partners with three out of every 10 of them. She'd heard that on those rare occasions when a partner left the Firm, sometimes for a general counsel position, sometimes (though rarely) for a different firm or solo practice, that partner would soon become the repository of all of the Firm's discontent. As Jill had learned when she'd left to teach, many partners harbored secret desires to do something else or to be somewhere else or both. This day, four different lawyers told Kathleen, behind her closed door, of dreams of teaching in the inner city, running a small hotel on St. Lucia, writing a screen play and opening their own law office. Each peppered his dreams with the names of individuals he no longer wanted to be partners with. She took their confessions as absolution for her own disloyalty.

Towards the end of the afternoon, Brian made a rare appearance in her open doorway. No matter what she might say to other nosy partners who might ask, she would tell Brian exactly what she thought. In an odd way, she trusted Brian more than any of the others. He was sometimes impolitic, but he was always up-front and honest. If his narcissism was unfettered, it was also unconcealed, a known danger rather than an ambush. That knowledge allowed her to see Brian as her best friend still at the Firm. For better or worse, she considered herself a member of Brian's team, and she had enough pride in her own judgment not to lie to him. She would tell him what he didn't want to hear: the Firm was going to lose to Ann Rose.

"Because of your testimony?" he said gravely. He pulled a guest chair closer to her desk and sat down.

She leaned back in her chair. "I prefer to think it will be because of the facts of the case."

"What are you going to do?" Brian rested his elbows on her desk, his right hand propping up his chin.

At first she didn't take his meaning.

"I suppose you could go in-house somewhere. Ever think about going inside with Anthony?"

She straightened. She'd thought the Firm would treat a loss to Ann Rose as a slap on the wrist. Officially, the Firm would deny any wrongdoing, and when it got around to making amends, it would make a huge splash of its promotion of a woman. The thought that the Firm would need to polish its public image sometimes had given Kathleen the faintest glimmer of hope that perhaps Management Committee was not entirely lost to her. While the next most senior woman was two years behind and the Firm could wait for her to come of age, it had never occurred to Kathleen that perhaps her very partnership was at risk. Brian seemed to assume it.

"Can they do that to me?" she said, leaning over her desk towards him as if to speak confidentially.

"An eye for an eye? It's not that the Firm cares one way or the other about paying Ann Rose some cash. But we care *immensely* about disloyalty."

"We?" Her right temple began to throb.

"Lookit, Kitty. I'm not the most popular guy around here. They think I'm grabby about billings and I've sometimes played it fast and loose in that area, but they know I'm a hundred percent loyal to the Firm. They respect me. Even when I'm beating them at their own game, they might cry foul, but the truth is, they respect me for playing. You throw an elbow under the hoop, you get called on it less than half the time—so what? You're aggressive but you play by the rules. But if you tell them you don't play by their rules, then, my friend, you are out of the game. Your best move is to pre-empt them."

"And transfer my billings to you, no doubt!" She didn't want to believe that Brian's judgment might be as accurate in this regard as it was in others. Brian was paged, and as he left, she dialed Jill's number, but got her nanny. Jill was at the health club, the woman said in broken Polish, adding that she would give her the message.

In the cab home on Friday afternoon, Kathleen told Marshall what Brian had said.

Marshall raised his eyebrows and then looked out the window. "You don't need to decide today," he said.

Had she not been so tired, she would have fought him on that. If Brian was right, then by all means she wanted to decide today. She would want to act immediately, to do it to them before they did it to her. She *wanted* to decide, to know what was going to happen.

She looked at an unruly curl on the back of Marshall's head. She'd done her best at trial and she'd been honest. Surely, the Firm couldn't openly punish her for that! Perhaps Marshall was right. She wouldn't have to confront the issue right away.

Despite the fact that each of them felt compelled to go to the office Saturday morning, by noon they both were sufficiently caught up with administrative matters to treat themselves to the rest of the weekend off. They dumped their briefcases at his place and went to a neighborhood diner for lunch. Marshall paid but told her to leave three bucks for a tip. She had a few singles in her pocket and slipped them under her coffee cup. There'd been no big discussion about going Dutch or whose turn it was to pay. Obviously, they both had more than enough money. She herself could retire on what she'd saved so far, if she continued to invest well. It wasn't about the cost of tuna salad. What got her attention was Marshall's assumption that they were on joint funds.

We really are a couple, Kathleen thought. It had happened so easily! She tried to remember how this relationship had started, and she couldn't pinpoint a beginning. They'd had a dinner; they'd been on trial together. It seemed to her now as if they had always been together. Maybe men who have been married once just act married sooner, she thought. Maybe they forget they are dating. Since she hadn't yet said yes to his proposal, they were technically dating, weren't they?

They started walking south, just to be moving after a week of sitting and listening and thinking. They found themselves on Michigan Avenue. At Tiffany's, Marshall gave her hand a tug and without hesitation, pushed through the revolving door first with the confidence of a gentleman to whom etiquette is never a quandary. He strolled deliberately to a display case on the right. He didn't say a word, so neither did she. The salesman, in a suit so expensive-looking it had to be counterfeit, dragged his half-eyeglasses off his nose and let them dangle on a black chain. Looking at Kathleen's naked left hand, he asked if he could help them.

Marshall said they were just looking. "Need some ideas for our designer," he said, pumping her hand below the counter, out of sight from the salesman.

"Designer?" she shook her head in a hearty laugh when they were back outside.

"You don't want some garish three-carat cut glass, do you?"

"Let me see, three carats from Tiffany's. That would be too what—stereotypical?"

"Much too ordinary! I got an 'A' in art in college. I'll design something. I have a friend who has a studio here, and he can make it. It will have great sentimental value."

"I thought maybe we should decide first."

"Jury's still out?"

She smiled.

S he was pouring herself a scotch Sunday evening in her kitchen while they waited for a pizza to be delivered. She dreaded the tension of the coming week, everything feeling so suspended until the jury came back. In theory, in order to make up for weeks of unbillable time, she should throw all of her waking hours into billable matters, the next big thing she could find to absorb her nervous energy. But she couldn't focus her attention on something new until the Ann Rose matter was resolved. Marshall was sitting at the kitchen table with the remnants of the Sunday newspaper. She asked him how litigators handled the wait.

"Same way," he said. She didn't know what he meant. "They drink at Italian Village during the day and on Rush Street at night."

She scowled.

"I thought you wanted to do something about that," he said, his tone even.

"I'm OK," she said brightly. "I'll be a lot better when this thing is over."

"It worries me," he said and picked up a section of the paper.

"What?"

"What will happen," he said slowly. He put the paper down. "You know Blake will make your life miserable, no matter what. In all those subtle, quietly unfair ways that drive you crazy. And then, I'm afraid, I won't be enough. You'll still think that's the answer." He pointed to her glass of scotch on the counter. She hadn't left room in it for water or soda.

Her heart was pounding and her neck was covered in a red and prickly heat. How dare he criticize her! She picked up the glass, and took a long, slow, mean drink, daring him with her eyes to say whatever it was he dared to say.

"You're the one who said you wanted to quit, remember? I know it's none of my business, except that I love you and I want you to be happy. It's just that simple," he said.

"Nothing is that fucking simple! Where have you been the past two weeks?" She slammed the glass down so hard the liquid splashed over her hand.

"I guess I don't do Darby very well," Marshall tried to retreat. "Of course it's complex. That's why I thought this person I know could help. You said you would talk to someone. How could it hurt?"

"It can hurt to have one more man telling me who and what I should be," she screamed. "You!" She exhaled. "You don't want to marry me! You want to marry some idea you have of who I should be." As she said that, she knew, perhaps for the first time, that deep down where she kept all her secrets, she in fact wanted to marry him.

"Forget it! You don't tell me what I want out of my life! I don't change for no man, no-how!" She grabbed her glass and went to the living room, where she faced out the window in the dark. He waited a full minute, and then followed her, turning on a lamp to announce his presence.

"Get out! Get out of here, now!" She wanted to pound on him with her fists.

"It's not about you and me, Kit. It's not even about you, really. It's about a habit you said was making you miserable." He sounded neutral, calm, oddly unaffected. Her back was to the room. She swallowed the crying noises that rose in her throat.

"You've never seen me really drunk..." she said between her teeth.

"No, I haven't."

That was some relief to her, anyway. Even when she'd had too much to drink, she'd maintained an appearance of control. She usually didn't slur her words, or stumble. She'd never been really drunk at a Firm event. She behaved within bounds with Anthony and Jimmy—in fact, was the champion of sobriety among them. It'd been years since she'd thrown up after a party. At worst, these days, she'd chew on antacid tablets at work the morning after getting a little too drunk the night before, and a glass or two of wine at lunch would set her straight for the rest of the afternoon.

It didn't seem abnormal to her. Everyone she knew, practically, drank the same way. Jill and Steve, for instance. Well, no, Jill never did like the taste of it. Brian? A very short-hitter. Well, Harry, then. Yes, Harry. Of course. Fondly, sadly, Harry.

It was the image of Harry, staring into a dark mirror at the bar at the Drake, that made her hold her breath. "Are you saying you think I'm an alcoholic?" she whispered, still not turning to face him. He didn't move. At least he knew her well enough to know she didn't want right then to be held or hugged.

"I've never used that word, Kit. I don't know. I don't care if you are or aren't. I love you, remember? If by some biological accident you are, I want you to get help, to get relief. Talk to someone professional, someone who might know. I just know that most people—if they don't have a problem—don't say they want to quit. They don't even try to quit. It doesn't occur to them. But it's your call. Talking can't hurt, can it?"

She took a deep, regulating breath. Her tears had stopped. "I want you to go home," she said quietly, her anger spent. "Let me think this through."

He readily agreed, and for a moment, she wasn't sure if he meant to save their relationship or to save himself from their relationship. When she heard the door close, she went to the kitchen and poured the last of her drink down the sink in a gesture more symbolic than sober.

The next morning she found a professional card, "Mark P. McNulty, Ph.D.—Clinical Psychologist" on her kitchen counter. Marshall must've put it there on his way out, but she hadn't noticed it the night before. She put the card in her purse. What would happen if she called? The address on the card was a high-rise on Michigan Avenue which housed both offices and residential apartments. It would not be like walking into a place with a sign in front screaming, "Liposuction" or "Drug Addictions" or "Bankruptcy Filings." No one would have to know. McNulty—whoever he was— would probably tell her not to drink for 30 days, and she could say okay just to move things along. If she were careful, how would he know if she had one or two? She was not convinced that talking would help, but it would get Marshall off her back, and she really didn't have anybody else to talk to—Jill was always so busy these days, and her mother, preoccupied with the aches and pains of aging, had long ago stopped understanding how a fabulous career and a marriage proposal could constitute any kind of issue worth discussing. Marshall himself, as much as he might consider himself the solution, was, in that very assumption, part of the problem.

In the bathroom, she took a little extra time with her makeup, paying special attention to the darkish circles around her eyes. Sometime during the day she would, no doubt, have to see Marshall. She put on her best suit and her leopard heels.

She arrived at the office on the late side, about 9:30. A huge bouquet of red roses towered over her desk. She closed the door and counted. Twenty-four.

"So extravagant," she said out loud. She opened the little white envelope tied to one of the stems. Inside, on a plain white card, were two ink drawings, a side view and a top view. On the left, the side view showed a circle braided of three strands, which had a Celtic feel to it. On the right, the top view outlined an oblong braided in a figure eight with an extra loop in its middle. In the bottom right hand corner, he had printed a legal notice of copyright: "© M. Long 1991."

She called to thank him for the flowers, actually forgetting the argument that prompted them. In her own mind, the issue had been resolved. She'd poured half a glass of scotch down the drain and had decided to call that McNulty character.

"The little loop is for the stone," he said. "Your choice."

"Ooo," she giggled, sounding to herself as adolescent as she momentarily felt. "Have I told you I love you?" she asked. It occurred to her that for all the times Marshall had said those words, she may not have said them. In fact, she hadn't been sure of them before last night.

She dialed her mother, but there was no answer. Later, her mother would congratulate her, and Kathleen could tell that, for all of her mother's pride in her other accomplishments, the great unspoken weight of Kathleen's spinsterhood had been lifted from her shoulders. She hadn't yet met Marshall, but if he were in love with her daughter, he had to be, she said, a wonderful man.

At 4:00, Darby called Kathleen. He'd first asked for Marshall, but Marshall was busy. The jury was back. They were due in court at 4:30. Darby would meet them there.

"Show time!" Kathleen appeared at Marshall's door, where he was on the phone talking litigation strategies with someone who seemed to be doing most of the talking. He stood up, stretching the phone cord while he reached for his suit jacket on a chair on the other side of the desk. He blew her a kiss and got one arm into one sleeve before he cut off the caller with the somewhat officious announcement that he had a jury back.

"At court," he said to his secretary, and Marshall, the litigator, rushed ahead of his supposed fiancée to the elevator.

"Hold that elevator, please!" she called after him, as if he were a stranger.

H elen Bornstein and her client were already at their table when Marshall and Kathleen swung through the double doors of Judge Jasper's courtroom. Ann's back was rigid and her head was faced straight ahead, but Bornstein, her legs crossed into the aisle, was making small talk in the direction of Darby and the four or five people gathered near him. He paced in place, his head bobbing up and down, perhaps in agreement with Bornstein, perhaps absently. When Marshall and Kathleen arrived, he waved his arms wildly, as if he were in a crowded airport lounge rather than a relatively empty courtroom.

Marshall greeted Helen in a perfunctory way and turned his back to her to face Darby. Kathleen and Helen said hello and lingered for a moment in mutual curiosity. Kathleen nodded and turned towards Darby. A few reporters sat in the audience, but most of the court watchers had gone home. They cared more about the drama than the results, and liked to leave the Loop before the late afternoon rush.

Quickly, with one eye on the bench, Darby introduced his secretary and two paralegals who had come over for the verdict. She smiled to herself when she noticed the little beads of sweat which had gathered at Darby's receding hairline.

Darby's support team moved back from the table to the front row of the gallery, making room for Marshall and Kathleen. Marshall sat, but Kathleen stood. She felt terribly alone. It was incredible to her that not a single member of the Management Committee thought the announcement of the verdict was important enough to attend. Or that they could deny their involvement by leaving only Marshall and Kathleen to face the jury. She stared at the bench and tried to imagine what a defendant in a criminal case would feel. "Ladies and Gentlemen of the Jury, how do you find?" What would it feel like to hear yourself sentenced to death?

There was a flurry of activity at the front of the room.

"All rise," the clerk said.

The bailiff ushered in the jury and they took their seats. Later, the litigators would say they could tell. There was a certain bounce in their collective step, a new camaraderie—or so one side would say. Kathleen could almost hear her heart ricocheting off the walls. The judge asked the foreperson to identify him or herself. A man in his late fifties, perhaps early sixties, stood up.

The foreman cleared his throat. In pointedly neutral tones, he announced the jury's unanimous verdict: Albright & Gill had violated Ann Rose's civil rights, as set forth in Title VII of the Civil Rights Act of 1967. Helen Bornstein turned to hug Ann, but Ann sat impassively, and Helen quickly retreated. She turned to the defendant's table and smiled broadly at Kathleen, as if she were a co-plaintiff. Kathleen nodded ever so slightly and looked away.

The judge thanked the jury for its time. They were free to go. Kathleen could read neither joy nor satisfaction into their appearance. Many seemed anxious to go. When the judge left, Darby's associates went back to try to talk to the few who lingered. Bornstein and Darby shook hands.

"You'll be in touch, I trust," she said.

The issue of compensation was to be tried later. Helen Bornstein had everything she needed to make sure that number would be high. She knew Albright & Gill would sooner settle than put its financial information—gross revenues and expenses and most importantly, personalized partnership information—into evidence in a new trial on damages. Blake Mills would not want his clients to know how many thousands of dollars he made each day.

"Come on, Philip, we'll buy you a drink," Marshall said. Kathleen looked at him with a question caught in her parted lips. "Hey, life goes on," he said.

Darby accepted the invitation and, in a generous gesture, asked them to wait while he gathered his associates. The young man and woman were obviously pleased to be included as part of the team. The young man followed his boss's lead and ordered a Stoli martini, straight up. The woman ordered a chablis.

"I'll just have a Coke," Marshall said, although it was rude of him to order before Kathleen.

For a long, considered moment, Kathleen resented Marshall's directive, but she pictured the roses and remembered the drawing of the ring. She hoped that Michelle, Darby's associate, wouldn't think she was a goody-two-shoes for not even having a glass of wine, but then kicked herself mentally for caring what one of Darby's associates thought—if she even thought—about it. She would deal with Marshall later.

"Me, too," she said.

By way of apology, Darby proposed a toast. "I'm sorry, guys. We gave it our best shot," he said. Then he added, "under the circumstances."

Marshall, who as a litigator had lost a few he should've won, and no doubt had won a few he should've lost, rushed to save Darby's face. "If it helps at all," he said, "I doubt that Blake is surprised. Any jury, given half a chance, is going to find for the underdog. A quiet settlement may have looked to our associates and recruits more like we were guilty, and so hurt us more in the long run. We're not going to buy off every person who doesn't make partner. Most people wouldn't have the stomach for litigation that Ann had, and they probably wouldn't have as good a record to go on, either."

Darby wasn't the kind of lawyer who could easily excuse himself because the jury felt sorry for underdogs. He opened his hands, palms up.

"Blake said he was pleased with the defense," Marshall said, and finally Darby brightened. Marshall continued, "He realizes he held you back some, like with the expert, and he appreciated that you followed his wishes. He also liked the way you handled our problem child here."

"Problem child?" Kathleen struggled to contain her mounting aggravation. "When did he say that?" Kathleen ignored Darby. If Marshall was talking to Blake about her, the least he could've done was to tell her.

"At the urinal," he said. "Where all important Firm business transpires."

Kathleen grimaced at Darby's young woman associate. Marshall had a knack for defusing her anger by admitting the absurd. "I'm afraid it's true, Michelle," she confided with a sigh. Still, he could've told her.

"Well, you always hate to see one get away," Darby said. "We're not used to losing."

"Comes with the territory, Philip," Marshall said.

"Yeah. You know, my own associates weren't too happy with me for taking you guys on. A third of our youngest associates are women. Maybe half our first-year class. We're not as big as you guys, so we're not as likely to run on stereotypes. Being smaller magnifies our differences, but also makes them more tolerable. You'd think it would be the opposite, but it isn't. We know the guy behind the outside appearances. I have one partner who is so wacko, I'd hesitate to be alone with him in a dark room, but I know him well enough to know he truly is a fine attorney—maybe our best—so we tolerate his idiosyncrasies. And don't quote me, Michelle," he pointed to his associate.

They had a second round and then split up. As soon as they were in the cab, Kathleen turned to Marshall. "You can't do that."

"What?"

"Either. You can't order for me," she said, still resenting that he had ordered a Coke when in her mind a martini was clearly more appropriate.

"I didn't order for you," he said, holding her gaze.

"Technicalities," she said. "You might as well have."

He didn't defend himself, so she continued. "And, the second thing is, if you ever have a discussion with anyone at the Firm about me, without telling me, we are absolutely, without question, finished. I don't care if it's the day before our fiftieth wedding anniversary, got it? You're out!"

Marshall exaggerated a gulp. "Yes ma'am. But...."

"No, buts."

"I was trying to protect you. You had a lot on your mind, and a lot of pressure, and I didn't want to complicate things."

"Thank you," she said, exaggerating a smile. "They've been so simple."

B ack at Kathleen's place, she and Marshall ordered a pizza with extra cheese and lots of onions and watched television mindlessly. She wasn't in the mood to talk to anyone, not Marshall, Jill or her mother. At 10:00, Marshall got up to leave, and she didn't ask him to stay. The logistics of two professional people—maybe engaged, maybe not—trying to live together in separate apartments was a bit baffling. Sometimes, he could go home without being kicked out, couldn't he? She didn't want it to be a big issue to her if sometimes he went home to his own place, or to him if sometimes she didn't beg him not to.

"We're grown-ups," he said, laughing. "We can work this out. Shall I call you in the morning?"

"That's what they all say." She kissed him good night and, although she was exhausted, as soon as she lay down she was wide awake. She could hear her heart pounding with an unexplained urgency.

Before the trial, and even up to the moment of her testimony, she'd known what the rest of her career should look like. She should hit the million-dollar mark in annual billings in two or three years, and then, by the middle of the '90s, certainly, the Firm should elect its first woman member of the Management Committee. It was a realistic goal. She was smart, ambitious and a hard worker. She had a needed expertise and a way with people. She wasn't too feminine or too unfeminine. There weren't many women with her seniority, and, while it was immodest of her, she didn't consider them much competition. Hers was a future almost every young lawyer in the city thought he or she aspired to, with the rare exceptions of the unusually committed or independently wealthy, like Rachelle Fineberg.

She sat bolt upright, her forehead damp. Brian had said—even before the Firm lost—that what she imagined to be her future was no longer possible. How had that happened?

Tentatively, she retraced her steps. It hadn't been her fault that Ann Rose was passed over. Her evaluation hadn't been the one to tip any delicate balance. In fact, it was the same as several others who thought the woman needed to improve her interpersonal skills. She wouldn't have been faulted, even by her own feminist conscience, for not standing by Ann Rose. At trial, her opinion of the Firm's process had been called irrelevant.

Then why had she done it? Why had she answered Helen Bornstein's meaningless question in a way that indelibly would mark her as disloyal? Why had she put her own Management Committee ambitions on the line for Ann Rose, a woman who wasn't even a friend?

Kathleen tallied a mental ledger. She liked what she did for a living well enough. She liked the fast pace, the non-serious nature of the oddball questions clients asked her, the proximity to the entertainment business. She especially liked making more than a quarter-million dollars a year, enough to be comfortable and generous, to not have to worry about her future and to be independent. She liked that being a partner of Albright & Gill gave her a certain instantly recognized status, even in a city as large as Chicago.

But it was not her passion.

She'd said as much to Marshall any number of times. She wanted Albright & Gill to the extent it didn't want her: not just to prove that women in general were capable of it, but also to make it one possibility among many for women who came after. She didn't want Albright & Gill for its own sake. It neither fulfilled her sense of self nor satisfied her soul. Perhaps she'd always known that, but never so much as when, on that stand, she'd said "seven out of 10" and had known in her bones that was not good enough.

She simply had not known a better way to leave them without feeling that she wasn't doing what she was so eminently capable of doing—establishing a precedent for women in the law. If *she* didn't set that precedent, she knew now, someone else would. Ann Rose had set one kind of precedent, Rachelle Fineberg another. There would be others, each in her own time. The burden of the movement was not hers alone. She'd done what she could do. She couldn't do more without a sacrifice of self that she was not willing to make. What, precisely, would give her the meaning she desperately craved she couldn't say for sure, but she knew this: to save herself, she would have to leave Albright & Gill behind. Perhaps Ann Rose had known something similar when she had said, "I am who I am." By taking her chances, Ann Rose, who wanted in, had shown Kathleen a way out.

SIXTEEN

Overruled.

T he next morning, the *Tribune* carried a front page story in the lower left hand corner with a picture of a rather grim Ann Rose leaving the courthouse, and the *Sun-Times* ran the story on page three, in the bottom right, with a similarly grim Ann Rose but a shining Helen Bornstein. Neither Marshall's nor Kathleen's name appeared, much to her relief, in either story. Both stories said the case stood for the proposition that judging someone according to sexual stereotypes was a form of employment discrimination and quoted testimony from the social psychologist. The managing partners of several of Albright & Gill's key competitors allowed themselves to be quoted in self-serving ways that conveyed, "it couldn't happen here."

When she arrived in her office, the Firm's internal "all-personnel" memorandum was waiting in her in box. It read:

> As some of you may be aware from the morning's newspaper reports, the jury yesterday returned a verdict in favor of the plaintiff in <u>Ann Rose v. Albright & Gill *et al.*</u> Although the expected financial implications will be minimal, the Firm regrets the jury's decision and will be considering its options. Since this is still an open matter, please do not discuss it with persons outside the Firm. All press inquiries should be referred to Leonard Stonehill.

There was, of course, absolutely no chance that the lawsuit would not be discussed outside the Firm. Blake's primary use for the memorandum was to signal Helen Bornstein surely, but indirectly, that her demands for financial compensation (which would come in part two of the trial) should be reasonable.

Ann Rose herself had been assistant general counsel at a venture capital firm for a year and so was not strapped financially.

Judging by her lack of visitors, Blake's memorandum had the desired effect of calming her partners. Most were satisfied to know that there would be no overwhelming impact on their individual financial statements. The Firm had weathered other storms in its 100 year history, and while the Ann Rose controversy had demolished Kathleen's future plans, for most partners, it had barely registered on their personal Richter scales.

For the rest of the week, Kathleen turned her attention as best she could back to the practice of law. The newspaper stories had reminded some clients to check in with their lawyers, and so her phone was busy and she submerged herself in other people's problems. In the evenings she and Marshall cooked spaghetti or chicken and discussed plans to get away for the weekend. All she wanted, she said, was sunshine. She didn't care where.

On Wednesday night Marshall mentioned that he'd heard Kraft Foods was looking for a chief trademark counsel, and Kathleen got up from the dinner table to get herself more coffee. "No commuting," was all she said, and was relieved that Marshall didn't pursue it. She was still miffed that he'd huddled with Blake about her being a "problem child" and hadn't told her. She wasn't a child, and she was not, she repeated to herself, the problem. Marshall could read the want ads, if that's what he needed to do to feel like he was helping, but it was her career, and she wanted him to stay out of it. Perhaps, during the trial, when Jill was so unavailable, perhaps then she'd relied too much on him for comfort and support. Perhaps she should slow the whole thing down while she got things straight. She could talk to that therapist, and she could decide, without Marshall's urging, what to do next.

She poured him some coffee and suggested New Orleans for the weekend. The future would take some time. Part of her felt an overwhelming failure, and she wailed on her knees before the pyre of her career. In the next instant, she saw "Hannigan, Streeter, Alton & Fineberg" in brass against an historic brick building, and inside, a rough-hewn, high ceilinged loft space where the lawyers—all women—worked cooperatively and casually and sensibly. She kept both to herself, a form of retreat from the intrusive side of intimacy with Marshall. She didn't feel like talking to him about her future right now. What mattered was what she wanted to do, not what Marshall thought she should do. When they got under the covers that night, he held her hand lightly, and she knew that even as she pulled away, he wouldn't panic. He wouldn't tug too hard, but he would be there. She could do whatever she wanted.

On Friday morning she got a call from Blake's secretary to come to his office. She assumed he wanted to discuss post-verdict and settlement options, but when she entered his office, Jimmy Logan, who was not related in any way to the case, was standing, staring out the window, while Ernie Gordon paced nearby. Jimmy didn't turn when she entered the room. There was an empty chair, and Blake nodded to it.

"We have been discussing an opportunity," Blake began. "Jimmy?"

Jimmy shrugged. With a hand outstretched in Blake's direction, he deferred.

"Anthony would like you to be his general counsel," Blake said. Not waiting for her to react, he added, "and, after due consideration, we believe that it would be in the best interests of the Firm if you were to accept."

She smiled a wry smile.

"We believe it would be in your best interests as well."

She rocked back in her chair, rolling with the punch. How stupid did he think she was, not to have understood that the latter was implicit? Of course the Firm expected her to serve its interests above her own. She couldn't take her eyes off of Blake, who sat motionless, his hands folded on top of his desk. Even though she had suspected it would come to this, she was genuinely surprised that the Firm had acted so quickly and so directly. She'd thought they wouldn't have the audacity to strike so closely on the heels of the jury's decision. She'd miscalculated Blake's arrogance. If he felt it necessary to defend himself—and it was unlikely there was anyone to whom he would have to answer—he would say that this had been in the works for a while, that there'd not been time, since Monday, for it to be retribution. Nonetheless, there was no doubt in Kathleen's mind that—despite whatever price tag, perks and prestige they would attach to Anthony's offer—this was recrimination for her testimony.

She glanced at Jimmy, who didn't look at her. They both knew that had she wanted to be general counsel of Anthony's empire, Anthony would've created that position for her long ago. In his own disloyalty to the Firm, Jimmy had offered it to her numerous times, usually someplace over Cleveland, when he said he needed some and was going to make her rich. Just last night, she had admitted to herself how little passion she felt for the group enterprise of Albright & Gill. It was absurd to think that she would give herself over instead to the greed of Anthony's sole proprietorship.

She stood.

"How convenient for the Firm that our interests suddenly coincide!" She laughed, resting her hands on Blake's desk and leaning slightly in his direction. A flicker of confusion may have crossed Blake's forehead. "What exactly about my leaving the Firm would be in its best interests?"

She waited. He could give her a trivial answer, some polite talk about solidifying the Firm's relationship with an important client and succession planning for Jimmy's not imminent but foreseeable retirement, or he could treat her like he would treat an equal, the way she guessed he would treat a man in hand-to-hand combat.

"The Firm has a legitimate interest in being certain of its partners," he said.

"You question my competence?" she said, still trying to force him to be honest about the retaliation.

"That they not exhibit disloyalty."

She was relieved, in a way, that he had at least articulated the rule. It made all the more clear in her mind her rejection of it.

"Unless they do so quietly or in quiet desperation."

"You've set a more public precedent," he said.

"I hope so," she laughed. "Otherwise it's been a lot of hoopla for nothing! Do you think Ann Rose really cares if she joins this Firm or another? Do you think we are so desperate that either of us would play by all your rules just for the privilege of playing a game that's rigged against us? Do you really think the game is worth that much? You can't tell me, Blake, what is in my best interests. You have no idea who I am, let alone what's good for me. You can only say you no longer want me as a partner. And, since Monday, you better be damn careful how you say that."

"Ha! That's my girl!" Jimmy was animated. "You tell 'em, sons of bitches!" he said. He batted at the air with his right hand and spun around, knocking an imaginary one out of the park and steadying himself at the end with both hands on his knees. No doubt his world was still spinning when he started to run the bases but Ernie caught him at the shoulders. Startled, Jimmy remembered where he was, and Ernie guided him to a chair behind Kathleen. She turned slightly so that her rear end would not be directly in Jimmy's face. His outburst had given her the moment she needed to swallow her rage, and she continued her own tirade in a controlled, almost dispassionate voice.

"The rules are going to have to change. Not as quickly as I would like, but not as slowly as you would have it, either. I admit I was naïve. I thought for a while that if I had the same credentials as the guys, I would be on an equal footing from the get go, all the way up the ladder. I didn't think it was going to take 20, 30, 40, however many years for it all to be equal, if it ever can be. I know today it's not going to happen just because a few women become partners or one is on the Management Committee. It's a much longer, cultural process. To get to the point where we are not aware of gender first, or race, or whatever, where we are not women lawyers or African-American lawyers—that's going to take a lot more patience than I have."

"Albright & Gill has been in existence since 1877, Ms. Hannigan. I trust we have the requisite forbearance."

"I imagine you do. Despite the Firm's distinguished history and its long tradition, it's going to change—one lawyer at a time. I know I was just one partner, but I hope I made some kind of difference, in my own way. As did Ann. As does Jimmy, even if he doesn't want to. And Randy Randolph, even when it didn't show. We're all just making it up as we go along. We have no precedent."

"Nor did we," he said. "Until now." The corners of his lips turned up. She thought he meant to acknowledge, however reluctantly, that she'd played a good game.

"I'll have my attorney contact you regarding the financial aspects of my severance," she said, thinking she would call Helen Bornstein.

"Isn't there some spousal immunity which pertains?" he asked, the hint of a twinkle in his eye.

"Not yet," she said brightly.

"The Firm will be fair, Ms. Hannigan. I doubt you'll need the services of Helen Bornstein."

"She knows the relevant precedent."

"It is *our* precedent, Ms. Hannigan, as well as yours. Your contribution, financially as well as with respect to these other matters, is noted. We have both benefited from our affiliation. I trust we won't forget each other." With a final but respectful solemnity, he stood and extended his hand. It was, she knew, high praise.

She was almost at the door when Blake spoke again, "By the way," he said, sounding a little curious and perhaps disappointed, "Only seven out of 10?"

ABOUT THE AUTHOR

M ary Hutchings Reed, former partner in the Intellectual Property Department of Winston & Strawn in Chicago, is currently Of Counsel. Her practice is primarily in marketing, advertising, trademark, copyright and entertainment law.

In 2007 she was honored by her peers in *The Best Lawyers in America* for her advertising law practice. Among her numerous publications on intellectual property and advertising issues is the leading treatise on special events law, *The IEG Legal Guide to Sponsorship*. She is also the author of *The Legal Guide to Cause Marketing* and *The Copyright Primer for Librarians and Educators*.

Ms. Reed is on the board of directors of Lawyers for the Creative Arts and the Legal Assistance Foundation of Metropolitan Chicago. In 2005, she won the Thomas R. Leavens Award from LCA for Distinguished Service to the Arts. She has also been a director for the YWCA of Metropolitan Chicago, the Off the Street Club, the Chicago Bar Foundation and the Chicago Chapter of the American Civil Liberties Union. She has taught entertainment law at Northwestern University School of Law and in the graduate program in Arts, Entertainment and Media Law at Columbia College, Chicago.

Ms. Reed began her law career at Sidley & Austin, becoming a partner in 1983, and joined Winston & Strawn as a partner in 1989. She received a J. D. degree from Yale Law in 1976, an M.A. in Economics and a B.A. in Public Policy, both with honors, from Brown University in 1973, where she was a member of Phi Beta Kappa.

Her novels, *Saluting the Sun* and *An Educational Experience* (*The City Girls*), were Semi-Finalists in The William Wisdom-William Faulkner Society's Novel-in-Progress Competitions. Her most recent novel, *One for the Ark*, was a Short List Finalist for that award. She has also won honors from Pariah Publishing, *Writer's Digest* and *ByLine* Magazine.

In 2006 her musical, *Fairways*, a stage play about golf, honesty and love with music by Curt Powell, premiered at the Steel Beam Theatre in St. Charles, Illinois, to 12 sell-out performances. An avid golfer herself, Ms. Reed also enjoys sailing, and is presently at work on a musical about the cruising life.

Ms. Reed lives in Chicago with her husband, Dr. William R. Reed.

www.maryhutchingsreed.com